A Seemingly Unstoppable Dawn

ALSO BY BILLY TOOMA

Shin's Shadow & Other Stories
The Great Obesity Crisis & Other Poems

ALSO BY OZYMANDIAS MELANCHOLIA PRESS

Skyline Worlds: Collected Stories

A Seemingly Unstoppable Dawn

A Novel

Billy Tooma

Ozymandias Melancholia Press
◆
New Jersey

Copyright © 2014 by Billy Tooma

First Edition, Trade Paperback, Ozymandias Melancholia Press, LLC

Original front cover artwork by Laura Chew

For more information visit www.osmapress.com

ISBN-13: 978-0-6158-6074-9
ISBN-10: 0-6158-6074-5

Always do sober what you said you'd do drunk. That will teach you to keep your mouth shut.

– Ernest Hemingway

Britney Spears' "Oops, I Did It Again" was playing on the radio as the bus crossed the Delaware-New Jersey border. God, I wish that this story could have started better, but the truth of the matter is that Britney Spears really was playing over the speakers and I won't cut that part out. I never cared for authors who fudge on truths because they are embarrassing, or, really, they deem them to be so. Me, well, I won't do that. I can't. The whole purpose of putting my story to paper is because it's therapeutic. I've lived for too long with a careless lack of restraint, much like the rest of my compeers. Now I know what you must be thinking, "Oh, no, he's one of those crazies you hear and read about, and I shouldn't take a word he says seriously," and, up until a few months ago, I would have wholeheartedly agreed with you, given you a shiny silver dollar, or one of those pretty gold-plated Sacagawea ones, and sent you on your merry way. But that isn't the case anymore.

You see, I am just getting over what one might call a bad habit. Okay, I call it that. My doctor and his pretty young nurse with fiery red hair, but wait, I'm getting ahead of myself again. I'm notoriously known for doing that, and for trailing from the subject at hand, but, I promise, I always manage to bring it around and back to where it, the story, belongs. Well, I have been clean for about three months now, and let me tell you, it has not been an easy road. Looking back at that bus ride, I can tell you that I never thought living without drugs and booze was possible for me. The problem is that once you start using them both early in life, you really aren't left with much of a past to look back on in order to remember happier, actually, cleaner, times.

It has astounded me to this day how bad a person behaves when they first come off the drugs. The alcohol is easy, at least, for someone who inhales, injects, and however else you can get it, to come off of, but your liver will more than likely get the better of you during withdrawal. I don't remember much of mine. What I do recall though, vividly, is a time when I thought my whole life was about to turn into something significant. Don't have the slightest clue as to what got me to think that way, but when you live in a cloud, like I did, you tend to ignore the logic of the Houyhnhnms and embrace the savagery of the Yahoos. In my short intervals of normalcy, I read, I wrote, but usually ended up burning it all. Kafka may be jealously rolling in his grave over my very proud declaration. Well, I seem to have danced away from the music, so let me see if I can't bring it on back.

I said that the pop princess' song was playing on the bus radio. I remembered this song's video so well because of that goddamned TRL, Total Request Live, on MTV, Music Television, to be sure. A lot of abbreviations back in those days. Truthfully, it was the dawn of the Abbr. Age. We all started becoming too lazy to say or spell words, so we made things easier. The text messaging era was on our doorsteps, and, poor us, we hadn't a clue. But that video of Spears' had her dressed up in this tight little red body suit. I wondered if she'd made a conscious decision when choosing that piece based on the fact that in her very first video, she'd been wearing a short little schoolgirl outfit. I had never been one to want to make sure I was home for TRL, but I made it a point in those days. Pathetic? Yes, but at the time, when I had a bottle of hand lotion next to me, and a tissue in my hand, it didn't really matter to me what anyone would think. She could hit me as long as she wanted, and I would have been just fine with that. Correction, she could have hit me as long as she wanted so long as I might get to hit, well, slap, her in return. Quid pro quo after all.

I'd been on the bus for a little over a half-hour, but I was ready to hurl myself through the window into greener pastures. Now I was never one to use public transportation but when in the rare chance I did, I always managed to sit near or next to a mother and a crying baby. This time was no exception. She, the mom, looked like hell. I can think of no flattering words for this woman because none would fit. In my thinking, she must have been up for hours before boarding that bus. That couldn't have been her only child, not unless she had gained over a hundred pounds during its incubation. Long before they started charging people for taking up more than one seat, you had to suck it in, plop yourself down, and pray to God the person next to you didn't complain. At least I wasn't that poor bastard. From where I was sitting, I couldn't see the guy, but I knew he was there, suffering like a true championship-level traveler.

As far as the kid goes, I have to say that was probably the ugliest baby I ever did see. I am not entirely positive if it had been a boy or a girl. Its mother, of course, had dressed it in a neutral-colored, unisex outfit, so without a standard splash of blue or pink, I was helpless to come to any concrete conclusion. Screaming is a term I will use, because I am not sure screeching works. When you think of the latter, you might get a sense of intermittent moments of loud sound followed by similarly-lengthened periods of silence. No such luck. That little shit machine, and shit it did, constantly, with a smell that would make any toxic waste dump alongside the Jersey Turnpike envious, whaled for the first half of the ride. No amount of bobbing or cooing on the mother's part would do any good. It was all I could do to not rise up, declare a revolt, and stage a coup that would rid everyone who was suffering from all of that terrible noise. Not knowing where I stood with the other passengers, however, caused me some concern, and I knew I couldn't end up like Che Guevara, a poor, half-naked former godhead of revolution, dead, along the asphalt banks of the Garden State. I wouldn't let myself go out like that.

Sleep was no use. I suffered from a terrible insomnia that might very well have been cured if I had stopped taking drugs. But if I stopped taking drugs, I would be able to sleep, and I might continually sleep in, so, by that reasoning, I would never be on time for any job that might come my way. Sadistic reasoning, I know, but at the time it made perfect sense to me. All I could do was rest my head. I have always considered buses quite comfortable. Unless you land yourself in a two-bit piece of shit, you never really get the feeling of anything but relaxation. The seats are always cushioned, the back never stiff and hard. I was Goldilocks, that bus was my just right porridge, but I could only pray for the mama and papa bears to come and swallow that noisy little brat whole. It's a horrible thing to grow up and realize those were only tales of fiction, and to rely on them would be foolish. You may call me a fool.

So as the infant's symphony of screaming continued on, I looked to try and have a conversation with the young girl sitting next to me. She was wearing tight jeans, which didn't complement her at all. When a person has a little more girth to them than they should, I don't think that is an invitation to showcase it. Nobody wants to see your fat hang out, flapping in the wind. But I tried my best to stave off the urge to commit double murder by talking to her. "Going to New York, too?" I asked in my not-so-subtle flirting voice. Hey, give me a break: yes, she was a little on the hefty side, but it would be a long bus ride, and, in between, I figured, if the opportunity for travel-buddy fondling came up, a deal could be worked out.

Initially, she gave no response. She had a pair of headphones on and was looking out the window. I'm not sure what she was looking at, but I had every reason to believe that I was being ignored. That muffin-eating bitch didn't even have the common courtesy to acknowledge my existence while here I was trying to establish the possibility of a heavy-petting scenario. Where's the appreciation, I wondered, in people? I attempted to restart the initiative. "Hey, where are you headed to?"

I had said that one a little louder so that she had no choice but to admit that I, in fact, was a living, breathing human being. Okay, that I was at least living and breathing. "Where are *you* headed to?" she asked back to me in a voice that told me she had a deviated septum and had blown her share of cocks in her short years. God, I was praying she'd line me up next.

"I asked you first."

"Well, the bus' final stop is Penn Station, New York City, so wouldn't it lead to reason that I am headed there?"

"Is that sarcasm? See, I only ask because if it is, it's the same thing I might have answered just a second ago, but I'm not sure you would have taken it as well as I have just now."

"Was that supposed to be a witty remark?"

"Did you take it that way?"

"Maybe." There was a hint of a smile in her fattened pink lips, and I knew that this long ride might not feel so long if I kept it going.

"So," I said, this time slowly moving over half an inch towards her, "what's waiting for you in the city?"

"I'm supposed to be starting college there in September. My father wanted me to go up early and experience the place beforehand."

"Experience the place? What the hell does that mean? What happens if you have a bad experience? Does that mean you crawl back home with tears in your eyes and say, 'Daddy, the bad, bad city hurt me?'"

Right after I had spewed out the words, I wished I hadn't. I tend to get so over the top that my initial message is lost in a sea of words no one should ever have to listen to. But this chick laughed and finally took the headphones off. Her ears were big. I noticed that right away. I wondered though, if I could get past it all and seal the deal. If I had been telling this to a bar full of vagina-starved bikers, they'd have begged me to tell them I did her in the ass. But I'll let you use your imagination until the time is right.

"My dad's a douche," she said. "He wanted me out of the house as quick as possible. Just married him a new little slut and wants to probably spend the summer humping her until she realizes she'd be better off with my purple dildo. And I told her as much before I left."

"I honestly don't think I have one thing from my bag of tricks to use against all that," I said. "Look at it this way, you've got freedom now. Granted, freedom dependent upon if your dad's money continues to get flushed up your way."

"He can screw. I'm getting a job ASAP. I'm Gerri by the way."

"Ash."

"Really? Ash?"

"My father named me. He said that when I was born, I was so small that I reminded him of the little ash that hangs off a cigarette."

"You've got to be shitting me."

"I am, but, for a second there, you were totally at a loss for words," I said, smiling.

The banter of the sexually-frustrated youth continued on until the driver, who was a hulking brute of an Arab, I don't know, maybe Iranian, pulled into a rest area. "Hokay, hokay, folks. Tek half hour and meet bek here."

The cattle that we had become slowly shifted body parts in and out like contortionists in order to free ourselves from the stockade that our bus had become. Some of us, not me, kind of smelled like we belonged in a barnyard. And that still crying little bastard should have been the Thanksgiving turkey. Plucked and tossed into a fiery pit to quiet its nonstop noise making. I still can hear it if I think long and hard enough, which isn't exactly easy for a person like me to do.

Gerri took off ahead of me. My thinking was that perhaps she'd gone to freshen up her female parts for the eventual touch-fest I was aggressively cultivating. As I made my way into the building, I took notice of the name of the place: The Walt Whitman Rest Area. Really? Did the State of New Jersey really go and name a rest-stop after the father of free verse? Let me tell you, I hope that when I am dead and buried, possibly cremated, that I get a place like that named after me. I am kidding of course. How in God's name do people even begin to consider naming it after a person in the first place? We like names and titles and all other kinds of fancy shit to associate things with. News flash, Whitman lived in Long Island, New York, and died in Jersey. Yes, a fitting tribute to the overtly sexual poet of the 19th century; have him forever linked to the king of the cowboys and his fried chicken, which, by the by, I was after the moment I stepped off the bus.

I come from the land of Hardee's where Burger King plays second fiddle to the shining, smiling star. But in all my young years, I had never had Roy Rogers chicken. There had been stories passed to me by those lucky fools who were fortunate enough to escape the confines of our little state and partake in the golden-fried joy. There were doubts in my mind. I figured that if you kept getting hyped to about something that when you finally got to experience it yourself, you'd be let down. I took my chances, ordered two pieces, a thigh and a leg, but waved off the curly fries and biscuit. I would later learn that I had been a moron for having waved my hand to those delicious side orders.

After taking just one bite, I realized that the Colonel could go screw himself and if he's spinning over in his grave, I hope he takes this as a lesson from a fried chicken connoisseur; you can take your Kentucky Fried and shove it. Mr. Rogers, God bless you, wherever you are.

Once my foray into sexually-themed gluttonized eating was finished, I looked around for Gerri, who would help me transition over into full on, true sex. She was nowhere to be found inside, so I took a shot that perhaps she'd made her way back onto the bus. I was right. There she was, sitting alone, no one else around. Not even our driver had come back. Serendipity was calling to me. "Get everything you wanted done?" I asked.

"I took care of some things, ya."

"You know, we do have a little while before people come back on."

"What's that supposed to mean?"

To my credit, she had said that last part with what I thought was a raised eyebrow. To me, that indicated a sense of rebounded flirtation. Much to my later regret, I fell on top of her. It was a messy bit of body fondling, but, eventually, I got myself elevated above her enough to begin the standard unfastening of the pants. My libido was definitely calling the shots at this point, because Gerri's "no's" and "please, don'ts" were not registering with me at all. God, I wish they had been. After I was able to undo her button and zipper with one hand, I was quite talented in those, my younger days, I slid my digits right on down. Again, where was God when I needed Him? Perhaps it was karma or some other higher, crazy whacked out religious belief I can't pronounce. Either way, I got taught a lesson, and it was a firm one to match the stiff, hairless, and undersized dick that I found in Gerri's, original name, Gerald's, over-sized panties.

There wasn't a sound. Not from me, not from her, er, him, um, *it*. I casually, but with some quickened pace, retreated and recoiled back into my seat. I probably should have gotten up, but, wait, yes, I did in fact, get up. My mind was still in that seat, but I found myself outside, smoking a cigarette for all the wrong reasons. There would be many times in my life that I would smoke a cigarette for all the wrong reasons. And like that moment, I needed something more than just tobacco and nicotine. Nobody other than "Gerri" was around, so I took a little joint I'd been holding onto and lit that sucker right up. In went the weed, out through my nostrils via my brain went the smoke. I needed it, badly, and I hoped to Jesus that what had just transpired would be my only foray into that kind of alternative lifestyle. One can only hope, right?

The rest of the farm animals began to shuffle back out to the bus, and I knew I'd have to climb those stairs and enter back into the house that Satan had crafted for me. When I got in, I noticed "Gerri" sitting in another seat, tears streaming down "her" cheeks. It must have been the aftermath of a terrible ordeal of emotions and memories of "her" daddy doing "her" in the backend, pretending, and wishing, he had had a little girl so that the abuse and rape could make sense sexually to him. Poor, misunderstood-by-his-own-mind bastard. I didn't feel sorry for him, but I did for "Gerri." Wasn't "her" fault. Not that I said as much to "her," because I walked past where "she" was now sitting, not acknowledging nor even attempting to breathe in the same surrounding air. I was truly a piece of garbage, but I was high now, so it didn't really matter a bit to me.

When mommy dearest and her devil's spawn sat back down, I saw "Gerri" cringe a little, but I ignored the obvious pain "she" must have been feeling. Then I saw the front of the man who had been exiled to the land of whaling diapers. I'm positive that when he saw "Gerri" sitting in his seat a large part of his soul had its faith renewed in a benevolent creator. He walked over to me, where the only empty seat would now be. "Looks like I'll be sitting here. Would you like to take over the window?"

"Ya, sure, thanks," I said, shifting one over. "You don't happen to have a vagina by any chance?" My words were slurring, but I think I got the message over and clear.

"Last time I checked, I was void of one."

"Then by all means, my good man, enjoy yourself here in the kingdom of my own design."

"You're an interesting fellow, I must say. Much better here than over there," he said, pointing to the mother-child-transsexual triad.

"I'm not entirely sure how you didn't rise up and strangle the kid."

"If it hadn't been for the coke I brought with me, I probably would've."

My eyes lit up with the gaze of heterosexual love. "Coke, eh? I suppose you've gone and snorted that all up?"

He laughed. "Actually, I have about half a saltshaker left." He reached into his jacket pocket and revealed the holy grail of that bus ride. "I'd be happy to share the last of it with you when this thing gets moving again. Oh, I'm Stuart by the way."

"Stuart," I said, "I think this is going to be one smooth going ride from here on out."

He, of course, agreed. In all honesty, the guy was just grateful for not having to sit next to that kid again, and he might have thought that I had made it all possible. I would have let him have thought anything he wanted so long as I would have gotten my fix. The weed I had was decent, not great, but decent. But just knowing there was white powder in my presence, made me fiend like one of those drug-starved maniacs from a 1950s Public Service Announcement. I let Stuart go on and on about himself. None of which I personally cared about, nor continue to, because the relevance to any of it has been lost to the brain sparks of time, and I am not sure if I'll ever recollect them to their fullest extent.

From what I picked up, Stuart was from Rhode Island, originally. His entire family had moved down to Long Island when he was ten. After attending Hofstra, he moved himself down to Florida. It was in the Orange State that he lived for three years. His initial plan had been to open up a construction company, but things didn't work out for him. He spent his days working as a plumber's assistant, which made him crazy with depression. I didn't say it to him at the time, but I was thinking of what could possibly be in the job description of a plumber's assistant. Needs to be able to work on his knees? Needs to be able to handle large tubes? Needs to know how to pull underwear back up to conceal ass crack? All those questions circulating throughout my mind when all I wanted was that saltshaker to work its magic, which, eventually, after the longwinded babble of Stuart's had settled, it did.

"Not your first time doing this, I hope?" Stuart asked, smiling.

I took the little glass beauty right from his hand, ripped off the small piece of Scotch Tape he'd affixed to the top, and proceeded to dab a line across my left wrist. As I handed back the shaker, I inhaled the stuff right up. It burned my throat, but once it was down, in, and all around, even that baby's crying became a minor concern to me. I could tell Stuart was impressed with my natural ability. His mouth continued to remain agape even after it was his turn to snort. "I guess this *isn't* your first time," was all he could say.

"Practice makes perfect," was my response. "This is pretty decent stuff, Stu. I don't think I've ever had stuff so fine. Must be nice to be able to afford the best."

"Well, I won't be able to anymore. God knows what I'll be doing tomorrow or next week. Brother's telling me he can find me work. Why did I piss four years away in college to do odd jobs?"

"I'm kind of hoping that's one of those rhetorical questions, because my mind is quickly leaving this place." I turned to look out of my window. "I've never been to New York, Stu. I have never actually been anywhere before. It's scary and sad."

"New York City is a place where dreams can come true if you know how to please a hot shot in whatever business you're trying to break out into. But it can also be a nightmare for you. I escaped the nightmare only to end up meeting it again down south." That bus of ours contained all his belongings; he was going back to live at home as it turned out. Our initial plan was to grab a beer once we had reached our destination, but it never happened.

Stuart asked what I was going for, but I began to leave him behind me. Truth was, I had no real reason to go there. It was all about escape for me. And escape I did. But a person can't run forever.

I had hopped onto the bus the day after my mom's funeral. How many twenty-one-year-olds can make a statement like that? I guess too many these days. Mom was a lovely woman, but died far too young. At the wake, when I approached the casket, I could see that she was finally at peace, and that made me happy inside. It might have been the line or two I had taken up beforehand, but I chalked it up to emotional distress at the time.

After my dad left, it was just me and Mom. I could've been a better son. Actually, I just could have *been* there for her at all. Our big problem was that because Dad had gone MIA, I became the target, the proverbial punching bag. That's how I saw it, but, in her defense, my perception was always a bit biased for one reason or another. Everything did seem to be my fault, and, half the time, it more than likely was. There was the time when I was fifteen and stole a car. It wasn't premeditated or anything like that, but when I saw that blue Mustang, it spoke to me. Really, it *spoke* to me. It said something like, "Hey, baby, you want to go for a ride, cowboy?" Yes, it was a girl.

There hadn't been any kind of high-speed chase, though Mom's reaction would've led someone to believe there had been. Looking back, I should have taken that bad girl out on the highway, given the finger to the law, and burnt tar until dawn. Lucky as I might be sometimes, that incident proved to be a bad one for me, but really, it would plant the seeds for Mom's own personal misery. Only reason why I got out without charges was because the sheriff had always had the hots for my mom, though I didn't think he'd ever have a shot in hades with her. No pun intended on that last part. Well, actually, yes, pun intended, and I wish he had shot himself a long time ago.

My mom, first name Mary, lived and died in our tiny town outside of Dover, Delaware. She was the only daughter of a hardware store owner and a homemaker. Like any parents, they wanted the best for their little girl. If you grew up in that town, you knew better. Almost nobody ever got out, and in the off chance you did, you were looked at as a betrayer along the lines of Judas Iscariot. Mom was a beautiful girl with blonde hair, eyes of sky blue, and a wonderful complexion that got passed to me. She once mentioned that being an actress had been her dream. All the school plays saw her in the leading roles, and she held onto every single program.

The dreams Mom may have been harboring were completely obliterated the day she met my old man. He was the typical rural badass who peaked before the age of eighteen. They dated for a year, got married, and her parents cut her off. When the asshole left, she told me the only decent thing to come out of the whole debacle of her failed marriage was me. Even after I fell down the ladder of life, and our verbal arguments escalated, she never took that remark back. Working two jobs hadn't been easy for her. She was always tired. Weekdays, she worked as a secretary for an ambulance-chasing lawyer who probably had wet dreams about putting her over his desk. I had met him once and got that impression just from the way he looked at her. I wanted to cut it off of him right there and then. From Friday to Sunday night, she was a waitress at a tiny truck stop where the patrons probably had the same thoughts as the lawyer but at least you'd expect as much from their breed. After I graduated high school and it became clear that college wouldn't happen, Mom just stuck to being a secretary, getting back her weekends, which weren't that glamorous anyway.

Drugs came into my life shortly after my stunt with the Mustang. Marijuana and I got along very well. Problem with living in the kind of town I did was the local police had nothing to do, no action. Those lousy pigs were always itching for a little bit of trouble to come their way. Well, I gave it to them one October night. I had just picked up enough weed to last me a week when I got stopped. Since the car incident, ole Sheriff Richie made sure to keep an eye out for me. Bastard had a plan in his head that would involve Mary and her delinquent son. When I got brought to the station, the sheriff saw me, saw the pot, smiled, and then took me home.

Mom wept as ole Richie described to her the kinds of consequences I could face, having been caught with drugs. "I'm telling you, Mary, he could face up to ten in prison or maybe even life. I brought him home because I know how much you love him."

Half of what he was selling was complete bull, but Mom didn't know. I couldn't believe what my mother did next. She knew the sheriff had liked her since their days in high school. He was the football star, who, like my old man, climaxed his life on the field his senior year. When he realized that he couldn't be an asshole anymore, he found a way to cheat the system of social order by becoming a cop. Now that I had been caught, though not yet charged, in possession of narcotics, Mom would make it go away. Her and Richie went out that night. I didn't say a word. I sat there, in my living room, on the chair that once had been the possessor of my father's imprint, and waited. I don't think I moved the entire night. All I could think about was what my mother could possibly be doing with ole Richie and when I kept coming to the same conclusion, I wanted to vomit the thoughts out of my head.

She came back the next day and proceeded to tear me a new asshole. "What in God's name were you thinking? Drugs? Are you out of your mind? I want you to understand where I'm coming from. Look at your father, that good-for-nothing piece of crap. He drank himself stupid every night. Don't you remember?"

"Of course I remember, Mom."

"Why would you ever want to end up that way? Keep doing this stupid shit and you will be even worse off than he was."

"I don't know what to tell you except that I won't let it happen again."

"Is it that you won't do it anymore or you'll do whatever you can to not get caught anymore? I'm not doing this again, Ash, for you or for me, it isn't going to happen again. Rot in jail for all I care, because as much as I love you, if you want to mess your life up, I obviously can't do anything about it."

She slammed her bag down onto the table and sauntered into her bedroom. I'd been yelled at before, but she had never, and I mean never ever, compared me to my old man. Mom was cranky. That much was made clear to me. I guess she hadn't gotten a lot of sleep the night before.

When Mom was diagnosed with cancer it was too late to save her. The doctors gave her the "You have Six Months to Live" speech, but she suffered for an entire year. This event brought her parents back into her life. We moved her into their house, while I stayed at home. During this period, my drug use was a constant act of daily life. From weed to coke I went as my mom lay slowly deteriorating in a bed, being cared for by parents who knew they were simply playing babysitter to the dying. To pay for my nasty little habit, I delivered pizzas for a guy who used to pick his crack right before making the cheese. Whenever I'd catch him, he'd shrug his shoulders and just say, "Don't judge me." Needless to say, I never ate the food there. The rest of the bills, for the house, my grandfather took care of. I hardly ever visited Mom. Maybe just once or twice in those final months. It was obvious to my grandparents that I had been no Jesus to their Mary.

The last time I saw her alive was the night before she died. A month before, the doctors had suggested admitting her into the hospital so she could be made as comfortable as possible. I had no real intention of going there to see her, because places like that make me feel uneasy. I have always believed that when a person goes into a hospital, they are signing their own death certificate. Those institutions of legal narcotics only make a person worse.

My grandfather found me sitting on my ass at home. "Get up," he said, "off your behind and get to seeing your mama."

"I went the other night," I said, lying.

The old codger was fast, I'll give him that. Strong as a bear, too. He lunged at me, and, in one swoop, I was pressed down in the recliner as his hand choked down on my throat. "Listen to me, you little piece of worthless trash. Your mama needs to know you were there at least once. Don't go lying to me, you little scumbag. I'm gonna leave here now, and if I find out you stayed in this chair all night, I will get my hunting gun and teach you a real lesson."

Gramps was a persuasive man to say the least. I didn't blame him for the physical way in which he told me; in his mind, it was more than likely my father he had been talking to. I smoked a blunt after he left, in pre-gaming fashion.

It was late, way past visiting hours, when I stumbled into the hospital. Took me a while to find the right wing, but with a little concentration, I found it. The attending nurse saw the state I was in, and thought I had wandered away from the emergency room. As she escorted me to the door, I began calling my mom's name, and the nurse realized what I was really there for. Knowing there'd probably be a scene if she tried kicking me out, the nurse showed me the room, 104, and walked away as I went in. Mom wasn't just lying there; tubes and machines were hooked up to her. Her eyes opened, but I'm pretty sure nobody was listening on the inside. Too much morphine. She was lucky, didn't have to feel the pain.

I sat there in silence, eventually holding her hand. Maybe it was what I was on, I'm not sure, though in the back of my mind, I knew. I started crying. I cried like a small child who might have been caught playing with a kitchen knife, without malicious ideas, only because it looked shiny, then got yelled at and spanked for it. I knew that I had been a horrible son. I knew that even though she never said it, I was what held her down in that town. Because of me, her youth had been wasted away at an office job and at a two-bit diner after the deadbeat left. I could've been a son who deserved her love, but things just hadn't turned out that way.

She never said a word, but when I was talking to her, I thought I heard a mumble or something, and I lifted my head up. I started speaking again, but until I'm in heaven by someone's, probably St. Peter's, screw-up, I will never know if she heard or understood any of it. "Hey, Mom. It's me, Ash. I wanted to see you just in case you got up tomorrow, decided you wanted to go on a vacation or something, and I might not be able to go with you. I just wanted to tell you that I love you and that if I did anything to hurt your feelings, I'm sorry. I don't know what else to say except that I'm sorry. So sorry. Sorry. Sorry. Remember when I had that birthday party, not mine, remember that kid, Chuck? Ya, he had a clown, and I said I wanted one, but when I didn't get one, I said I hated you. Mom, I never hated you. Okay?" For an hour I just kept telling her how sorry I was for being who I was and that I loved her. When the sun started to come up, my high had been long over. I leaned over, kissed her on the forehead, and left. Around twenty-four hours after that, she was gone forever.

A springtime funeral is always bittersweet. The air is warm, flowers are blooming, but those wonderful colors clash with the black attire of all the mourners. I stood next to my grandmother. At one point I thought about holding her hand, but that feeling went away before the rest of the people even arrived. The priest spoke his words. People wept, but not me. I'd done my crying a few days earlier. Back at my grandparents' house, I was informed that the place I called home was going up for sale. It didn't take me long to figure out what I would do. Nothing was keeping me there. I stole whatever cash my grandfather had in his wallet, packed a bag, and left. Looking back, I probably thought I was doing what my mom had yearned for: to get out. I wouldn't be tripping the light fantastic on Broadway, but I would at least make it out of that godforsaken town that had consumed my mother's soul and was slowly nibbling at my own.

Couldn't say exactly why I chose to go to New York. My mom had told me that's where my dad had probably run to, but I wasn't going there looking for him. New York just seemed like the kind of place I could escape to that was far enough away from home. Philadelphia had been a possibility, Baltimore too, but New York is the city that never sleeps, and I wanted to experience that adrenaline-driven trip. There was a game plan; I wasn't going into the Big Apple without knowing anybody already there. In a way, having known this person was in the city probably helped me in my destination decision-making process.

His name was Ricky Donnardo. He had a nickname, too. If you knew it that meant you were "in" with him. It was "Veps." What it meant, I had no clue whatsoever. Now Veps and I went back to our sophomore year in high school. We had a couple of the same classes, but schoolwork wasn't what brought us together. When it was apparent that smoking weed had become an integral part of my life, I needed to get it from someone. Veps provided me with a steady flow of product, and we liked hanging out with one another. He had the area under his thumb. It was the perfect job for a teenager. His clientele ranged from middle-schoolers to the people attending the local community college.

Being Veps' friend had benefits, to say the least. He always had money on him, of course, and was the kind of person who'd punch someone out if he felt they had insulted his friend. There's this one time I can remember when Veps and I got into a little bit of trouble. At school, he had gotten sweet on this girl named Shannon Trundy. I say at school because there was no way Mr. Trundy would have ever allowed his little girl to date him, but Veps, well, he was a slick kid.

He came up to me one Friday afternoon in the hall by my locker. "Okay, listen, and listen very closely. What we have here is a very promising opportunity for both you and me. Shannon's aunt is in town along with her daughter, Karen. Shannon's folks are taking the aunt out for the night and won't be back 'til late. Them two young ladies are gonna be all alone for hours tonight. Us two, we're gonna be the one's keepin'em company." Veps' smile was always a broad one when he talked about getting pussy.

"I got no problem being a wingman," I said, "but is Karen at least some kind of pretty?"

Veps slapped me on the back. "Well, I've seen a picture of her, and I tell you that if Shannon wasn't gonna be putting out, I'd sure as hell hope her cousin would!"

I'm never one to be the killjoy, so I told Veps I'd meet him at the Mobil Station at seven that night. We walked over to Shannon's, pounding back a six-pack. Veps had one of his college customers purchase it for him. Before we got to Shannon's, he stopped me. "You got rubbers on you, bro?"

"Um, no, I don't," I said.

"Not to worry, killer. Here ya go!"

I held in my hand a condom. Not just any condom, mind you, but my first condom. I'd never had sex before, but it appeared as though Veps had set me up to get laid that night. Not too sure why I was still a virgin then, but I guess it had to do with not being very cool with the girls. At that time, I was still more into smoking up than getting with the opposite sex. Don't get me wrong, I flogged the log on a regular basis and had a fair share of chicks do it for me too, but I hadn't yet been able to seal the deal with one. Holding that Trojan, I remember feeling nervous and hoped Karen, if she was willing to do *it*, wouldn't laugh at me if I screwed up somehow.

We got to Shannon's and went to the back door. The girls let us in, and I got my first look at Karen. She was thin, tan skin, with brown hair, long and straight. They both had on mini-skirts, and I could tell Veps' were raging as crazily as mine. This was proved correct when he and Shannon took their leave of us into her room. Karen and I decided to take the guestroom where her mother would be sleeping while the cousins shared Shannon's room later that night.

The two of us sat on the bed in that dark room for ten minutes in complete silence. "I wonder what Veps and Shannon are doing in there?" she asked, with a voice lacking innocence. I immediately knew she was just being polite. A young lioness ready to pounce.

"I'm pretty sure they aren't swapping cake recipes," I said, cringing. It was the smoothest line I could muster up. God, I was an awkward youth. I was probably lucky that I could figure out how to masturbate without hurting myself. Or did I want that? One could never truly be sure. Some more standard small talk went on, then, eventually, and inevitably, we started kissing. Karen's tongue moved its way inside my mouth, and when she let me start feeling her up, I knew we were going to go to the wall together. My hand soon went up her skirt, and when I was certain which hole was which, I proceeded forward. She began to moan with pleasure. We started undressing one another. The next thing I knew, I was in her. It was an odd sensation at first, but not entirely unlike when a girl goes down on you, except with this way, you're the one, depending upon position, creating the friction.

    The first real sexual experience of my life didn't get far, because as we bumped against each other a car pulled into the driveway. I remember hearing Veps and Shannon scrambling in the next room. Karen threw on her clothes, but her mom and Shannon's parents had already entered the house. With no other option, I slid myself under the bed. There is where I remained the entire fucking night. Karen's mother eventually came in. I watched as her pants dropped to her ankles, and she slid into her pajamas. If she had been wearing underwear, I would never know. I fell asleep with the pressure of the woman a top me, and, just in case anyone was wondering, yes, gas all night. Around one the next afternoon, Shannon woke me up. Karen and her mother had gone. I got up, cramped and disjointed, but capable of walking. I met up with Veps afterwards for some food. We had our laughs about it all, although I think he had a few more chuckles than I did. He'd gotten it in, and finished, of course.

    I hadn't seen him in over four years. Veps dropped out when we were seniors and moved up to Manhattan. Once I got into town, my goal was to find him. Last I heard was that he might be living in the Village, but for all I knew, he could have been up in Harlem, although I doubted that very much. On my ride to New York all I thought about was what kind of crazy stuff Veps and I could get ourselves into. It hadn't been a mistake, me going to the city, because I knew this was living.

That May afternoon, as my bus drove up the New Jersey Turnpike, I caught my first live glimpse of the world famous New York City Skyline. The Twin Towers were the first things that I immediately saw. They shot up high into the blue skies over the island. Those two superstructures dwarfed everything around them. It was hard to believe that there were still buildings taller than those two. They were the perfect example of man's ability to shape metal into godlike proportions. After downtown, there were hardly any high rising buildings, but that changed when the bus got closer to the Lincoln Tunnel. Soaring above all else around it was the Empire State Building, the granddaddy of them all. It was a sight I've never forgotten. Even my bloodshot eyes could see the beauty in the architecture.

The tunnel freaked me out. When we entered it, I felt trapped. This whole concept of underwater travel still doesn't sit well with me. Knowing there were tons of pressure pushing against the encircling walls made me sweat. I'd never known myself to be a claustrophobic, but that structure was killing me. My heart pounded, blood rushed to my head, and I wanted nothing more than to be rid of that place. Even though the bus only spent about five minutes in the thing, it was enough for my taste. From that moment forward, I was officially a bridge man, unless I was in a state of not knowing my ass from my elbow, in that way the tunnel was okay. Go figure, right? I'm not sure if it had been the drugs, but I think the ghosts of those Irish construction workers spoke to me from beyond those tiled walls. They might have been telling me to get out while I still had a chance. My summer of 2001 had begun with me ignoring the voices of the damned. Punishment would not be swift.

I don't think anyone plans on being homeless. It just happens to them. I think it starts with money, or actually, the lack thereof. That's how it happened to me. It wasn't until my bus had driven away, and I was left standing in the middle of Penn Station alone, that I realized I hadn't thought my plans out very well. Maybe a small part of me figured Veps would just magically sense me being there and sniff me out. Such a fool was I.

Homeless. That was my station in life at that exact moment. Checking my pockets did nothing, because I knew I'd only find a hundred dollars, which, one might think, was enough for a cheap hotel, but I didn't know where to find a safe one. A sudden urge came over me. An urge I had felt many times before, and one that had been building from the moment Stuart's cocaine had run out. I had kept the saltshaker as a memento of our bonding on the bus, but it was empty, and that depressed me. Weed or coke? I could never decide, but I figured the decision could be made when I came across the first dealer. Whatever they had, I was buying. Food? Shelter? Those were things a person could go days without. Drugs were something I couldn't, hard as I tried, which, wasn't that much.

I walked around the bus depot for a while before making my way into the concourse of the station. It was the crossroads of tri-state civilization. Escalators ran up and down, and there must have been twenty of them. Men, women, and children alike were hustling in and out while vendors hawked their many precious heirlooms of commerce. A person could lose their mind here. They could get lost entirely without realizing it. I was no exception. That main entrance eluded me the entire first night.

I spent a week looking for Veps. He was nowhere to be found, but that didn't stop me from searching. It wasn't hard to score at all. Back home, I'd have to actually try, once Veps left, but in the city the only question you had to ask yourself was which dealer would you want to buy from. When my days turned up no Veps, and night settled in, I would take in some product. It was good, not great, but good, got the job done.

With no place to stay, I wandered around Penn Station. No one ever bothered me. I learned quickly that most city-dwellers didn't care about anybody but themselves, a fact that worked to my advantage. Everything I needed was right there in the terminal. There were food stands and bathrooms. The one thing I did lack was a shower. That didn't bother me all that much as I had nobody to impress, so my eventual stink didn't faze me. If the body odor became too much I always had the option of a Puerto Rican Shower: douses and douses of cologne.

As far as sleep went, I didn't get any the first three nights. On the fourth, I had been walking down one hallway with a recently refilled saltshaker. Just as I turned a corner, I saw a cop. I've never been sure of it, but I think he had taken notice of me. Without panicking, I backed up slowly, and, rounding the corner, I proceeded to haul ass. Whether or not the pig was following me, I wasn't taking any chances. When I saw the men's room door, I stumbled in. There wasn't anybody inside. I was alone.

My nerves dictated to me to remain inside that bathroom. In case anyone came looking for me, I ducked into one of the stalls. I plopped myself on the toilet and spun around. Trying to get comfortable, I propped my legs up onto the wall, using my backpack as a pillow. The smell in there was disgusting. New Yorkers should know that the taxes they pay are definitely not going into the cleaning of their public restrooms. I snorted up. The bathroom stall walls were very distracting. They were covered in graffiti. Different shades of ink and marker were strewn across them. Some markings showed names and dates, but there were also phone numbers and messages about loose women. Eventually, I did fall asleep, didn't even fall off the seat once. Those forty winks did me good, because my mind needed the break. The rest of the week I made sure to slip into my stall once I was ready to go and call it a night.

It was on a Monday night that I finally found Veps. Down to my last five dollars, I was beginning to doubt my chances of lasting another day in the city. I had walked up to Times Square. My eyes moved around like crazy. All the lights, the noises, even the huge tele-screens flashing commercials are enough to make a person go nuts. Never before in my life had I ever been so freaked out while not having an ounce of anything in my system. If you're able to pass up Madame Tussauds Wax Museum without thinking you're going out of your mind then you're doing just fine. It's always been beyond my comprehension as to why people enjoy those kinds of places. They stand there with static shiny sculptures and somehow feel themselves becoming closer with the celebrity who offered up the mold. Like I said, make it past there and you're in the clear, but not for long.

That low, muffled sound of speeding traffic is nothing compared to when you're finally face-to-bumper with it. Taxi cabs run in and out of slow-moving nine-to-fivers and make turns on a dime. Not even Michael Knight with his trusty car, K.I.T.T., could hold a torch to those foreign devils behind the wheels. My immediate move of self-preservation was to make it to the island in the middle of the three-ring circus. After several narrow escapes I found myself in the middle of neon-lit hell. Where Satan was, I couldn't say, but his influence was obvious.

On the island that once was the sight of that all too infamous sailor-kissing-nurse photo, I strained my neck to take in my surroundings. I wasn't too sure where the buildings ended and where the sky began. The notorious conjoining corner of Times Square stood before me in all its horrific glory. What started with a pink bulb ad for Yahoo! moved up to a news screen that displayed the stock exchange numbers for the day. Those figures might as well have been written in Swahili, because there was no chance I would ever understand them.

Above the Pepsi logo, beyond the Discover Card plug, laid dormant the location of the New Year's Eve Diamond Ball. For as long as I could remember, ringing in the new year always meant watching Dick Clark, who I am convinced had died off long before his official expiration date, being replaced by a cybernetic replica, counting down the final minute before the ticker-tape fell from the heavens. A slight feeling of light-headedness overtook me for a moment, but I chalked it up to lack of proper food and my unplanned withdrawal from narcotics. Baby aspirin might've even helped, but without any strollers in plain sight, I knew I'd have to grin and bear it.

When the feeling of nausea came up, I tried taking my eyes off the towering inferno of "Eat At Joe's" advertisements, but I was only to be struck with the obnoxious, golden arches of god-like proportions that by all means could've stretched three city blocks. The McDonaldization of America had reached Times Square and the great obesity crisis of the early 21st century was just beginning. Right next to them stood a fifty-foot tall M&M, the red one, milk chocolate. For a minute I thought I almost heard him whisper straight at me, "I'll melt in your mouth." If I had survived living in Penn Station's bathroom without anyone's "chocolate" melting in my mouth then things were looking up for me. Sad as it sounds.

Without my having realized it, the light had turned red and a sudden influx of pedestrians forced me into their collective. I found myself being shuffled from my safe haven towards Toys R' Us. When Dante was describing his seven circles of the underworld, he had no idea that some sick, sadistic CEO would turn it into the country's largest toy store. Through the spinning doors I went, which continuingly scare the crap out of me, and I finally became jealous of psych-ward patients who are jacketed and kept in small quarters away from people.

Children ran around me like I wasn't even there. Tyrannosauruses stood erect, roaring horrible sounds towards me. As I stumbled away from the indoor Jurassic Park, I somehow managed to discover Candy Land. Since then, I have never been able to look at a single piece of confectionary without the image of a large, green, hairy plumb-plucking creature appearing before me. Not wanting to make a scene and get locked up, I knew I had to make my way out of that cesspool of plastic.

The shakes began when I finally fell back onto the sidewalk. I *had* to find Veps, there was no question about it, but there was no possible way in which to do that in my current state of being. Times Square is one dandy of a trip, especially if you're tripping, but the fact of the matter was that I was nowhere near any higher state of being. After browsing the Virgin Megastore out of sheer boredom, I came out to the street and saw him.

There he was, Ricky "Veps" Donnardo, standing there all cool and collected. He hadn't changed physically all that much: skinny, clean-shaven, but with this really homo-looking haircut, think they call it a faux-hawk. Anyway, there he was, in ripped jeans wearing a Nirvana t-shirt. When I walked up to him, he just looked at me with business on his mind. "What's good, my man? What can I do for you?"

"Veps," I said, using the secret nickname of our schooldays, "it's me, Ash. Ash Grishin."

"Ash?" He looked puzzled after hearing his nickname and mine.

"High school. Ms. Argy's English class. I was the one who got her skirt to rip clean off her by hammering those tiny nails into her desk."

"Argy? Ya, ya! The one with that ass we all wanted to grab hold of and squeeze 'til she'd cry!"

"Ya, bro, her!" I saw that he remembered.

"Ash, shit, man!" His connecting synapses were giving off sparks. "Holy fuck. What the bunk you doing here?"

"Got into town less than a week ago. Been looking for you."

"Well, goddamn, son! Us two are gonna have one hell of a time tonight! Listen, here's what we're gonna do. I still got some 'usuals' scheduled to pick up, so come back in about an hour. Good times to come! Woo, buddy!"

I left Veps and found some little diner called Spoonz. With my last bit of change, I bought an order of fries with a side of gravy. I didn't have enough for cheese, but I did scrounge up enough for a cola. Waiting there on my stool, I glanced around the place. It was a typical diner void of any kind of elegance. The light fixtures were old; they flicked like the ones you'd find on an old subway car, not as bad, but the similarities were there. The counter was long, wrapped all the way around the place. There were booths laid out along the windows. I saw some couples, but mostly a lot of guys, just sitting alone.

Seeing them made me think of my old man. I hardly ever thought about him, but my head suddenly was filled with him. His name was Tom, not Thomas, just Tom, plain and simple. He left eight years earlier when I was thirteen. Most of my bad habits, boozing and drugs specifically, I got from watching him. His best friend, Jack Daniels, and him were out on the town almost every night it seemed. Took a toll on my mom. Two of them fought all the time, but he never hit her, never even made an attempt. I guess even alcoholics have principles to live by.

Alcoholic. Was that what I was becoming? No, I don't think so. Beer and liquor were big parts of my life, but to say I had a drinking problem would've been stretching it. Drugs, now I was faithfully addicted to them. Dad smoked pot, just a little, but got hooked on painkillers after a rear-ender broke his arm. When he left, I swore I'd never be like him, but the sorry part was that I was farther down that road a lot more than I would have liked to admit. Addiction to anything can screw your life up, either very quickly, or slow and agonizingly.

If my dad was in the city, I hadn't a clue. On that stool, my few strong memories of the guy came to the forefront. There were two things I remembered very well. One was bad, the other good. The bad one had to deal with when I was nine. Back then, I had been on a recreational soccer team. We were the Stingers, wearing black and yellow uniforms to mimic the appearance of a little swarm. It had been a Thursday night in April, and we had practice from five to seven. We did our drills then scrimmaged. When we were all wrapped up for the evening, I sat there, waiting. Dad had promised to pick me up as soon as practice was over then go for ice cream. I waited until it got dark out, but there was no sign of him or his blue pick-up truck.

When it became apparent that I'd been forgotten yet again, I started on a three-mile walk home. Before the first mile had been finished, it started raining. I walked alongside that old road for over two hours until I made it to my front door. Mom took one look at me and freaked out. She undressed me and wrapped me up in warm blankets. When Dad got home, of course drunk, the two of them went at it for over an hour. Dad broke a lamp against the wall and left. He came back after the weekend was over. I never did get that ice cream.

Our good time together was one of those *Leave it to Beaver* father and son moments. One day, at the junkyard, when I was eleven, I found an entire mountain-bike, albeit in several pieces, with most of the parts missing. Never underestimate the possibilities of shifting through a garbage dump. I had a friend once, Stanny Jones, find this little old metal statuette that he ended up getting five hundred big ones for. The bike wasn't worth anything, but I still brought it home with me. With no clue of what I was doing, I found myself in the garage with a jigsaw puzzle, the finished product eventually being the bike.

Don't know what possessed him to help, but when the old man took notice of what I was trying to do, he walked right into the garage, smiling. We drove to the hardware store to pick up the pieces that were missing in action. Two of us spent the weekend putting that bike together. This was the only weekend I can remember when Dad hadn't touched a drink; his mind was preoccupied on the task at hand. Mom was happy. She made her boys food and brought out sodas. For one weekend, we were a family. When Monday morning came, I rode my bike to school. Guess it was fitting that the day he left, the son-of-a-bitch ran the thing over as he backed that blue pick-up out of the driveway.

My attention turned back to the waitress. She was a sweet old lady, probably had her share of kicks in her time. Her name was Flora. Silver lay where possibly lush jet black hair once grew. Eyes were brown, and in those few minutes we shared, Flora had been more of a grandmother to me than I had allowed my own to be. With a smile, she dropped my fries right in front of me. Now those greasy potatoes were just outstanding. Combined with the brown gravy, I was in heaven. The cola, which happened to be of the cherry persuasion, put the icing on the cake. When my fingers were licked clean, I threw my money on the counter. I knew I'd be short a few dollars, so I waited until Flora went into the back before walking out of there.

The night air was warm. I knew my little evening of fun was going to be interesting. Veps was where I had left him. He came up to me, flashing that big broad smile of his. With a slap on the shoulder, he laughed, saying, "Oh, man! Can't believe you're here! Well, I got my business for the night taken care of over here. It's time we got our drink on. You ever been to the city before? No? Don't worry none. We got the finest dope, and I got me tabs at all the best bars from downtown to uptown!"

We hopped into a cab that took us far enough away from the lights and tourists. We were in Veps' world. I stepped out of the cab; the sign was in old neon, Elroy's, plain and simple. Veps threw some bills at the cabby, put his arm around me, and we walked in. White Lion, hair metal, was blasting on the jukebox. Smoke filled the place, and I'm fairly certain I was picking up the subtle scent of marijuana.

Some people sat at the bar, while others stood in secluded groups. Tables were scattered around the place, and there was a tiny dance floor being utilized by a small number of people.

When we got up to the bar, Veps started us off with two shots of Cuervo, then he had to hit the head. I leaned against the bar, my left elbow resting on a soggy coaster. These were my kind of people, just looking for a good time. There was one girl though, just sitting at a table by herself. She had brown hair, long, a little past her shoulder, and snow-white skin. I couldn't immediately tell, but her eyes were hazel, little things that I just happened to notice. Right before I was about to go talk to her, Veps shot back into the room. "Woo, buddy, did that piss feel good! My God that needed to happen! Just blazed in there, too." He held an unlit blunt. "Try this when you head to the toilet, some Bluff, it'll be religious!"

"Thanks, bro. Yo, that girl over there, the one by herself, you know her?"

"Oh, her. Name's Marci, cute thing, close to forty, maybe over, but tight in all the right places. I'd stay clear of that one. Her language is the green kind."

"What is she, a hooker?"

"Hooker's an ugly word. Let's just say her time is valuable. I've never seen her with anyone who couldn't pay her rent. Just trouble if ya ask me. Now, come on, let's down a few more shots, this time Jäger, then you should go and spark that stick up!"

Three shots, and blunt later, I was wrecked. Veps was a marathon man in the world of binge drinking. He was untouched by the stuff and functioning fine. Elroy's was crowded to capacity by midnight. For a Monday night, I was astounded, and no one looked ready to call it quits. Music was blasting, and Veps walked up with two people, Christie and Mike. To say these two were a couple is pushing it, more like fuck buddies who shared a place sometimes, no real commitment or attachment. Situations like that never last very long, but to each his own.

Veps introduced us all, and we ended up bullshitting for over an hour. Mike was an electrician, but private, no union membership. He worked for some old timer up in Yonkers. This guy seemed crazy, even to me, which says a lot. It was plain to see he enjoyed smoking crack; a couple of his teeth were missing. Made sense to me why he kept sucking up to Veps, he wanted the good stuff at a low price.

Christie, now she was one of the finest things the trailer park ever produced. She couldn't have been more than eighteen. Whether or not she was still in high school, I never asked. Her hair was dirty blonde, freckles scattered across her face, but her tits, man, woo, let me tell you, they were melon-shaped and natural. Most of the time she spoke, my eyes were fixated on those orbs.

Veps kept having drinks brought over, and I started getting worried; I didn't have cash on me anymore, just a backpack hanging on the chair. "Don't worry about the bill," Veps said, reassuring me. "This is your night out with me! Besides, I've been coming to this place for two years now and I ain't paid for a thing! Nutty Tony, behind the bar, takes care of me, while I keep his nasty little dope habit going."

"Nice little gig you got going on," I said.

After a few more drinks, Veps pulled me aside. "Ya, man, so whatcha think about a little Christie over there? Nice little ass to go along with those jam-bags. I'd like to motorboat them until my lips go chapped. Man, I've been itching to get her."

"Won't your boy, Mike, get pissed off?"

"Please, he ain't my boy. He's not even a good customer. Frequent, yes, but let me ask ya, would you like a taste of that sweet little thing?"

"I don't know, man. Doesn't seem to me like she'll be up for something like that."

"Nonsense! Come on, just look at those fun bags."

Against my better judgment, due to the pressure Veps was putting on me, I said, "Hey, I'm up for anything, I guess."

"That's what I like to hear, kid!"

Veps took off for another round and brought Mike with him. I sat back down next to Christie. There was an awkward silence before she asked, "So where ya from?"

"Delaware, outside of Dover. How 'bout you?"

"Upstate, but I ain't been back up there in over a year. Mike takes care of me real good. We'll get married one day soon. I just know it."

The guys came back with beer, and Veps, whispering, said, "Mike and I came up with an arrangement. I stock him for a week at half the regular price and we get Christie tonight."

"Ya, but you think *she'll* be okay with your little arrangement?"

"That's what the alcohol is for, my boy!" Veps said, crying out with a sinister laugh.

By the time we were set to leave Elroy's, I was blitzed, Mike was dying for a fix, and Veps showed minor signs of being tipsy. He truly was an alcoholic god. Christie, well, she was gone, not one ounce of her tiny body was sober. In the final hour before we left, Veps fed her a couple of beers then whipped out the cherry-flavored schnapps, and that was it for Christie. We all stepped out onto the street. The city was still buzzing. Crazy town, New York City. Veps told me we were going to head back to Mike's apartment, which wasn't too far, so we walked, well, more like stumbled, to it.

The building wasn't glamorous by any means. It was an old brick, probably not renovated since the 1930s. Mike said the doorman had taken sick earlier that week, but there was no chance that building ever had a doorman. We climbed the stairs to the fifth floor, which was no easy task in the state we were in. The apartment was nice, not extravagant, but nice nonetheless. There were two bedrooms, a bath, kitchen, and living room. When we were all settled, I looked to Veps for our next move. He passed some powder to Mike, who took it up quicker than I'd ever seen. I'm sure, though, the rest would be in crack form, but at our present state of being, him handling an open flame wouldn't have been such a good idea.

Veps made the gesture to Mike, who led Christie into their bedroom, the other one, it turned out, was full of boxes filled with Mike's stuff. I was impressed with how Mike's addiction superseded any feelings he might have been harboring for his chick. His only condition was that he'd have to stay in the room with us. That rule was cool with Veps; he didn't mind an audience. I, on the other hand, didn't know just how comfortable with all this I was, but continued going along with it.

Mike flipped on his Super Nintendo and sat on the floor at the end of the bed, playing it. Now I have already mentioned how wasted Christie was when we left the bar and our walk hadn't sobered her up one damn bit. She was lying there on her back, right on the bed, all dazed out. Veps didn't waste any time. He unzipped his pants, whipped out his dick, and shoved it right into that broad's mouth. Since she had no idea where she was, she simply started servicing him, which made me feel a bit more at ease.

Since everything had gotten going, I would've gladly waited my turn, but as Veps skull fucked away on Christie, he turned his head to me. He motioned for me to start up on her. Something inside me thought not to do anything, to just stand there and watch. The booze and weed were in control, though. So with *Super Mario World* music playing in the background, I crawled up on the bed. What I proceeded to do next I knew wasn't at all a good idea, but I'll admit I was horny, and Veps is a hard person to say no to. I pulled off Christie's pants, at first halfway, but when I realized she made no effort to stop me, I took them clean off of her. She had on this little pink thong with tiny hearts on it. I cautiously slipped that piece of string off her. I remember being impressed by how neatly trimmed her pussy was, just a little landing strip right above the lips.

By the time I had come face-to-beaver, Veps had positioned himself fully over Christie. His hands were holding tightly to the headboard, and he was fully thrusting his piece in and out of her mouth. My initial choice would've been to start drilling the chick, but I didn't have any rubbers on me. There was no telling what she might or might not have had, so there was no shot of my cock going into her. Veps could take his chances, but not me. I decided to get my kicks by finger blasting her. I used my right pointer and middle fingers to do the job. She was pretty loose. When I started working her over, you could hear the moaning coming out of her cock-filled mouth. Dumb tramp was so drunk she couldn't comprehend how Mike, whose dick I'm sure she thought was down her throat, could be making her blow him while fingering her pussy.

This girl was pulsating, I mean really twisting. Her vagina was totally soaked. After fifteen minutes of fun, Mike, who had just lost his last life on the game, I guess got horny listening to his girl. He dropped the controller and climbed up on the bed. Three guys and one chick is not my idea of a good time, so I took my fingers out, wiped them off on the comforter, and told Mike she was all his. Crazy fool shoved his dick right into Christie; he was pumping her hardcore. This is where things kind of went south. Everything sort of clicked for the girl as she began gyrating to the piece between her legs.

Christie's buzz kill came when, well, when both Veps and Mike busted their loads into her two occupied orifices. Some kind of brain spark must have happened, because Christie started screaming. I guess she realized that not even Mike could possibly have two dicks. When she spit out the cum in her mouth and tried wiping her vagina, the frenzy began. Whatever she could grab, she threw at us. We flew out of the room, slamming the door behind us. Christie was screaming bloody murder at Mike. Veps was laughing his ass off. "My God, my God, Mikey boy, hell of a night! We'll leave you to tidy her up. See me this week for your stuff."

Mike gave an awkward smile and we let ourselves out. It was 3:30am, and my high was dropping. The alcohol was settling down into my system. The morning hangover was pretty much guaranteed.

Veps hailed a cab. We were inside the car when he asked where he could drop me off. "I got no place, man," I said. "I don't have a cent to my name right now."

"Uh-huh, mhm, I see, yes, sir, I see," he said, mumbling on, "it's plain to see how to handle this. Driver," he gave him his address in the Village. "Ash, friend, you're crashing at my pad. I won't take 'no' for an answer."

Of course, there was no way I was turning down the offer. The long nights of sleeping at the station of all stations was not something I had any desire to continue. Our cab ride wasn't long. We got out of the car and took the lift up to the studio loft that Veps called home. Place was big, makeshift walls separated the bedroom from the rest of it. Veps grabbed a briefcase and sat on his sofa. He opened it up, placed a bit of coke on the table. Next, he proceeded to make lines with a joker's card he always kept on him in his wallet. I must say that I always thought myself an expert in the art of line making, but Veps was masterful.

When he felt he had done an acceptable job, he moved over one spot. "Come on, man, a nice line before lights out is the best way to secure a proper dream state. Now sit down so you can enjoy the only decent export the fine country of Columbia has ever produced!"

I'm a self-respecting addict, so I plopped my bony bottom next to Veps. He took out two one-hundred dollar bills. "Gotta take it up with good old Benny, ya know? Ah it's just an arrogant thing, but, oh, feels so good!"

We rolled up the bills together, but he was much faster at snorting. It's not that I didn't know what I was doing, not at all, spent years perfecting my technique. I've only got one good clear nostril if I'm lucky. Up the coke went, and, it felt good. Veps was right, one hell of a nightcap. When the clock hit five in the morning, Veps called it a night. He wandered into his room and crashed. I didn't last very long by myself. Without much effort, I laid my head down and 'assed out cold. My first night out with Veps had come to an end, but not the smell of white trash upon my finger.

Morning came and went. It was sometime around two in the afternoon when I finally woke up. There was a note from Veps taped to my forehead. It said to eat whatever I found in the kitchen and that he'd be back by four. Food was the last thing on my mind. My brain pounded around in my head, but I'd had worse hangovers, and more were sure to come. What I desperately needed was a shower. I could *feel* the stench of a week's worth of sleeping in a toilet come over me, though the scent of Christie's pussy juice still lingered as well. Couldn't tell which was worse. I gave myself a scrub down, almost used up the entire bar of soap. Veps had some blue shampoo, but no conditioner, so my tattered long hair would have to go another day without the proper care. Sometimes it feels like I predated the metrosexual.

There wasn't a great food selection. Seeing as how I'd just recently awoken, my immediate choice was cereal. Fruit Loops were the only choice, and that was all right with me. I should've known better than to eat, because it turned out that the milk had recently spoiled. After my frenzied round of shitting out and throwing up the curdled dairy, along with whatever alcohol hadn't already joined with my system, I took yet another shower. Oh, and I lit a candle I found, assuming that it was there for when Veps used it on bitches to come off as romantic.

I watched television for a while until Veps came back. He was dressed in a suit and tie. This confused me very much, because I had been unaware of any possible office-type job he could have had. Who would hire him to do anything but push? Obviously, I questioned him about the getup he was wearing.

"Ha, ha, man, I didn't tell you? Ya, I got a corner office downtown with a secretary I bang every hour on the hour." He smiled, almost bursting out laughing. "Just messing with you, man. This little diddy is what I wear when I do business at the Trade Center. With this thing on nobody even gives me a second look." It made perfectly good sense to me.

Veps explained his entire technique in detail to me; he must've been either bored or really impressed with himself. I think it was a combination of the two. He'd get down to the Trade Center at 8:00am. Over the course of the first three hours, he kept "appointments" with his customers. The way he spoke down there was nothing like the way he spoke regularly. He said he added a long-winded, and increasingly annoying, monotone sound to his speech pattern that blended in well with the suits around the place. At noon, he broke for lunch. There was some Chinese place in the area he was obsessed with. Once 1:00pm hit, Veps was back in business, and onto the second tower.

"And, because I look and sound the part, no one's the wiser." Veps said, beaming. "Sweet lil' deal I got going, huh?"

"How often do you, um, conduct business down there?" I asked.

"Oh, I'm down there once a week, usually a Tuesday. One day more is too many and paranoid mooks start asking stupid questions."

The conversation shifted next to my current, or lack thereof, living and monetary situation. I had nothing planned out, and I told that to Veps. He lit a joint. After a minute of walking around the loft smoking, he snapped his fingers. There was a diner close by whose owner was a customer of Veps'. When he had finished the joint, he took me to the place. I was hoping to have found a job a tad bit above the level of a diner, but beggars can't be choosers. Veps was a good guy to me, why exactly, I didn't know, probably because we had shared some childhood experiences only slackers remember.

The diner was a five-block walk from Veps' place. Sign on the front said Pappy's 24-Hour Eats. Fantastic, I thought, I'm going to get the graveyard shift deal. I had done the midnight run once back home, and it sucked. Veps told me to wait outside while he went to speak to Pappy. Standing there with a cigarette, I could see Veps talking to Pappy through the window. How a place like that cropped up in the Village, I'll never know, but shit like that flies into my mind and out quickly. Five minutes after having finished the cig, Veps came strolling back out to the street.

"Okay, okay, everything is squared away with Pappy. I told him you were my cousin who just moved into town. Said you were a decent guy, wouldn't steal nothin' from the place. You got work Mondays through Fridays, but I ain't even told you the best part. Since last night was so wicked of a time, we gotta have the nights for more good times. You're working the day shifts, washing dishes, but he said he might even move you up to waiter if he likes you. It's a minimum-wager, but that'll be a good amount in your pocket."

"What about a place to stay?" I asked.

"Stay? Man, you gonna crash at my place. I won't take 'no' for an answer. Sleep right on that couch, better yet, open it up, it's a bed, too, 'case any lil pretty things follow you home."

"That's great, bro, thank you." I said. "Work starts tomorrow, I guess?"

"Yessiree, but tonight, tonight, we get our kicks off again!"

I couldn't argue with the arrangement Veps had proposed. He wasn't looking for rent provided that I cleaned up after myself and helped buy the food. Things were coming together pretty well for me. Only thing I was dreading was work. I'm lazy, I hate working, especially doing menial labor like dishwashing. Wish I could live in a world where money meant jack. It'd be a happier place, believe you me. Kept my complaining to myself though, didn't want to make Veps think that I was being ungrateful.

When we got back to the loft, Veps tossed me some pot and a Dutchie. He went to get some shuteye while I sat on the couch. I'm not too sure what kind of weed he'd given me, but I didn't really care. I stripped the cigar, laying out the pieces down on the coffee table. Worst part of putting a blunt together is licking the dried tobacco strips, because they make your tongue crust up. Since the end result of rolling is always a rewarding experience, I continued. Right way to do it is not to completely soak the strips in your saliva, but don't just give them a quick swiping either. Trick is to imagine you're licking envelopes.

Once you've got the strips ready just drop the right amount of weed down onto the starting one. Don't think you're out of the woods just yet, because rolling is where the real skills are shown. More or less, you're born with the ability to perform the perfect roll, although if one pays close enough attention, it can be picked up. Soft and gentle hands play a large part in the process. Just when you're ready to secure at an end point, you squeeze, while being mindful of your applied pressure. Following these words will leave you in a good place.

Whenever I light up, I go through the same thing. As I hold the unlit blunt in my hand, my mind spins about with all the possibilities that could happen once I'd spark up. After I play down all those crazy notions, I simply light the little sucker. The first hit is always the special one. That first long drag tells you whether or not you've succeeded in rolling properly. I'm ashamed and embarrassed for those of whom I have seen light up only to watch their blunts fall apart due to negligence. Poor dumb bastards.

So once the first hit was completed, and the blunt seen as secured, I went into my building high. What I was used to smoking was nothing compared to the stuff Veps was toting. The weed he'd given me the night before was good, but what I had there on the couch was outstanding.

I must have fallen asleep after the blunt was finished because the next thing I knew, I was being shaken. My eyes opened, the sun was down, it was 8:30pm, and Veps was in full-blown party mode. "All right, all right, all right! Tonight we are getting paid and laid. Well, maybe just laid; ain't much scheduled for tonight. We're gonna get fucked up, son, no doubt. Get up, up, come on! Whole city is waiting for you."

No one could argue with him when he was in his nightlife rage. We left the loft to get something to eat. Veps kept raving about some Mexican place, so we hopped a cab over to it. Its name was Poncho Villa's and was a little hole-in-the-wall place. We walked inside and sat down. The place was dark, and the lights they did have on flickered, a lot, which kind of annoyed me. There weren't many tables. The bar seemed to be the main feature. Posted up along the walls were pictures of the place's namesake, ole Villa himself, the great firebrand.

Our waitress was a cute little thing straight out of Mexico City. Her name was Maria. She couldn't have been older than twenty-five, but her age wasn't what was on my mind. Her breasts were well-rounded spheres of brown beauty, and her ass met the same description. Hair black as the night with a voice so soft that, for a quick minute, I saw myself with her forever. What caught me off guard about her were her eyes. Not brown as one would have assumed, but piercing sky blue, a total shock to say the least. More than likely there had been some gringo blood mixed in her family, but goddamn if it mattered to me if she hadn't been Mexicali-pure.

My little Maria brought out tortilla chips and salsa. I've never tasted better in my life. This concoction was no store-bought crap, but rather homemade, best ever and spicy as all hell. Veps put in an order for some margaritas and made Maria assure him the tequila would be Jose Cuervo. I laugh whenever I'm in a Mexican-type place. The menu lists over a dozen kinds of meals, but when you get right down to it, they're all the same. They're always some form of rolled-up tortilla, a load of beans, and some kind of meat. Burritos, tacos, enchiladas, the list goes on for like a mile.

The drinks came, and Veps had decided we should get a platter of assorted tacos. As I poured in my tequila, I ingrained in my mind the sight of Maria's south-cheeks bouncing up and down, opposite of one another. I kept my thoughts about Maria from Veps. A part of me knew that had I told him our waitress drove me wild, he'd come up with some scheme for the two of us to get her. With that in mind, I kept silent about it; I'd never share Maria with him or anyone.

The margaritas were good, so we each had three of them. When the food came out, a mountain of heartburn was laid out before us. That was some of the best food I've ever eaten. You've really got to hand it to Mexicans, because they can cook amazingly. Not just their own ethnic food either, they're very versatile in the kitchen. I've seen them prepare Italian, Asian, fast food; it's an endless scroll of cuisines. It makes me feel bad when they have to smuggle themselves across the Rio Grande. Doesn't seem fair that we'll let in any Canadian into this country even if they're a self-loathing, wife-beating, pedophile, but God forbid a Mexican father wants to find a minimum-wage job cleaning toilets just to send the money back to his family. The grandiose United States: In Hypocrisy We Trust.

During our feeding, Veps kept raving on about how great of a city New York was and how he couldn't have found a better place to make a life for himself. I asked him how exactly he'd come into the good fortune he was in. He took a big gulp of his drink and told me, which I'll never be able to forget. Veps had decided on NYC after dropping out of high school, because he knew it to be a city where big things could happen for a person. Those buildings, the people, the city's history in general all represented to him the ever present, but usually hard to touch, American Dream. Like poor Willy Loman, Veps assured himself that the Big Apple was his Treasure Island, but unlike the old salesman, he eventually found what made him happy.

When he first arrived on the island, Veps had enough money to stay in some dump hotel for a week. With the way he spends though, he was out on the street within two days. On his fourth homeless night, he came upon a row of young male hustlers standing outside one of the many porno-houses that call Manhattan home. He bummed a cigarette off of one named Shemp, who, according to Veps, resembled nothing of the famous Stooge he took his name from. With no place to go, he just stood there until a green Cadillac pulled up.

"So this sixty-something-year-old redhead asks me how's things. I tell her bad 'cause that was the truth. She says her name's Greta, but it could've been anything. I asked what I could do for her, and right up front she told me she could use a good fucking. Now I'm not one to simply jump into the car of a complete stranger, but when she flashed five hundred big ones, I wasn't turning it down.

"Goddamn if that car's heat didn't feel outstanding! The whole ride over to her place was a wild trip. Old bitch kept reaching for my dick, telling me she wanted me ready by the time we got to our destination. All that was on my mind were the green bills she'd stuffed back into her purse. So we get the car parked, and the place of hers is in some fancy little high-rise overlooking Central Park. Poor dumb doorman tipped his hat to me by sheer force of habit, which more than likely pissed him off to high holy heaven. Now her place had the look and feel of a museum. It crossed my mind once or twice to knock the broad out and run off with whatever I could pawn, but I figured I'd ride the train to a complete stop.

"Sweet old Greta, who had on way too much make-up and a yellow dress that had probably seen the Johnson administration, told me to stay put and that she'd be right back. When she left, I moseyed on over to the mantle: pictures of kids, grandkids, and a wedding shot of her and her 'soul mate.' I'm not one for shock, but the next thing I know, there's Greta, completely naked! Up until then, I'd never seen anyone older than twenty-seven nude, but she wasn't half bad. Her skin was wrinkly, but her tits didn't sag, definitely store bought if ya know what I'm saying.

"Greta walked over to me and told me to undress. I complied. When she took notice of my limp dick, she sucked me like a Hoover, top ten best blowjob I've ever gotten. We walked over to her white sofa where I proceeded to finger her old, worn-out, but unexpectedly shaven, pussy. After a couple of orgasms, I asked her if she wanted to go into the bedroom. With a sharp tone, she explained that the bed she and her husband shared was no place for the two of us, so the sofa would be the spot. Didn't bother me none, sofa, bed, floor, I didn't care."

Before he went on, Veps downed another drink, this time a Corona as we had moved on from margaritas. He let out a beer belch that reeked of tacos and continued. "So I ask Greta if she wants me to shove it in her, and she bends over with her ass in the air. Before I made a move, she informs me that shoving it into her vagina would be useless. According to her that late husband of hers had done her pretty hard over the thirty-something years they had been married, so that made her vagina too loose to enjoy anything except the custom-made vibrator she had. I then took notice of her freshly lubricated asshole.

So without being asked outright, I rode the Hershey Highway and I did it raw!"

I almost threw up my dinner, but Veps kept laughing through his story. "Her and I spent over three hours butt-fucking, and when she felt satisfied, I was allowed a shower to clean up. When I had finished and dried off, I found her fully dressed with cash in hand. We said our goodbyes, and I took a cab back to the hustlers spot in front of The Horny Toad."

What Veps said next I never would have guessed could've happened. He said it in a calm voice. It turned out that Shemp and some of the other guys hadn't appreciated Veps taking a potential client from them. They lured him into an alley, there were four of them including Shemp, and they worked Veps over pretty bad. He got punched, kicked, and, what's worse, raped by all four of them. They hadn't gotten his money, though; he'd hidden it in his sock. As he lay bleeding from his face and rectum, someone from The Horny Toad had found him and brought him inside.

"Well, it turned out," Veps said, "the place was owned by a guy called Boss Denham who just happened to have been a bigwig in the world of narcotics distribution, if ya catch my drift, and he took a liking to me. Helped me get fixed up and made me a dealer, said I had a knack at communicating with people. So ya see, Ash, my boy, I started out the night homeless and ended up employed!" Veps had a funny way of looking at things.

When we left Poncho Villa's, Veps held out his arm to stop me. As I took my final glimpse of Maria, the next thing that crossed my vision were blotters of acid. "This will send our night up a couple of notches," Veps said.

Those little patches of magic held so many possibilities, none of them good, of course. I'd done acid only once. It was the summer after high school at the beach. A bunch of us were sitting there in the sand just bumming under the sun. Someone, a guy whose name escapes me, though it may have been Greg, decided that we needed a different kind of high. From his personal stash, he handed out the acid. I tripped balls and somehow ended up stark naked on the Dairy Barn roof. After I found some pants, I had a morning milkshake. So in retrospect, it hadn't been all that bad.

Ignoring commonsense, I threw the memories of my one and only trip to the back of my mind. With one swift motion, I ingested the acid, allowing its power to take me wherever it felt I should go. The night from five minutes after that is completely distorted when I look back. I will do my best to describe the events of it, which saw the invention of a new sex game, but leaving out the obvious things I know to have not been real, such as the two-headed blue pig Veps swore was following him. Anyway, after the restaurant, we cruised over to a bar called Frederick's Pub.

The place was small, but there was a decent amount of people. There was an Irish theme to it. The bar had been designed after those old-time bars you'd never find back in Dublin. A live band was performing some crazy native mick music, and I'll be damned if I could understand any of it. Of course, it didn't help that through my eyes, at the time, I saw the musicians as leprechauns. Now that I think about it, I may have even asked them about their lucky charms. Acid, nutty.

Veps and I started drinking immediately. There were shots flying through the air at one point, I believe. Two girls kept staring at us. By no means were they hot, but in the altered state of consciousness we were experiencing, it hardly mattered. Doing them justice, though, the two had some kind of drunken cuteness going for them. It may have been their voices. I've always felt it cruel for a girl to have a beautiful voice but nothing else going on for her. Their bodies, those were credible, but their faces could've been improved with brown bags over them. I might be being overly critical, but, oh well.

I alerted Veps to the chicks eyeing us, and his mind made itself up. He ordered a pitcher, and we brought it over to the girls' table. A conversation was going on, but all I could hear was blah, blah, blah, and at one point I may have even said "blah" out loud. One girl's name was Tammy, and her companion just happened to be her older cousin, Kate. They were two dumb Midwest small-towners who were in the city for a week's vacation.

Tammy was tall, we're talking Amazon here. Had we found an all-night women's wrestling ring, she'd of won the title. Tits were nice, ass was fat, but not much else, I guess. She wasn't fat, but skinny would've been giving her too much. Any lesbian would've been happy to munch on her carpet. Kate was a brunette like Tammy. We soon realized that her right leg was shorter than her left, not by much, but enough that caused her to walk with a limp.

At one point, Veps pulled me aside. "Yo, man," he said, flubbing over his words. I guess not even he could win over the acid. "You wanna get these girls?"

"I don't know, bro, I think we could do better."

"Ya, but look around you. There ain't much action going on in here."

Through my fogged-up mind, I said, "Your call." Thinking back, I probably should've said "no."

Veps made the suggestion that the four of us to head back to the girls' hotel. They were, of course, against the idea, but Veps' dick basically had a mind of its own. I didn't know he had done it until the day after but in the last round the girls got, Veps had thrown in one blotter of acid each. It was only a matter of time from there on out. Within the span of ten minutes, Kate's pupils were dilated and Tammy's soon followed. Had we been any kind of clean, Veps and I would've probably screwed the hairy bartender before even thinking of touching those broads, but you work with what's thrown at you.

An hour after the girls drank the acid-laced beer, they were tripping hardcore. Tammy started dancing on the bar, much to the horror of the establishment's patrons. When she fell on her ass, I suggested we should all go back to their hotel. Slight problem arose with that plan; neither of the girls could remember the name of the place where they were staying. Veps heard this, and the wheels in his head turned at high speed. He shoveled us into a cab, and the next I knew, we were outside a place called The Teacup Hotel.

This hotel was what you would figure it to be: one of those pay-by-the hour joints. Its frequent clientele included middle-aged Wall Street hotshots who brought along their scantily-clad escorts for a night away from the trophy wives who had bore their children, but just couldn't seem to lose that extra weight they'd gained from the pregnancy. Being quite blunt, wives who had lost their luster. That's who Veps and I had at our sides, two sluts with no shine, an Amazon and a gimp. The elderly fellow in the cage knew Veps. I was fairly certain Veps had used the facility before. My theory turned fact when the guy asked Veps if he wanted his usual room. With key in hand, we went upstairs to room 214.

Had there been a black light in my pocket, I probably wouldn't have stayed in that place. There was one bed, a T.V., the essentials. No coffeemaker, though. The girls were giggling so hard that I wanted to slap them in the mouths until they'd shut up. Seeing as how at that point I didn't think I could raise my arm, I refrained from any kind of sudden movement. Veps had made it clear he wanted Kate the gimp. Tammy had been holding onto me, so it was all good. Something about a big mirror in the bathroom made Veps drag us all in there.

It was big enough for the four of us to fit our reflections in. What Veps was about to suggest, I would've never guessed would come out of his mouth, no matter how much was in his system.

"Okay, now listen very, very carefully. I got a little game for us all to play. Now we can see one another in the mirror, so listen closely to the rules. Kate, you're on my team. Tammy, you're with Ash. Girls, now I need complete cooperation from you both. You're both gonna bend over with your hands up over the sink on the counter. Ash, you and I will fuck these two young ladies from behind. You reading me? Picking up what I'm throwing down? First one who finishes loses!"

It took a minute to process everything Veps had just spouted out. By the time I had made sense of it both girls were assuming the position. I, of course, threw my hat into the ring. Tammy had a skirt on, so I didn't have much to remove. Her panties were orange. Pussy was hairy. Veps counted down. I inserted into her, and the game was on. Both girls went from giggling to moaning. Tammy's body flab flapped about while I rammed into her. If I had been having a good time, I no longer could tell. Minutes went by, but I couldn't hold out anymore. I busted a nut inside Tammy, whose legs gave out, bringing us both down onto the tiled floor. Veps declared himself the victor. At that point, I blacked out.

My eyes opened up the next morning only to have two bare breasts staring back at them. I had fallen asleep on the Amazon. We were both naked. She was snoring, obnoxiously. Slowly, I crept off her, found my pants, but the shirt was nowhere in sight. Next thing I knew, Kate came hobbling out of the bathroom, screaming about waking up with a cock in her brown-hole. The noise woke Tammy, and the two started freaking out, because they had no clue where they were or how they ended up naked with two guys without a single used condom in sight.

Veps stumbled out of the bathroom, looking wasted. Kate yelled her head off, but he just laughed at her. Tammy got dressed, and the girls left in a hurry; I'm almost certain tears were coming out of them. Part of me felt like a monster, but just a small part. My warped reasoning was that somehow, since the acid and alcohol had been controlling me, I'd been absolved of all wrongdoing. I sat on the bed, looked at the time, and realized I had to be at work in half an hour.

Working at Pappy's turned out to be one loco experience. My time there saw some of the weirdest people cross my path. Pappy, a big black man whose beard was thicker than a haystack, well, he was a funny old bastard. He used to tell me stories about his life growing up in Harlem. Don't know why he told me things, guess he just liked to talk. And talk he did.

Joe "Pappy" Thompson was born in the home of his parents back in 1946. His mom, Loretta, died giving birth to him. When he told me this, I mentioned how mine had just passed. Tears swelled up in his eyes. Said that everyone used to tell him how much of an angel his mom had been. I think there was a lot of guilt resting on his shoulders. Man had it in his head that he caused his mom's death. Crazy ass, was probably the mid-wife's fault, but I kept my mouth shut when he spoke about his mom.

Pappy's dad's name was Roy. Man drove a bus his entire life. He was a drunk who used to beat on ole Pappy whenever he happened to get in his way. Fathers. Most of them end up messing their kids' lives up more than they help. I think that Pappy loved his father though, no matter what he did to him. It probably had something to do with the fact that the dude was Pappy's only parent. I remember something Pappy said his father had once told him. "No matter how many bum-brownies life plops on you, there's bound to be some turnaround one day."

Our conversations shifted one day to Vietnam. Pappy had been drafted in 1967 into the army. There were thoughts he had before reporting of fleeing to Canada. They were nothing but pipe dreams. I probably would've headed straight for the border, crossed over, and not have given turning back a second thought. Fuck war. War is why the world we live in is so screwed up. Human nature, destroy ourselves, the code our species lives by. We're so stupid, but that's obviously a part of our nature, too. Bunch of ignorant fools.

Pappy reported, got sent to basic training, and finally was thrown straight into the shit. He remembered beer, music, and faces of his friends blown fifty yards away from their bodies. How this man was as stable as he was, I had no idea. During one of our rap sessions, I asked him if he ever actually killed anybody. He wiped some sweat from his bald head and started in. "Well, I tells ya, son, that my old rifle got herself a long workout in them jungles. Some days, the heat was so bad that I could swear a part of me must've died out there in hell. I do remember one day that I never will quite forget. We was patrolling what was supposed to be some abandoned Charlie outpost. Well, them dumb asses up in the choppers evidently weren't paying no attention 'cause when we got there, them rice-loving gooks had us surrounded!

"You could tell they had been caught off guard just like us. Tell ya the truth, both our sides could've maybe talked our ways outta the situation, but in a place like Nam, talk would get ya dead quicker than a slug to the gut. I don't remember who shot first, but it was a blood bath. I got my black booty outta there and into the trees as fast as I could, but one of them slanted-eyed rice eaters followed me.

"Two of us got into it real quick. Got off a couple of shots each then the guy charged me. I pulled out a buck knife from my boot, and when the gook made contact so did the blade. We fell to the ground, and I had the son-of-a-bitch die right on top of me. That night, once my unit's remnants made it back to base, cocaine went up into my nose for the first time. Only thing that would help me sleep after that."

Nice to know Veps, and by then myself, weren't the only ones who enjoyed an evening-closing snort of coke. Pappy came back home in time to close out 1971. His father had died while he'd been gone, but Pappy said it didn't take him long to get over it. After a few years of jobs that brought him nothing but troubles, Pappy pulled together enough money to open up his diner. Since 1978, Pappy's been serving the oddest New York City has had to offer.

The first waitress hired, Justine, was an ebony beauty according to Pappy. The two got together, but it ended two years later when Justine gave birth to a baby girl. Pappy named her after his mother. Quicker than Pappy knew it, baby mama took off on him, but left the kid. The husky-voiced bastard kept the girl and she became his greatest achievement. By the time I'd gotten there at the diner, Loretta was down in Georgetown, studying to be a doctor. Good going for the parents who actually care about the children they bring into the world.

But that name, "Pappy." I always wanted to know where it had come from. I knew he'd been using it long before he was a father. On one of the slower days, I remembered to ask him about it. Story led him back to a day in Vietnam. For all the faults he had, the man was a bit of a neat freak. I imagine that trudging through the mud must have driven him out of his mind. Anyway, it was at his base camp, and his fellow anti-commie commandoes were laying their crap around wherever it fell. Pappy started lecturing them on order and putting things away. Naturally, they dubbed him their surrogate father and obviously the name stuck.

Nicknames. The whole city was full of nicknames. Where I come from taking "Benjamin" and flipping into "Benny" was extreme. There, in the Big Apple, yet another nickname, nobody seemed to want to use their real name. I always wondered what my alias might've been had I been bestowed one. And that's the trick right there. A person can't just make their own nickname, it has to be given to them by someone else. Just try and inform friends you wish to be called something like "Diesel" and if they're intelligent enough, they'll instead refer to you as "Mimi." Voyage on, sailors.

Perhaps the craziest asshole that ever came into Pappy's had to be Eddie Shabeck. He'd come in every day after the lunch crowd had headed on out. Never sat anywhere else but the corner booth. All that extra room gave him space for the books and notepads he would carry around in his backpack. Ate hamburgers, mostly, with fries drowned in ketchup. I've always felt that too much of it takes away the natural flavor of the grease. People, I think, just enjoy unnecessary additions.

Whenever Eddie would come in, nobody ever bothered him. He seemed to be troubled about something. One day, he hurled a coffee cup across the room. It shattered against a wall and Nicole, the waitress who had a nasty habit of shooting up on the job, nearly loafed in her panties when the ceramic pieces went flying about. Pappy hadn't been there. If he had been, I'm sure he'd of cracked Eddie's head open and watched him bleed out.

I walked over to Eddie's booth and saw he was crying a little. "What the hell's the matter with you?"

He wiped his face up with a napkin then looked up at me. "I'm sorry about the cup. I'm just so frustrated. Do you see this? All this? All these books, none of them help me, none of them!"

"Exactly what do you need help for?"

"I'm a writer. I'm a grad student, too. I've been trying to write this novel for three years now! This writer's block's been kicking my ass. Grad school doesn't help either. No one in those classes wants to help one another. You bring in something you think is good, and they tear it a new asshole."

I did my best to get away from him, but Eddie was now on a soapbox with no end in sight. "I have seen the best and worst minds of my generation do nothing with their lives! I have watched them wither into nothingness! How could young minds become so lost at such an early age? This is a question I find myself asking over and over again. Seems to me that something happened to the world a long time ago. To put it bluntly, it changed! Our world, or more specifically, the one before we all arrived, was a better place. Things weren't necessarily more simple, but, rather, things were laid out right in front of you. Nowadays, no one looks out for one another. It's a dog-eat-dog world of backstabbers and phony faces."

If I thought any kind of drug could help this lunatic born of the 70s, I'd of given it to him. This was a different kind of person. This was a man who had seen enough of what's out there. For reasons still unknown, I wanted to hear the rest of his rant. "The Beats weren't like this. They helped one another grow. No Cassady meant no Moriarty! Without the 1950s there'd be no 1960s. Jim Morrison and Hunter S. Thompson could never have existed had their predecessors been selfish. I look now at my contemporaries: the artists, writers, and filmmakers of this so-called 'Indie Generation' and I put my head down. Sorrow fills my extremely crowded mind, and I'm left with even more questions than I had at the start of all of this."

At this point, I actually sat down. Aside from Veps' sex and fart stories back at the loft this, sadly, was the most intelligent conversation I'd been involved in since I had gotten into the city. Most of what this guy was talking about I hadn't a clue as to what any of it meant, but he obviously was uber-passionate about it. Eddie took in a deep breath and kept going. "Nobody cares about the works of others. No one wants to understand their peers' writing. Read aloud your work in a room of people who consider themselves to be writers. The criticism will come down on you like crashing waves!

"'Why didn't you write it like this?' is a question you'll get almost every time. What they're really saying is 'why don't you write exactly as I do?' Where in the hell is the sense in that? Could we enjoy Hemingway, Fitzgerald, or Salinger if they all wrote the same? The reason why we love those authors is because they were very different. This current generation of ours is far too wrapped up in themselves. Most of the time, they're only looking inwards. How can this bullshit continue? This has got to stop. They all need to quit thinking so selfishly. These bastards all too often critique rather than enjoy. I wonder sometimes if I were to take a passage from Kerouac's *Big Sur,* and read it to colleagues of mine, would they rip it apart thinking it was my own work? We're far too critical of one another, because we all want to get to the top first. Hate to bring up the old saying, but it's very lonely at the top of the mountain."

Now after a while of listening to this guy, my opinion of his situation quickly started falling apart. What I had in front of me was a whining little bitch of a boy struggling to be a man. Since the patience that I do have while not high as a fiend is usually thin, it goes without saying that the blow-up came suddenly and unexpectedly. I leaned back, gave the knuckles a crack, and looked him straight in the eye. "Listen, Eddie, you've got to get the jammed tampon out of your vagina and calm down. You're wound so tight that if I were to bend you over, a cork might come shooting out of your asshole. Dude, if you want to be a writer, then quit reading all this. You can read about writing, but if you don't actually do it, nothing's going to happen for you. And as far as your buddies in your classes go, who cares what they think?"

I must've sent the poor tulip for a spin dry, because he sat there speechless as if I had gut checked him full force. No response came. Lord knows I was ready to go if this guy started swinging, but my chance to put him down didn't come. He packed up and walked out in silence. With a little bit of luck, I just might've given him that kick in the hindquarters he desperately needed, without question. Far too many complainers live among us. Not that I didn't agree with him on certain points, but self-loathers make me ill.

It'd been a Tuesday afternoon when this pretty young girl walked into the diner. She looked somewhere in her late teens, but whether or not she was legal, I couldn't decide. Wish these sluts had been growing up during my teenage years. Back when I did the school thing, getting a girl to put on a miniskirt was the most difficult task. These days it seems that a fourteen-year-old can look twenty with little effort. Well, this girl was a member of the Jailbait Club of America, if such an organization truly did exist. Pappy had me bring her order out, and I could tell she'd been crying. Why do all the crazies find me? One of those questions that will never seem to be answered, I suppose. She took her food from me and handed me a note. I felt like I was back in the 7th grade, but I accepted it and walked back into the kitchen. Not going to lie, those few seconds that I held the note unopened drove me nuts.

Once I had settled myself back in the kitchen, I opened the piece of paper up. The girl, who signed her name as "Mallory," was requesting that I meet her in the alley beside the diner once she'd finished her food. I was intrigued but hesitated a little to meet the request. For all I knew, this broad could have had three huge mamalukes out there ready to pounce on me for some money. Against my better judgment, which almost never ends up winning if it hasn't been made obvious already, I let her finish her meal, waited five minutes, and went out the back door into the alley.

I stood up against the wall with a joint I'd been holding onto since the morning. Veps had come into some Thai buds and kept pestering me to try it. As I came to the stick's midway point, Mallory showed up. She looked more distressed than she had inside. I held up the note. "Said you wanted to see me?"

She had on faded blue jeans and a man's oversized white button-down. Her hair was dyed blonde, but brown roots were emerging. With tears building, she looked up at me. "I need some money."

"So would I, but it ain't gonna happen."

"No, you don't understand," she said, sobbing. "I didn't make enough last night and my boyfriend, Marty, is gonna be fucking livid."

"Boyfriend in this case meaning pimp?" My big city terminology had been improving with each passing day, and I chose to not point out the oddly cute relationship between their names.

"He loves me!" I obviously had hit a nerve. "But he'll smack me around if I don't bring him another fifty bucks."

"Well, why are you peddling your ass around this neighborhood?"

"More clean people here," she said, starting to approach me. "I'll do anything you want."

"I'm working, I ain't got the time to go anywhere." Of course, had I disappeared for the day, Pappy wouldn't have given two shits.

"Right here," she said, desperately. "I'll blow you right here."

A part of me wanted to give her the cash and tell her to hit the road, but Veps had been slowly erasing my voice of reason. Only one question really entered my mind. "How old are you?"

"However old you want me to be."

"No, really, you want the money, and I want to know."

"Sixteen."

"And what the fuck are you doing here?"

"It's none of your business!"

"No?" I started to turn around. "Hope Marty doesn't do a lot of damage to that pretty little face of yours."

I didn't even make the complete turn before she let it out. "I ran away from home last year, okay! Marty takes care of me now."

"How come you left home?" I wanted to ask where home was, but I knew I wasn't getting that information.

"My parents hate me. I was never good enough." Her voice got stern. "So are we gonna do this or not?"

Before I could respond, she had me against the wall. Her knees bent, and she was now at crotch level. Like the pro she had unfortunately become, she got my dick out of my pants with the quickness. It got hard instantly in her hand, but right before her lips made contact, I plucked it away, and tucked it back in. I stood her up, threw the money in her hand, and walked back towards the kitchen door. Mallory, confused, asked, "What's this for? I didn't do anything."

I sighed as I answered. "Just go and be safe, okay, kid? But don't come around here again."

She hightailed it out of there. I went back inside and sat at my sink; the dishes had been stacked for me. As I washed the crap away all I could think about was what stopped me from letting that girl suck me off. I started remembering my old man. Even though he'd been a dumb drunk, somewhere inside his head there were principles he lived by. Like him, which pissed me off to accept, I had my limits when it came to being what society would label me: a Class-A scumbag druggie. My moral compass had pointed me to where I'd ended up, but it may very well have been magnetized, which would have explained a lot. About a week later, I found out that Mallory had gone missing. The optimistic side of me hoped she'd gone home, but the reality was she'd probably be laid to rest out on Hart's Island near Peter Pan.

When I finally did quit my job, I tried to do it with as much courtesy as I could. After the lunch crowd left to eventually deal with indigestion, and possible diarrhea, I walked over to Pappy. The big bastard was in the kitchen up against the grill, just looking into the grease stains. I saw him eyeing, in particular, an unfortunate fly that had flown too close. Dumb little bug got too curious and was now lying there, cooking on the black surface. Pappy, horribly mesmerized by the sight, just stood there. "I don't think I'll be coming in tomorrow," I said.

It took a few seconds for him to respond. "Got something planned, do ya?"

I realized I would have to be very blunt with him. "No, Pap, I mean, I quit."

He looked at me, his first break in concentration from the frying fly. "Does that mean Veps'll charge me full price again?"

"I'll talk to him, see what I can do."

Pappy cocked back his head, gargled, and hocked a loogie into the trash bin. "Take care of yourself, kid, don't get done dirty by life, and for God's sake, no Czechs," he said, scratching his crotch, forcing himself to forget some unfortunate decision made in the heat of the moment.

I dropped my apron off on the counter and walked out onto the street. With nothing planned, I walked back to the loft. I had told Pappy that I would talk to Veps about his product charge. During my walk, I kept thinking about the whole concept, drug dealing. Why not get in on the ground floor? Veps did very well for himself, why not me? I hadn't any experience with the profession of selling narcotics, but I had been an all-too-often user of the stuff. If I could get myself a piece of the angel dust pie, I'd be completely self-sufficient. Not that I wasn't grateful to Veps for putting me up, and taking care of the outrageous bar bills we had been accumulating, it's just that I wanted to have some security. By the time I'd reached the apartment, two things were decided. First, I needed a fix of something, didn't matter what, and second, I would tell Veps that I wanted to be a part of his product-pushing world.

He was awake and about when I got in, wrapped up in searching for something, never bothering to ask me what I was doing home so early. I sat down on the couch, and, for a couple of minutes, just watched him go from his room to the closet and back. After a few repetitions, I finally spoke up. "Where's the coke?"

Veps stopped dead and looked at me. "When did you get in?"

"Little while ago. Now how about the coke."

"Coke? Got some in the fridge."

"No, jackass, *coke*."

His mind was obviously overworking. "Oh, oh! Check the bag in front of you."

I reached for it, and he went back to searching. There was a decent amount of product, but I only needed a line or two. I spread it out, formed the duo, fat ones, and took up the first one. As my head went up and back, I asked, "What are you looking for?"

"I'm trying to find my, ha! Found it!"

He came in wearing an Ahab's Animals band t-shirt. I took up the second line and asked, "Didn't those assholes die in a plane crash or something?"

"What? Boy, you've got to be outside your mind. These guys are alive and rocking."

"Veps, I can safely say, I don't think anyone but you remember those guys."

"If that were the case then they wouldn't be playing tonight at the Garden, would they?"

"The Garden, huh? Well, have fun with that." My next move was to talk to him about my possible dealing future but he sidetracked me.

"*We're* going to have with that." As usual, his method of explaining himself was impaired, so I could only imagine just how much coke had been in the bag before I got home. Veps held out two tickets. "You and me, pal, we gonna party tonight!"

Within three hours, I got my lazy ass up and ready. Veps got us a cab, and we were on our way. Had someone that morning told me I would be seeing Ahab's Animals in concert that night, I'd of said they were on a strand of pot that I would like to have some of. The band had formed in the early 90s. Their very first album attempted to sustain life to the dying era of the 80s hair bands. When it was obvious that girls weren't flinging their panties at them, the boys decided to become the east coast version of Nirvana. They had a few minor hits and got coverage on MTV, but things went south quicker than Vanilla Ice's career. Well, it looks like Cobain had the better idea, because once the pop princesses and boy bands changed the world, alternative rock, grunge back then, got kicked in the nuts.

Ah, those pop princesses. Every day on MTV, you'd see them and their mini-skirts. Watching their breasts mature basically became a new spectator sport. God, the things I would've done to those little pieces of tail. Their music was meh, but that's what the mute button on the remote control is for. The boy bands, dear Lord above, if I could have shot them all down dead, I would have. Seeing young hos, older ones too, throw themselves at these dudes with testicles that had yet to drop made me vomit in my mouth a little bit. Half the time, no scratch that, almost all of the time, those frosted tipped Streisand-lovers lip-synced and put all their show's emphasis on dancing. Like I gave a misfart about their ability to grab their dicks and bob their heads.

During the latter part of the Clinton decade, gothic punk was starting to come up on the horizon. Turned out that Ahab and his crazy beasts had decided to adapt to the times. I didn't understand it, but Veps was into it. I'll never comprehend how a band can just forsake their morals, but money always ends up being the root of all evil. If the ticket hadn't been given to me there was no chance in perdition I'd of gone.

The cab dropped us off near the Garden. MSG, a place I had definitely wanted to take a look at. The patriarch of all the modern-day sports and show venues. The concert wouldn't start for over an hour, so Veps suggested we get something to eat. We found some rinky-dink bar near the venue. The two of us stepped into the place. The usual bunch of commuters were nowhere in sight. This surprised me. On a Wednesday night, out in the city after work, those kinds of suits were in desperate need of downing drink after drink until they had enough courage to go to their homes and bone their rapidly decaying wives, while imagining they're doing some skanky young thing. At the time, I couldn't make sense of their absence.

We sat at the middle of the bar, ordering some beers, wings, and potato skins. The meal was pretty good to say the least. I've always been a fan of Buffalo wings, but the suckers have to be spicy. To me, no spice equals bland chunks of chicken, good enough only for a starving dog. Veps threw mounds of sour cream onto his skins. He was a man who liked his spuds covered in tons of melted cheese along with numerous pieces of those tiny bacon bits. Over our food and drinks, the two of us talked about, of all things, movies.

"Brando is the greatest actor to ever step foot onto the silver screen," Veps said, testifying, loudly. "There's a man who can play anything."

"Ya, Brando had his moment in films, but now he's a fat old coot who looks more like Nero than Augustus, if you catch my drift."

"All right, smartass, you tell me, who's the new Brando? Which actor's gonna usher us into the 21st century of film?"

"One name," I said, snapping my fingers, "Johnny Depp."

"Oh, shut the fuck up."

"Are you kidding me? Depp is by far the most amazing actor today, maybe even of all time."

"How much did you snort before? You're talking about the dude who had scissors for hands!"

"And who kicked ass in *Fear & Loathing*. It was Thompson playing Thompson."

"Next thing I know, you'll be preaching how *Showgirls* should've won an Oscar."

We both stared at one another for less than two seconds before we burst out laughing. "Ya, it should've!" we said, screaming out in unison.

Veps was beaming. "Gershon's full lips and nips man, good Lord, I'd take a life for those!"

That got me going. "Goddamn, bro, Jessie Spano buck naked and full of slutty intentions."

"Oink, oink, mama!" Veps said, his nose pushed up in full pig imitation.

The conversation shifted to other celebrities who had appeared nude in the movies. Veps was obsessed with Annette Bening. "And all of a sudden she's there in the hallway, tits all over and a trimmed bush. I'd make that baby bone dry."

I decided that right there was my chance to ask Veps about dealing, but he quickly stalled my attempt. "Two more pitchers over here!" he said, calling out to the bartender.

How the two of us tore ourselves away from the bar is beyond me. We had usually been the closing out crew wherever we went. The concert was about to start in twenty minutes, but the bartender had just brought us the beer. To make the show, Veps and I smiled at one another, held tight a pitcher each, and chugged. With full stomachs and buzzing heads, we paid the check then hopped over to MSG.

That place would've made the Romans who designed and built the Coliseum proud. Even though no one's throwing Christians to the lions, not yet anyway, the building gives off that raw feeling of entertainment that one might get witnessing the bloodshed of monstrous feline incisors crunching down upon a soon-to-be-martyr. When you hand your ticket to the taker and pass through the turn-style, you've entered a whole new reality. The feeling of knowing you're in the same building where Ali solidified his legendary status as the bad, bad man sends you on a whirlwind spiral. Inside those walls, you become a part of history. Too bad we were there to see one of history's forgettables.

Our seats weren't terrible. They faced the stage from one level up; everything was in clear view. To my surprise, the place was filled to capacity. There was a wide array of fans. Old-school grunge culture was represented by the long-haired, flannel-wearing, used-to-the-rain Seattle worshippers of the early 1990s. But there were punks and Goths. I've never been sure as how to distinguish the two. Most of the time, I judge them by who has a multi-colored Mohawk and just go from there. And if you can save yourself from that distraction long enough to actually pay attention to the warm-up bands, you're in a better class of people than I ever was. I had no idea who any of them that night were, and I'll be hard-pressed to say they were any good. "Warm-up" shouldn't be the term given to them. In my opinion, they should be referred to as the "please don't throw tomatoes at us, we're only here because the main event needed to sound better" band. Take that and reword it but you'll get to the same point. Be wary though, because one out of a hundred of them might end up being the next Aerosmith.

After the grueling amateur hour ended, Ahab's Animals came on. The Garden erupted in cheers; it was out of control. Well into the first hour, I took notice of Veps talking to the girl sitting next to him. I think she was a punk, but, oddly, cute as a doe. Short black hair, dyed obviously, brown eyes, a tan, store bought more than likely, which in and of itself was a contradiction to her people who seem to always mirror the complexion of a porcelain doll. She had on this one piece, black, that came up way too high to fall into the skirt category. My guess was that she had on a long t-shirt. The belt, studded, hugged her tight-looking hips. Her legs sported knee socks, pink and blacked-striped ones. Converse sneakers finished the outfit. Another slight contradiction, but without that Mohawk, I could never be sure.

Veps and her kept whispering to one another. I began to wonder what kinds of lines he was feeding her as I had come to the quick conclusion that Veps could shovel the bull faster than any patriotic agrarian. It must've worked, because eventually, they started making out. I expected them to start going at it right there in their seats, but it didn't happen. When Veps came up for air, he turned over to me. "I've gotta take a leak, drain the ole canal. You need anything?"

"No," I said. "I'll just sit here with your new friend."

"Pretty piece of flesh, ain't she? Her friend's with her, too," he said, getting up. "Be back in a sec."

I leaned over to get a better look of the girls. They were giggling with each other like stupid girls usually do. When Veps' girl moved forward, I caught full glimpse of her friend. Anthropologists will tell you that the Neanderthal went extinct thousands of years ago, but one flew under the radar. This girl looked manlier than I could ever hope to be. Now that my dick had retreated far into my asshole, I knew that while Veps would most certainly get the pretty one, I'd be stuck with keeping Fred Flintstone's sister company. Why do the cute girls always keep ugly friends? I figure it's to make themselves look even better. You'd be surprised how easily a girl who's a six on the hotness scale can jump to an eight when she's keeping busted company. I wish Buddha or Confucius had lectured on things like that.

Veps came back with a red sneaker, an Air Jordan come to think of it, size eleven, in his hand. "Where the hell did that come from?" I asked.

"Found it on the men's room floor. Fifty bucks inside it! This is my new good luck charm!"

"You're out of your mind."

"That may be so, my good man, but I'm having a time of it! So what ya think of Cheryl's friend?"

"I think she's going to have a happy career with the circus, although I'm not sure if she fits the profile for the big top or just sideshow."

"Oh, come on. She ain't *that* bad." He looked at the two girls then turned back to me. "Okay, maybe she is, but Cheryl *needs* me."

"She *needs* you, huh?"

"Yes, *needs* me to show her how to do the horizontal mambo!"

"Good God, man, what are you planning?"

"Just promise me you'll be my wingman tonight."

With much reluctance, I agreed to play second chair to Veps right before Cheryl grabbed him to start going at it again. The concert went on. When the encore finished, the lights came back on, and everyone started filing out into the exits. Veps introduced me to Cheryl who introduced the caveman, Joyce, to us. That girl, and I'm being generous in using that term, even sounded like she was from the prehistoric era. I had never been more repulsed.

The four of us walked out together. As we shuffled out, I could hear the girls talking. "You don't even know this guy," Joyce said.

"Oh, shut up. He's hot, and his friend's cute," Cheryl said.

"We've got to go down to Florida tomorrow."

"The thing doesn't start until Monday."

Joyce stopped and looked at us. "Sorry, guys, but we're calling it a night."

"Oh, bull," Veps said. "Why?"

"We've got a funeral, our friend's father, down in Orlando." Joyce's voice and tone made me want to hurl my dinner and all the booze right on up, hopefully, having them mix upon her face. "So take care, bye!"

"Shut up, Joyce," Cheryl said, snapping at her supposed friend. "I'm the one driving, and I say we leave tomorrow." She grabbed Veps. "Let's go back to my place." Then she looked at Joyce. "*All* of us."

I knew that Veps was happy, but I was dreading the rest of the night. As we came to the exit gate some nut job came running up to Veps. "Yo, man, that's my shoe! Give it here."

Veps started laughing. "Hey, man, finders keepers."

"Oh, come on, bro, I'm gonna look like a moron walking outta here with one sneaker on."

"Twenty bucks," Veps said.

"Huh?" the guy was obviously confused.

"Finder's fee is twenty dollars right here in my hand," Veps said, explaining his own beliefs in the timeless saying where the losers shall forever be weeping.

The guy realized Veps wasn't kidding, and he coughed up the cash. He got his shoe and ran off, but as the crowd overtook him, we could hear him ask, "Where's my fifty?"

Veps laughed his ass off, and we all got out onto the streets. Cheryl kissed Veps. "We'll go get the car. Don't go anywhere."

The girls took off, and Veps looked over to me. "The things I'm going to do that girl...mmm, I can't even think about it, I'm getting hard." Something over my shoulder caught his attention. "Oh, man, come with me."

He pulled me over to a food vendor, but minus any conventional cart. More than likely, the man had no license to operate, and I came to that conclusion when I took notice he was selling pretzels out of a shopping cart. Veps slapped me on the back. "My treat, two of them, my man, mustard."

The vendor took them out of the cart. The whole bottom had been lined with tinfoil, and a layer of charcoal had been placed on top of that. Propped up over the heated rocks was a grilling plate where the pretzels sat. Veps paid the man and handed me over one of the knots. "You'll love it. No doubt in my mind."

"I'm not gonna lie," I said, "this looks disgusting."

"Bite into it, and you'll take that back."

I tried some. I'll be damned if that wasn't the best tasting thing ever. My God, I'd never expected something sold out of a greasy piece of metal that had rust stains eating away at it to taste so good. Yet another piece of city living I had spent so many years missing out on. I inhaled the pretzel. Veps and I then stood there, waiting. "You think they're coming back?" I asked.

"Please," Veps said, "that girl's down to party. No question about it."

We waited another ten minutes. The girls finally pulled up. The two of us got in. Veps sat up front with Cheryl, and I got stuck in the backseat. I asked where we were going. Cheryl said her place out in Queens, but first we had to stop and get coffee. The creature next to me needed a caffeine fix sorted out. As we drove, Veps and Cheryl spoke up front, but the radio was on, and I couldn't hear them. Joyce, who sat as far away from me as possible, suddenly jerked her head towards me. "Just so you know, I'm not going to do anything with you."

I wanted to tell her to go fuck herself, but I bit my tongue. In my most calm voice, I said, "Don't worry, you're not my type."

"Why?" she asked. "Not thin enough for you?"

"You said it, I didn't."

"Go to hell."

"Already there," I said. "Already there."

We got into Queens and stopped at some decrepit coffee shop. The girls went in, and I leaned forward to Veps. "I want a bag of super silver haze when this night is over."

"Don't worry, my friend, we'll toke up like fat cats all day tomorrow once this broad and I seal the deal."

Cheryl and Miss Flintstone came back and got in. "We're dropping Joyce off at home," Cheryl said, annoyed.

There was silence of the awkward kind all the way to the bitch's house. We pulled up in front, Joyce got out, took her bag out of the trunk, and went inside. I thought, "Thank the Lord above. This girl's not my problem anymore."

Cheryl took us to her apartment. When she parked the car, she turned to Veps and me. "Let's go up."

Her place was on the third floor. We got to the door and she stopped us. "Hope you guys don't mind cats," she said, opening the door. The floor was moving.

The lights got flicked on. The one or two cats I had anticipated on seeing turned out to be more like thirty. The smells tore at my nostrils, but I found myself walking in, and the sound of the door closing behind me gave me a sense of entrapment. Cheryl's apartment wasn't big. A living room, bedroom, kitchen, and bathroom. The essentials were represented. If the cats staring at me weren't enough, the kitchen brought a whole new definition to weird. Lined across the walls were gargoyles and demonic baby dolls. Veps and I had entered the realm of one crazy broad.

Before I could catch Veps' attention, Cheryl looked at us with a very serious expression on her face. "Now it's not like I've never done it before, but a threesome is out of the question."

"Oh, but bringing two guys you don't know back to your place by yourself is perfectly reasonable," I said, not realizing at first that I had actually been saying the words aloud until they were out.

Veps gave me a look to kill then put his arm around Cheryl. "No sweat, doll face. Ash here can keep himself occupied while you show me your room."

She smiled. "Okay, fine." She looked at me. "Eat whatever's in the fridge." There was a slight pause. "Don't look in the freezer, though."

Well, once she said that, I of course had to look. I opened the freezer then looked at Veps and Cheryl. "Oh, you've got to be kidding me."

"What's in there?" Veps asked, raising an eyebrow.

I reached in and pulled out a Ziploc bag, tossing it over to him. He held it up in his hand. "What are these?"

"Cat fetuses," I said.

I thought Veps was going to lose it right there. He threw the bag back to me and started wiping his hands like crazy. "Um, Cheryl?" I asked.

"Oh, don't be such a baby. It's not a big deal."

I just wanted to be a prick and mess with her, so, I put the bag in the microwave. "Mmm, can't wait for my snack."

"No!" Cheryl said, screaming. "Are you nuts?"

"Am *I* nuts?" I couldn't get the words out right away. "You're asking me if I'm...."

Veps cut me off. "All right, just put the thing back in the freezer," he said, pointing to me. "And you," he said to Cheryl, "go get ready, okay?"

She went off into her bedroom. "Are you kidding me?" I asked.

"What's the problem here?"

"We're in the middle of psycho-town, and you're still gonna go through with this?"

"I'm already here. No sense leaving without taking care of business."

"That girl is twisted six days from Sunday. You go in there and she's liable to cut you up into tiny pieces."

Cheryl's voice could be heard from behind the closed door. "Ricky? Are you coming?"

Veps put his hand on my shoulder. "Grab some food and here, do a line. I'll be out in a little while."

He left me alone. I looked in the fridge. I found some meatloaf then sat down in the living room. There was a PlayStation. Wished it had been a Nintendo. Would've settled for a Genesis. Anyway, I digress. I went ahead and played a few rounds of boxing. The cats circled around me. I had to hold my breath for extended lengths of time. When I heard Veps switch it into cruise control, I turned the television's volume up. About ten minutes later, he came out of the bedroom, zipping up his pants. "Let's get outta here."

I knew something was up by the tone in his voice, so I followed him out. Veps made sure to close the door quietly. When we got outside, he made me haul ass for two blocks. I finally got him to slow down. "Dude, what's going on?"

"Man, oh, man," Veps said. "I get in there and she's laid out naked. She spread her legs, I slapped on a rubber, and dove right in. I pull out and the thing had broken. She goes 'oh, that's okay, I'll just get another' then points out the scar. We cuddled for a minute then I started looking around her room. Total meth head, man, like, bad. I wouldn't be surprised if those fetuses were filled with the glitter."

"What's she doing?" I asked. "Trafficking?"

"I'd say yes, and, for her boyfriend, probably."

"She's got a guy?"

"Ha, ha, ya," Veps said, smiling. "Crazy broad. Good sex, though. But, ya, outta her mind. She thought we were gonna stay over. That's when I knew we had to get out of there. Right about now, she's probably realizing we split."

"I tell ya, bro, you sure do pick'em."

"Ya, ya, ya, let's get back home," he said, looking around. "Oh, fuck me, we're in Queens. We gotta find a train."

"What, no cabs?"

"You find a cab running through these streets, and I'll jump buck naked into the Hudson. Sober and straight."

"When are you ever sober and straight?" I asked with a smirk on my face.

"Don't go native on me, my boy."

The two of us walked for a couple of blocks. It was late, around four in the morning. Temperature was low, and I got a little cold. We had no clue where the train station was, but we were reluctant to ask directions from anyone we might run into. At that time at night, you don't want to associate yourself with anyone who might be lurking about. There were strange vibes all about us. I just hoped they wouldn't close in for the kill.

We rounded a corner and saw a group of big, hulking black dudes, I mean, African-Americans. Was that politically correct? I can never keep up with the times. They were sitting on a stoop, brooding. A block separated us from them, and I would've kept going had it not been for Veps. He grabbed hold of the back of my shirt. "In my opinion, it's in our best direction of self-preservation to turn around and go another way."

"They may know the way to the train," I said, obviously not thinking.

"We're not in my jurisdiction, bud," Veps said. "If we go over there, we'll get our asses handed to us if nothing worse."

The silverbacks, and I don't use that as a racial jab, they were just enormous sons-of-bitches, caught glimpse of us and started to slowly walk over. Veps and I turned and ran. For a second, I thought they might be chasing us, but more than likely not. I am not one for running. My lungs have been abused since childhood. All the sprinting going on made me cough up more phlegm than I would've like to. When Veps felt we had gone far enough, he jammed his brakes and came to screeching stop. The two of us, hunched over, tried to catch our breaths.

I looked up and saw a garbage truck. I hit Veps with my the back of my hand. "Can we ask them?"

"Uh, ya," Veps said. "Shouldn't be any problems."

We walked up to the garbage man, a Hispanic, and asked him if he knew where we could pick up the train back to Manhattan. He looked at us for a moment, then, in horrible English, said, "Chu gotta go over tu di station? Dos blocks, right, left, you ci di station ova der."

The gist of what the Hispanic had said, we understood. Following the directions, we came to the station. There was no one around, so we sat on a bench to wait for our ride. I decided to tell Veps my plan. "You know, I quit Pappy's today."

"Why'd you go and do a thing like that? It was easy money for bullshit work."

"I was bored out of my mind over there. Bunch of nuts for customers." I waited, thought about it, then just bit the bullet. "I want to work with you."

"With me on what?" he asked, looking confused.

"I want to deal, to sell, whatever the hell it is you professionals call it."

"Ya?" Veps got quiet for a second then said, "Well, ya, sure, don't see why not. Ha! Ya, this could be one funky situation. Monday, I'll go and talk with the big man, Boss Denham. He says 'yes' and you're good to go."

"Thanks, man. I appreciate it. I mean, you know, everything."

"Just more opportunities for good times."

The train came. We got on. It wasn't a long ride. There were a few people on it. Lord only knows why. Things looked up for me. A possible way to make good money hung in the air. Though the night out had its twists, it seemed like I was making it out fairly unscathed. Looking back, it was probably one of, if not *the*, strangest July Forths I've ever had.

It would be three more weeks of debauchery until I realized I needed a break. I had to get out of the apartment, without Veps, and find something that might entertain me. It wasn't that I didn't enjoy the time spent with him but after a night like the one we had just recently had, there was no shot of me enduring another one right away. With that in mind, I ventured out into the streets, looking for something to keep myself occupied. I smoked a blunt and out the door I went.

Of all the bars in the Village, I must say that one stands out. It's a place that when you hear its theme, you'd probably scratch your head and wonder why in God's name someone would create such a place. The KGB Bar was a joint unlike any I had ever stumbled upon. It's housed in this unassuming building, and if you survive the devilish stairway that is steeper than any double-black diamond out West, you're in good company. Darkened red lights give the place a look that's straight out of a bad Russian spy movie, but when you get over that, you begin to notice the little nuances that the room exudes. Between the Lenin and Stalin paraphernalia, I found a little cut out of baby bear Mishka, one of the mascots of a long-forgotten Olympics where the Soviets probably kicked our Uncle Sam-loving asses.

There was a decent crowd that night. A plethora of vodka bottles were stacked behind the bar. When ordering vodka that isn't a well-known stateside brand, I have always found it best to point. There'd be no chance in the Kremlin that I would be able to pronounce words with backwards K's. How does one even begin to do such a thing? I ordered a shot and a drink, downed both in a breath, and went for round two, then three. The night was shaping up nicely.

Around seven, one of the bartenders, although he was wearing a suit so I'm not sure if you could call him that, approached the microphone I had casually glanced at hanging on the wall.

"Ladies and gentlemen," he said, "if I could have your attention. Tonight, I'd like to welcome our poet of the week, Mr. Samuel Beton. I won't say anymore."

I had stumbled onto some kind of crazy off-the-beaten-trail poetry reading. Not the kind of place for it, I said to myself, but this bar was truly quirky enough to house all kinds of nutty events. Beton was a young man of skinny proportions. He had slicked hair to the side with thick-rimmed glasses. He sported a tight suit, but my immediate thought was not to think him gay. Even though this was the Village, not everyone was automatically a homosexual because of their exceptionally form-fitting attire. And if he happened to be a friend of Dorothy, who cares, right? His poetry turned out to be lyrical ballads that reminded me of a long lost, and misplaced, day of high school English class.

During the course of the reading, I took notice of a woman sitting alone in a corner of the room. At first look, I didn't recognize her, but something told me that I'd seen her before. Suddenly, sometime around Beton's final bow, I put it together. It was Marci, the older woman from my first night with Veps. I guess she caught me looking because during the applause, her eyes met mine and she smiled. Reminding myself that Veps had called her a hooker in not so many words, I resolved to do nothing more than smile back and return to my newly refilled drink.

So while the majority of people went over to pat the poet on the back and kiss his ass for being a maestro of the written word, Marci managed to find her way over. She sat herself down next to me. I couldn't help but notice her un-prostitute-like attire. A sundress. One with black and yellow flowers on it. I was obviously confused. Wonderbra on to give an extra boost to the girls but that was really the most scandalous piece on her. Of course, I wondered if she were a thong or panties kind of chick. I wasn't intending on putting up my money to find out though, so I kept quiet. Eventually, she began a conversation. "You look familiar. You been in here before?"

"No, actually. This is my first time. What about you?"

"Are you sure? I come here almost every Monday. Really? Because you look like I've seen you before."

"Ever been to Elroy's?" I asked, staring more at my drink than her.

"Yes, I have. But wait, I know you. You were in there with Veps. Right?"

"You got a good memory. Ash, by the way," I said, pointing to myself. "I guess you have to for your profession."

"What that does mean?" she asked, raising her voice a little. "What do you think I am? A whore?"

The tone in her voice raised red flags all around me where I had been sitting in a sea of crimson already. "I, I'm sorry. It's just that Veps had made a comment and I just thought that's what he meant."

"Well, your buddy should seriously know better than to say that crap. I have never taken money for sex, although, if I wanted to venture into that lifestyle, neither you nor he could afford me."

"A tad full of yourself for a woman in her, what, 40s?"

"Boy, you really know how to make a girl feel attractive. Before, I would have admitted you had a chance, but now there isn't one in hell."

"Not to sound like a complete scumbag, but, unfortunate as it may be, I don't think you'd even be able to get me hard, let alone off."

"Is that right?" she asked.

"Just being honest."

Before I knew what was happening, Marci's fingers had found their way down the back of my pants, into my undercarriage, and all of a sudden, I realized she'd given my asshole a quick fingering. I'm pretty sure it could have been constituted as rape, but no court in the land would have convicted her. "How'd that feel?" she asked, looking down at my suddenly hard member. "See ya around, kid."

I watched in utter amazement as she walked out of the room. After about ten seconds, I realized that if I didn't go after her, I would end up jerking myself off to her image for the next week or so. Throwing down some bills to pay the tab, I rushed out of the place, nearly broke my neck going down those goddamned stairs, and out the main door I went. Marci was standing there, smoking a cigarette. "Didn't think you'd be out here so quick."

"Why'd you do that up there?" I asked, trying to find some sort of meaning to it all.

"Come out with me, and buy me another drink. Maybe I'll explain, and maybe you'll get a little more, but, you gotta make the effort."

This woman was a vixen, and, possibly a sex-crazed nymph. While this was more like Veps' country, I felt it was my duty to uphold the ideals that the man had been trying desperately to instill upon me. Walking away from this situation would only represent me spitting in my best friend's face. I couldn't do that to him. No, I had to be the one to say, yes, yes, Marci, I'll buy that drink. "Sure," was my actual answer. "Where'd you want to go?"

Marci said she had a place in mind but that she wanted to walk there. I don't know why I followed her exactly. Maybe it was the curious sex inquiries I had regarding her. It was like asking why Alice followed the white rabbit down the hole. Mischief was at hand, that much was obvious, but how much and for how long would it last, I didn't know. This woman, who had to have been near twenty years older than yours truly, had a hold on me. The night and its possible outcome had to be seen through to fruition or ruin. Like I said, Veps wouldn't have had it any other way.

I followed Marci down a couple of streets. She was a Village goddess. I wasn't quite sure of which variety. It was clear, or at least it should have been, that she wished for me to be her Adonis. I watched her float over the curbs and back onto sidewalks, in and out of people; I don't know if she even had her eyes open. We came to an often-than-not-traveled street, although I would have called it an alley. There was a bar there. A cafe really. It didn't have a name that I could see. All that was shown was a little sign that could no longer be read without a terrible straining of one's eyes. That is either the mark of a cheapskate or a very brilliant and confident owner.

Upon entering, I came to the almost immediate conclusion that Papa Ernest's clean, well-lighted place had come to life. The smell of liquor-laced coffee filled the small establishment. Little lights shone a way to and from tiny tables for two. This place's maximum capacity couldn't have been more than thirty. A few tables were occupied. Marci led me over into an unoccupied corner of the place. The sounds of a mandolin played softly in the background. Sweet chords of Mediterranean passion filled my ears and a strange calm came over me. It could have been the several shots of vodka. I would have liked to have thought otherwise.

A tiny man, who might have passed for one of Kris Kringle's summer interns, came over to us. Marci mumbled something off in what I could only assume was Italian and the man smiled a broken smile, heading out of sight.

"What did you just order?" I asked.

"Why?" Marci asked. "Nervous that I might be poisoning you?"

"The thought hadn't crossed my mind, but now visions of paranoia have been given permission to rise."

"You're an interesting fellow."

"Did you actually just use the word 'fellow' in conversation? I have to tell you, that's a first for me."

"Have to keep you on your toes, don't I?"

"I'm gonna choose to not answer a lot of questions because, one, I'm drunk, and two, I don't know what to make of you just yet."

She smiled. "Oh, no? Not just yet? Well, I can tell you that you're not like your friend, Veps."

"I didn't know you knew him that well. Seems a lot of girls know him pretty well. Am I stepping on his toes?"

"He wishes you were. No, Veps has never had the pleasure. I watch him, I know him, enough, and I know you're nothing like him."

"You're kind but probably wrong. I'm more like him than I realized. My time here in the city has shown me that."

"Did you go to KGB tonight to listen to poetry?"

"Really, I just stumbled into the place. The reading was a bonus."

The could-be midget came back with two glasses filled with a strong, odious liquid. Marci raised one up, and I took the other. She thanked him with a "graci." As he hobbled off back into the kitchen, I sipped the drink. Strong. Best way I can describe it. My thoughts wandered back to why Marci had brought me there. Was she overtly coming onto me, or was this just a ploy by a well-educated prostitute, which she had adamantly denied being. But in the world we live in, a person can't take another at face value. Look at me. I probably looked to her like a burn out, speed freak, which, of course, I wasn't. Veps didn't dabble in speed, at least, I don't think he did. But Marci had a plan. That much I was sure about. And, because of my fascination with her, and, because I had noticed her that first night with Veps, I felt compelled to play along with what I thought she was proposing.

"Do you want to know why I wanted you to come here with me tonight?" Marci asked.

Holding back the first answer that popped into my mind because I wasn't sure if its delivery would be seen as wit or me being an asshole, I choked it down and said, "I just assumed you were interested. I mean, what you did back at the bar. It was...unexpected."

She took another sip from her cup. "It's all about the game. Do you know about it? I'll take the confused look on your face as a 'no.' Well, plain and simple, it's a game that has gone on forever. I've been a player in it since these," she grabbed her tits, "developed and this," she said, pointing to the warm spot between her legs, "realized it liked being penetrated."

"This is all entertaining," I said, "but let's be honest. You've just admitted to enjoying a good boning. I've been aware of it since the first hair on my balls sprang to life. What are you driving at? Give me the rundown without the bull."

"What you said at the bar. Your snide little comment about me not being able to get you hard. Did I?" She said that with her tongue emphasizing the word "little."

"Yank a snake long enough and you'll eventually get its venom," I said, trying, but failing, to sound metaphorically intelligent.

Marci adjusted herself, switching which leg crossed which. "You need to see what it is I'm talking about. You need to witness the game in play. It's one thing to insult a lady, because that's what I am whether you realize it or not. But it's another to question her ability to pleasure a man. That in and of itself is a slight at my gender. Pleasing men? Christ, we've been doing that since Eden. That Adam must've been crying and moaning for some food so poor little Eve had to go and rustle something up rather quickly."

"My interest in all of this is completely waning," I said. "To be perfectly honest with you, I only followed you over here in the hopes that you'd finish what you started back at the KGB. Does that make me a player in this stupid game of yours? I really don't care. My only true concern at this point is whether or not I'm screwing you tonight. The bluntness you're experiencing is the frustration of a dick that contracted blue balls about twenty minutes ago. If I wasn't such a gentlemen," that was my cute attempt at sarcastic charm, "I'd of rubbed one out right here at this table." And it's true, I probably would've. Didn't you ever once get the thought in your head about doing something like that in public? I have at least once or twice.

Finishing her drink, Marci placed it back onto the table and began to try attracting the attention of the tiny waiter. "Do want to see something? A small, and yes, there was a slight pun intended, showing of me playing the game? I bet you that I can make that poor guy love me then end up hating himself. Care to wager anything on it?"

"I don't make fool's bets unless I'm a tad nutty, which I may still be, but I'm thinking far too much. I also don't have the time to watch your great plan."

"Something like this won't take very long. Watch."

With that, Marci turned her attention away from me and to the waiter. He was busy stacking clean dishware and cups onto an old cart. She made no sound. Nothing. All she did was patiently wait for him to notice her. After finishing his task, the poor unsuspecting dwarf lifted his head up to make sure nobody needed anything. That's all it took. In one split second, possibly a nano, he and Marci made eye contact. His downfall was imminent. Marci had pulled her dress' bottom slightly higher than it had been, and it hadn't been that low to begin with. Her smile developed slowly from a squeezed smirk, and it all got sealed with a wink that if a stripper gave you the same one, you'd think you're about to get a free lap dance. "Watch this," Marci said through her teeth.

I sat there, sipping from my already empty cup to make everything appear natural. I watched as this unsuspecting waiter took all of this professional female player's signals and figured to walk on over. There were three table lengths between him and us when he started. One passed. The second went by. As he came upon the third, it happened. Marci, who hadn't broken her sitting stance, burst into tremendous laughter. There might have even been a direct finger pointed at the little guy who took no time in realizing what had just transpired. Marci continued her barrage of giggles as the waiter shot his head straight down. Gullible schmuck turned around, shoulders hunched, and I wish I were lying, walked back towards the kitchen but didn't take notice of the cart he'd just got done stocking. He tripped, fell on his face, and brought down a landslide of ceramic upon him.

No reaction came out of me at first. For a while, which wasn't probably as long as I remember it being, I just sat there, mouth agape. It was true what Marci had been saying. This game. One that has been continuously played since time immemorial. It had just taken me witnessing that show to comprehend everything. While Veps might go ahead and insult a girl to her face, Marci took pleasure in the destruction of a person's entire psyche. After coming out of my stupor, I found her to be lighting a cigarette as though she'd just entered the stage of post-coital delight. My fascination with this woman enlarged tenfold, and I knew there would be no chance of me wanting to escape my current situation. "No response?" she asked.

"I'm still coming to grips with what I just saw. Do you do this often? I don't just mean with that waiter but bringing guys like me with you to be a spectator. Is this your way of getting off after a life of sexually frustrating lovers who didn't pay for breakfast the next morning?"

"This is just me showing you that I'm as serious as I want to be. You're lucky to be sitting here. Do you know that? I could have ruined you at KGB, but I decided to have some fun. Are you having a good time?" She butted out her stick onto the tablecloth as she said that, and I remembered how much I wanted to strangle the patrons at Pappy's every time one did it.

"You truly astound me," I said, thinking of how badly I wanted to know what color underwear this woman was wearing and how nice they'd look on a bedroom floor just being lit up with sunlight after a night of heavy hitting. "You wanna get outta here?"

"Propositioning me are you?"

"I thought that was a hooker word."

"I told you, I'm not a hooker and if you keep thinking that, I'll leave you right here. Truth is, yes, I'd like to get out of here. Pay the bill."

Normally, I'd laugh at any dumb slut who thought just because they're brandishing a nice bottom that I would pick up the tab. But again, for some reason, this chick had me hooked. I liken it to drug use. You know that what you're putting into your system will eventually lead to your ultimate demise but you do it anyway without second guessing yourself. Marci was like a line of coke. Everything inside me, call it my often ignored commonsense, would tell me not to inhale that strip of white that Marci represented, but, fuck it, I was an addict to more than just narcotics.

Paying the check was not a fun experience. The tiny man, who had since placed a bandage on his forehead due to the fall, had to meet me at the register. Not a word was said on my part but as he handed me over the change, he said, "Pretty lady not so nice." Oh, how right the downtrodden can be.

The night's air had cooled. Not that the streets were by any means quiet for a little past midnight but when you walk through the city at that hour in the summer, and you're not getting slapped in the face with humidity, you remember to take it all in, cherishing the moment. Marci made it a point to occasionally walk a little ahead of me. She was smart. It was late, even for me. Bed felt like a good idea but each time she made her way to the front, my eyes caught sight of her backend bouncing up and down in that dress. Strategy was, no doubt, her strong point. "Getting tired?" she asked, making her way back to my side.

"Not gonna lie, a little."

"Maybe we should call it a night?"

"I said *a little*. I'm also a tad tipsy, and my high is coming down, but I could still hold my own with Veps if he were here."

"Do you need him to be here?"

"I don't know what you mean by that. No, Veps isn't required."

"Then just follow me through the wardrobe, Tumnus."

I ignored her C.S. Lewis-inspired jab at me, because I just didn't have an instant come back. Bitch. She had me by the balls. This night had all the possibility to drag on to reveal nothing. Me, being the curious party that I was and tend to still be, followed that white witch all the way to her building. This one had a doorman. Felt good to know that this chick had protection from the elements of the concrete jungle, because I had a feeling that those vintage doors the man opened for us might have been a disguise, hiding a revolving mechanism. The shit one thinks of as the penis takes over all normal brain functions. My God.

Marci turned the lights on in her apartment, illuminating a room of deep earth tones. Chairs, tables, the sofa; everything screamed children of the soil. Good taste as far as I was concerned, but this is coming from a guy who probably couldn't have told you the difference between pink and fuchsia. "Sit down and I'll be right back," Marci said, walking out of sight, into what I could only assume was her bedroom.

There was a picture sitting atop the end table. I picked it up, taking notice of the young girl in it. She was being hugged by a pair of large, hairy arms. Must have been her father. Marci, if it had indeed been her, couldn't have been more than ten or eleven. I can't remember if I had any photos of my old man and me. If they existed, Mom more than likely threw them out or burned them. Thinking of my mother standing there in our backyard in front of a fire-filled garbage can watching dried inked memories fade into nothing caused me to feel both upset and proud all at once.

"See anything interesting?" Marci asked, coming back into the room.

"Mini-episode of a childhood no one should ever remember," I said, noticing that she was now wearing a yellow teddy that came up to that special place on a woman where, if it went any higher, you wouldn't have to ask the age old question: landing strip or bald as a baby's behind?

"Do you want to see what I have for you?" she asked.

"It's a book," I said, sounding like I had just invented the word.

"This isn't just any book. This is my favorite collection of poetry. It's filled with the works of the Romantics. Blake, Wordsworth, Byron, and even little Sammy. Read much of them?"

"You brought me up here to look at a book of poems written by a bunch of dead guys who wrote about getting laid in decrepit old abbeys?"

"I brought you up here to do what I want you to do. Remember, it's all a game and you popped in a quarter a long time ago."

"A quarter won't get you much play time these days."

"And that kind of wiseass talk won't get you any of this," she said, sitting next to me. "I want you to recite a poem for me. Just one. A short by Blake. But I want you to read it with gusto."

"If I do this am I getting anything out of it?"

"Stand up, read it. If you break stride just once, you'll lose, and game over for tonight...quite possibly forever. I don't really like dealing with losers."

"Jesus-fucking-Christ, lady," I said, taking the book out of her hands. "Which poem am I reading with pesto or whatever it was you said."

She flipped the pages over with her finger until I saw "The Sick Rose" printed out in front of me. "Stand," she said.

I stood, which didn't make me terribly happy, but the reward I assumed was coming my way kept me in pretty good stead. "Ready?" I asked.

"Almost," she said, and before I knew what was going on, she had unzipped my pants and brought both them, and my boxers, down around my ankles. "There, that's better."

There I stood, my flaccid dick hanging in the wind, with a book of poems in my hand. What would anyone do in my position other than to just run with it? Right? "O Rose thou art sick./The invisible worm,/That flies in the night/In the howling storm." I had to stop myself briefly when Marci decided to start stroking my dick.

"Keep going," was all she said.

"Has found out thy bed/Of crimson joy,/And his dark secret love/Does..." I couldn't keep going. Marci had transitioned from a simple hand job to cupping my balls while fully sucking me off. I didn't know what to do.

She took a long slurp and said, "If you don't finish, well, you won't *finish*."

"Does," I tried to contain myself as best as I could under the circumstances, "thy," she tightened her oral grip, "life," here it came, literally, "des...des..." and like a shotgun, everything went straight into her mouth, down her throat, settling somewhere in the acidic cavity of the stomach to be with her forever in one form or another, "destroy." I was *finished*.

I didn't move at first. Truth be told, I'm still surprised that I hadn't fallen down. Marci wiped her mouth then her chin where a bit of myself dribbled on her. "You taste good," she said, which might be the greatest original compliment I'd ever received.

"You're an MVP of this game of yours," I said. "Give me like ten minutes and I'll be ready for the full injection."

Marci wiped her lips, stood up, and said, "There won't be any injecting tonight, killer."

In my somewhat unstable state of post-oral bliss, I stumbled from hearing her words, and fell to the ground, my bare booty brushing up against a rough patch of carpet. Only for a second did I bother to ponder as to why that particular spot's texture was the way it was before saying, "What do you mean? I can be ready in under ten if that's what bothering you."

"No, nothing is bothering me. I did what I wanted to do and that's that. If you need to clean up or something feel free to, otherwise, I'll be going to bed. Alone."

"You wacky slut," I said. "You can't just blow a guy like that then expect him to just be okay with leaving."

"Don't say unflattering things so soon after being sucked dry. My game. My rules. Now pull up your pants. Maybe we'll get together another time."

There wasn't much else I could say, I supposed. Marci had made up her mind, and I was sure it had been made up long before we ever reached the apartment. She'd won. I had been an unwilling player in her little arena. A gladiator, yes, that's what I was. A slave thrown to the lions, well, in this case, cougar, but you get the idea. Up went my pants, followed by the zipper. "No good night kiss?" I asked.

"I'd rather not," she said, opening the door for me. "Your smell is still lingering on me, and I'd rather just bask in it a bit longer."

Again, I had no response for her. Out I went and back into the awaiting city. Veps would never believe me. Okay, maybe he would but I couldn't bring myself to go and relate a night of failed sex. A fine blowjob is all well and dandy, but not crossing home is grounds for friend-on-friend ridicule. In the state I was in there's no telling how much, or how little, I could take. Best to keep it to myself was my way of thinking. That, and to ignore the slight itchy irritation going on in my pants.

By the time Veps had finished his morning run, and, of course, I don't mean on a treadmill, he barreled into the apartment like always. "My goodness, my goodness. Ash, where you at?"

I had been in the bathroom, showering. I'd just lathered up my hair when in burst Veps. "No worries, not an anal-bomb. I just had to drain the dragon."

This hadn't been the first time I had to listen to him pee while I was bathing. I just let it happen without reaction. As I washed the shampoo out of my hair, Veps flushed the toilet. After I let out a shriek from the instant hot water rush, he apologized through a barrage of laughter. "My bad, my bad, Ash. But I got news for you, oh, boy, do I."

"What's that? Make it quick. I'm not getting outta here with you in the room. I wouldn't trust you with a wet towel no matter how much you promised." I had been referring to a previous incident that had left me with a red streak mark across my bare ass. And, yes, it stung like a frustrated mother's slap.

"Well," Veps said, "I got a day planned out for the two of us. We're gonna get outta here, grab some grub, and eventually make our way over to Boss Denham's."

"What kind of a name is that anyway?" I asked. "He sounds like he should be in an old gangster movie."

"See, that kind of talk can get to you biting the curb real quick around Boss Denham and his boys. I don't know where he got the nickname, but I never asked nor did I ever wanna go wondering even to myself."

"Are my chances good? I don't wanna waste yours, his, or my time."

"Never hurts to ask. Besides, he's always looking to expand his enterprises. Might as well be you, the roommate to one of his best pushers. Well, he never actually would admit that, but it's obvious I'm one of his favorites."

Veps left the room, and I got out to dry myself. I nearly slipped on the floor, almost breaking my neck. It was one of those moments you thank God no one was watching because the sheer stupidity of it would kill you alone. Veps might be able to live off that one thing for months, never letting you forget about it. He was an artist in the craft of knowing how to make a person feel like garbage over things they did to themselves.

I got dressed. Veps was waiting for me. He was watching television. Another thing I should probably mention about the living enigma that was Veps: dude had a thing for watching C-SPAN. This guy could spend hours watching the stock exchange ticker at the bottom of the screen. Whether or not he knew what he was watching and could comprehend, I never asked. Best to leave some things unanswered. "You ready to head out?" I asked.

"Wait for it. Wait for it. And...okay, I'm ready."

"Did your stock shoot up or something?"

"Stock? Oh, no, that news lady's nipples were hard and I was timing to see how long those diamond-cutters would last. Little over a minute and a half."

"Right. Well, I'm ready to go when you are. Where are we going by the way?"

"First, drinks and food. But with the night ahead, you may want to load up on the booze. Boss Denham can be a real hard pill to swallow when you're sober."

Off we went, hailed a yellow painted, chipped, and peeling cab, with uptown being our destination. Manhattan taxi cabs are not something to be traveled in on a full stomach. I have called the drivers "devils" already, but "sadistic" should be an added adjective. No care for the human lives in their backseats. One would think that they had a death wish. This is all of them. I've never, in my life, experienced a pleasant cab ride. Veps had told the guy where to go, and at one point we neared entering the Queensboro Bridge, which even I knew wasn't right. The driver, an aged man of frail proportions, who happened to be of Rhine River Valley origin, had his own idea of American driving standards. I could never be sure but I swore to Veps later on that he had taken the car up and over a pedestrian, swearing it had just been the curb. Large part of me really wanted to believe the guy.

After eating three red lights in a row, the death trap came to a screeching halt. Veps paid the man, who hadn't really said much, actually, nothing, the entire ride. My hand had found a place to set itself on upon my stomach and all attention got put on just breathing without spewing everything in me all over the backseat. "Ash, my man," Veps said, stepping out of the car, "come on, brother, time to go."

He had to shake me to bring me back to the land of the living. "Right," I said as we walked away from the cab, the driver, and my near death experience. I was never one to be religious, but Jesus was probably laughing at me from all the way up.

Even today, I have to hand it to Veps for his ability to find the best random food joints. Trouble was, most of them were located in less than desirable conditions. Should a person feel that where they are eating is void of vermin and filth? I would have said, yes, but, with Veps, you had to rethink your entire concept of logic. This place was half take-out, half sit-down, but I never did see a table with a chair. You either walked through the one door to a small gray room void of anything except an ordering window, or you entered the second to congregate at the bar, which, by the looks of it could possibly have dated back to the time of the Five Points Gangs, but I kept that to myself when I saw the barbershop moustache being sported by the hefty bartender. All that was within me surmised that he could have pulled a razor blade on me the moment I made any sly remark. Being that I had just gotten my walking legs back after encountering the happy-go-lucky cabbie, there was not much chance in dodging any possible attack.

Veps pushed me aside. "I got this, my man." He tapped the decaying wooden bar top. "Keep, dear sir, four dogs with relish. And I mean I don't want to see the dogs. Cover'em up, buddy!"

The bartender nodded, bent over to where a little microphone was, and said, "Four corkers, rolled over." There was obviously some kind of secret language being spoken here.

"I gotta pee," I said, walking away from Veps.

I don't know why I did what I did. No one who has observed that the place they're about to eat in looks like the health inspector stopped bothering should attempt to use the bathroom. When I flipped on the light, an army of roaches scattered. Strike one. As I went to unzip my pants, I got a glimpse of a floater of mammoth-sized proportions. Strike two. After managing to ignore it, pee, and get a decent hand washing, I went to flush. Backed up. Overflowed. Strike three. I got out of there. "Don't use the toilet," was all I said to Veps upon my return to the bar where our food was waiting for us.

"Aha! Ash, my boy, sit your ass down and take in this golden secret treasure of our fair city. You thought those pretzels were outstanding, well, you're about to take it up another level."

Like most things Veps introduced me to, I was reluctant, but, after having been around him long enough, I stopped hesitating after just a second or two. In went the dog, which was covered in this hideous looking yellow relish. I don't know if it was just me, but I can't recall a traditional relish ingredient included anything even moderately resembling the color I was looking at. However, in it was, and down it went. Mustard. It had been the first flavor that hit my tongue, and, well, Veps had yet again succeeded in getting me to fall in love with another piece of food. Kind of always wondered how the crazy bastard wasn't an obese blimp of a man. Fast metabolism was my first guess, but it could very well have been the drugs.

As we chowed down, a pair of women had come in, gathering around one of the chair-less tables. I hadn't really taken much notice of them until Veps glanced over then grabbed my head, turning it in their direction. "Lesbians," he said, pointing to the girl sporting a mullet.

"That one, granted," I said, "but you can't expect me to believe the other one is." I had been referring to the redhead sporting a fine figure and tight jeans. "Not a chance."

"Ash, laddie boy, I will prove to you the truth of what I suspect."

"Dare I ask how you plan on doing this?"

"It's best if you just watch."

Veps sauntered over to the two, hands tucked into his back pockets like it would have made a difference which two ways he could've done it. He was under the impression that body language, no matter how dumb it might have looked, could be a great equalizer, or maybe, manipulator, if you did it with style. I never did have the heart to tell him that that particular pose made him look, and walk, like John Wayne. Although, I'm not so sure it would have bothered him.

The butch-looking girl noticed him first. "What the hell do you want, cowboy?" She obviously had seen what I had.

"I just wanted to buy this fine looking young lady here a drink," Veps said, whipping out his left hand to point at the pretty one.

"What did you just say?" the mullet-covered one asked.

"I said…."

Unfortunately, Veps couldn't get the rest of his sentence out. The bull dyke slugged him right in the mouth. Down he went, like a pile of bricks, and right on top of him she went. "You little dick weed!" she said, pummeling his chest in with her meaty fists. "She's *my* woman, you stupid fuck!"

I watched this without making an effort to intervene on Veps' behalf. A small part of me thought he'd just get up, smack her in the face, and jet out as quick as his legs could carry him. Then it happened. He started laughing. He laughed until the whole of the establishment, kitchen crew included, took notice of the would-be butchery being carried on. At first, it was a small giggle, but it gradually evolved into full out cackling. "Ha, ha! Come on, baby, give me some of that dyke-a-delic love! Woo!" I'm almost certain I heard him say it with a Texan accent.

When the girl finally decided his chest had had enough, she went for the face. That's when I finally felt it necessary to interject. Again, I'm not the best decision maker on the planet, and probably never will be, but I saw a friend in trouble, and I reacted. I'm an idiot. Without even getting within two feet of the scuffle, the skinny little redhead kicked me in the balls. Straight up to soprano for me. I still get weak in the knees thinking about it.

Eventually, the people in the place helped separate the butch from off of Veps. From what I could tell, he had a bloody nose but not much else damage. I, on the other hand, continued clasping my tender ones until the cops came. Yes, the fuzz entered with the quickness. No attempt was made to even touch the lesbians. Instead, Veps and I found ourselves in handcuffs. "Pigs!" Veps said. "Get your hands off of me. That goddamn carpet-muncher hit me. I didn't even touch her. I mean, would you?" Leave it to Veps to continue the funny as he was being put into the back of a police car.

Only one officer stayed in the vehicle. He drove on through the streets in silence, only taking moments to peer into his rearview to smile at Veps' busted face. I sat, holding my dick. The balls had gone numb. The pain had shot up into the shaft. "Why did you go and do that?" I asked.

"Proved a point, though," Veps said. "Told you they were lesbians."

"Your nose is probably broken and you're more interested in making a point of that you were right?"

"Never look on the dark side of things, Ash, my boy. Remember, everything works itself out in the end."

"It smells like piss in here."

For some reason that caught the cop's attention. "Hey, shut up back there. You two scumbags are in for a real treat. Friday night means you boys will be spending your weekend in the Tombs. All nice and quaint-like."

"If you want a blow job, Porky, just ask," Veps said, which brought the car to an immediate stop. Our faces smashed into the cage, and the cop laughed.

"Hey, short stuff," he said to me, "tell your buddy there to keep his trap sealed or there's gonna be a lot more stops like that."

I didn't respond, only nodded. Veps kept his cool the rest of the ride. He had felt the rusty metal against his nose, and I don't think he wanted to continue the experience. At last, something that kept him quiet, but alas, it wasn't to last. When we got escorted into the precinct, Veps put on a show. I had never actually seen the inside of a *real* police station. Boys in blue patting each other on their spam butts, thinking of ways to sodomize minorities and get away with it. Made me think of ole Richie boy back home. Made me sick, too. They were all the same, every last one of them. Their cocked, locked, and loaded pistols at their sides to compensate for their micro-penises made me chuckle a little, but I kept it internal. Our beefed-up tour guide held a tight grip on my neck, so I didn't feel like taking a private trip to the washroom. God only knows what kinds of broom handles might have awaited me.

We were sat down on a bench next to some drugged-out hobo. Of all people to be locked up with, Veps was most certainly the worst possible candidate. No one had searched us. All they had done was cuff us and take us to the slammer. But if *Law & Order* had taught me anything, I knew that we'd be patted down before the booking. Veps, at any given moment in time, was a walking pharmacy. A veritable cornucopia of uppers and downers. God, Himself, wouldn't be able to name everything my associate was carrying on his person. Nervousness grew in my belly, and suddenly that mustard-based relish didn't sit so well. I'd survived this far and my fall would come from a penis-envious lesbian with muscles bigger than Hulk Hogan's, and a gut like Earthquake, wailing on Veps. "What are we gonna do?" I asked. "What do you have on you right now?"

"Nothing," Veps said. "Just some bags of coke and a joint or two."

"That isn't *nothing*," I said, trying to whisper so that the hobo next to me couldn't hear anything. No need to rile up the cattle while they're resting in the barn.

"You worry too much," Veps said. "You think I'd get us into this kind of a mess if I didn't have a contingency plan? Shit, brother, how do you think I've lasted this long without being locked up?"

"Well, what do you call *this*? We're cuffed, cops are surrounding us like vultures to a dying dog, and you're packing twenty-five to life in one pocket alone."

"When Sir Bacon…ha, get it?" I gave no indication of being amused. He continued, saying, "Well, when he gets back over here, I get my phone call and everything will be taken care of."

"What are you talking about? We're screwed when they search you."

"You're like one of them claustrophobic guys, ain't ya?"

"I wasn't sure you could pronounce such big words," I said, uncharacteristically nasty towards Veps.

Before he could mount a rebuttal, the officer came back over, picked Veps up by the collar, and escorted him out of my sight. There I sat, just me and the hobo, who, to my great "luck," began talking to me. "You got any timber on you?"

My initial reaction was to ignore him, but when I heard what he had said, the better part of my judgment told the other part to shut up. "What do you mean, 'timber?'"

"I says," he gagged on some vented up phlegm, "you got any timber for me to have? Maybe, I even jus barow a whittle…."

The slurs in this man's speech made me wish that I had been the one the pig had taken to work over in the john. But here I was, and purgatory is where I'd have to remain for the time being. "I'm sorry, I don't know what you're talking about. Timber? What do I look like, a fireplace?"

"I ain't got nun firepiece, but I knows that I got *this*." He held up a cigarette in his black crusted hand. "So I needs some timber."

"Oh," I said, making the connection, finally. "You want a match. Sorry, I don't have one."

Almost right away, I grew horribly sorry that I, in fact, did not have a match or even a lighter. The hobo screamed something completely unintelligent, well, as if that was such a surprise to have to digest, and tackled me down to the floor. Bastard didn't even have one hand cuffed to the bench we'd been sitting on. Go figure, again, my luck. His raunchy breath, and rock candy-looking teeth, were up in my face. How death didn't come knocking on my door due to chemical poisoning, I'll never know. Eventually, although I'm pretty sure it could have happened quicker, a couple of blues hopped over to get the dumpster diver off of me. I'll never be positive about it but I swore I could see those donut-munchers passing around money afterwards. Betting on who was going to kill who, I wager. Savages, but, they're the ones with the guns.

I hadn't been placed back to my original seat. Instead, they shuffled me off into an interrogation room. There was Veps, of course, sitting there, with bags of powder, grass, and pills laid out in front of him. When I got placed, not so gently, onto a cold, hollowed metal chair, we were left alone. "We're screwed," I said, ready to throw up for the second time that night.

"Maybe one of them other poor gooch lovers, but not us," Veps said, although I'm not sure where he was going with that one. "I made my phone call. Now we just sit here and wait."

"Wait for what? Dude, I'm freaking out over this, I hope you know. I got no way to pay bail. No real lawyer. *Nothing*."

"Ash, in the time you've been here have you ever had to rely on just yourself? I told you I would take care of it, and all you're doing is whining." He took hold of the bag of powder, opened it, and stuck his head in.

"For the love of God! Veps, what is wrong with you?" I asked, grabbing the bag from him. "They're watching us through that stupid window right now and you're snorting up? At what point today did you lose your mind and neglect to mention it to me? We had a chance, but now we're definitely going to jail."

"Ah, man, jail isn't even in the cards for us. Besides, I'd have to make a break for it if they did throw me in lock up. I wouldn't last a day in the big house. Them gang-banger homies would pop a cap in my dome or do a 187 in my ass."

"Okay, you don't even make sense anymore. And what is a 187!"

"You know what, Ash, I'm going to sit back, relax, and you should do the same. Take one of the pills in that bag."

I eyed the table top, and for a moment I thought about it. I mean, why not? We were caught, red-handed, fingers in the cookie jar. What I wouldn't have given at that point to be back in Delaware. Silence then took over the room before Veps' snoring claimed it. Should've seen that moment coming but in the cloud-layered life that was mine, I had to just kind of roll with the whole show, freak-show, as it was turning out to be.

Nobody came in to talk with us. This went on for about an hour until the door opened. In walked a little bald man in an expensive suit he probably didn't deserve, carrying a briefcase. "-stein" was the last name suffix that I figured would be on his driver's license. Another suit, with legs, followed behind him. The man walked over to Veps, smacked him in the back of his head, and said, "Ricky, wake up."

Ricky? This guy meant business if he knew Veps but didn't bother making the effort to declare acknowledgement of the nickname. "What?" he asked, wiping dried drool from his chin. "Ah, ah! See, Ash, my boy, here is the answer to our prayers. Well, my prayers and you're butt-fucking-in-the-cell nightmares."

"Mr. Donnardo and Mr. Grishin are facing some serious charges, Mr. Eckstein," the woman said, verifying my initial read on the guy's membership as one of the chosen people.

Eckstein threw his briefcase onto the table but didn't make an effort to sit. Standing, he said, "What we have here, Ms. Cole, is one of those truly unfortunate instances of happenstance. Now no one is arguing over why my client and his friend are here. A bar fight, with a woman, which, I admit was stupid on their part," he said, eyeing Veps. "But no one can be sure just where these narcotics came from. Were they on his person? Yes, but again, completely plausible to figure on how they got there."

"I don't think they got there by magic," Cole said. "Would you also like to know that while here in custody, Mr. Donnardo was recorded using the cocaine we found?"

Eckstein took his glasses off, cleaned them, then, without bothering to put them back on, said, "Pamela, what is it exactly that you want?"

This is where my world of illusion came crashing down around me. Cole, still showing no emotion on her face, said, "Stanley, you know what I want. Anytime we pick up this one," she said, pointing to Veps, "or any other punk your boss has working for him, it's scratch our back, we scratch yours. Nothing changes just because we didn't catch him selling again."

The look on my face must have made me appear like I was on Valium, and I wish I had been for this. But I kept my mouth shut, and, much to my amazement, so did Veps. It was like when you're a little kid and you stay quiet because the adults are talking. That's what was happening. Grown-ups were chatting, doing business. "I do this for you, Pam, and I don't want to have to keep coming down here. If they work for Denham, call my office, but don't expect me to come. Let's make both our lives easier by not having to waste each other's time with bullshit banter."

"Give me the information we want and you can take these two losers out of here."

Eckstein reached into his briefcase, pulled out a folder, tossed it over to Cole, and said, "One of Denham's competitors has a shipment coming in the night after next. Enjoy."

It took less than ten minutes for Veps, myself, and Eckstein to exit the precinct. At this point, I was completely out of my head with what had just transpired. Eckstein put the two of us into the back of a town car, with himself plopping down in the front passenger seat. "Now listen up, asshole," he said to Veps, "Denham is not your biggest fan right now."

"You say that every time we gotta do this little dance," Veps said. "Just bring us to the boss so I can talk to him."

"Oh, you'll talk to him all right," Eckstein said. "He made me swear I'd get you to the club tonight."

"Nothing I wasn't planning on doing myself already."

"Don't talk to me for a while, Ricky."

With Eckstein's cold shoulder treatment enacted, the driver got us going. "Here," Veps said, handing me a pill, "pop it and relax now. See, I told you we'd be free and clear."

I held the tiny circular piece in my hand. This would make it all better. With what I had just experienced, I needed a little something to calm me down. "Veps, I, I'm sorry about freaking out back there. You gotta understand that I didn't know what the hell was going on."

"Apologies are for housewives who get caught blowing their dog walkers," Veps said. "Just trust me. Be cool."

From a nice shower to a cab ride of death. From tasty dogs to brutalizing lesbians. A potential weekend in the Tombs, getting jumped by a homeless man, witnessing corruption of written law, and now in a Lincoln, uncharged. What was going down in the city that never sleeps? Hell if I knew. And if I could figure it out, I would have forgotten it after that pill started doing its job.

The Devil's Den. That was the name of the club Veps and I were being driven to. It was one of those wanna-be upscale stripper joints that tries its damnedest to look professional like the ones in Las Vegas. This wasn't Sin City, but to a person like me who never had been to that desert oasis, The Devil's Den might just as well have been *it*. So much red and purple in my eyes that I thought I'd go color-selective at any moment. What Veps had given me was working its way slowly through, and I knew that if I didn't do everything I could to maintain myself, I'd be descending into Satan's causeway before I knew what hit me.

Men of all ages were represented in this pit of testosterone-fueled madness. They were bunched together by generations with very few gaps in-between. You had the straight-out-of-high schoolers who had just struck it legal and were out trying to experience what they perceived was the real world of sexual lust, the boys-trying-to-be men group who had college sheepskins in their drawers at home but were coming to the unfortunate realization that they might have been better off joining up with the Marines, the middle-agers who had finally figured out that their wives didn't really have so many new girlfriends, and the over-the-hill-and-through-the-woods pack whose dicks hadn't seen action since Reagan told Gorbachev to tear down that eyesore of a wall.

There were chairs everywhere. Filthy, disgusting seats of pure animal cravings that if you didn't check one over before you sat, you had all the likelihood of landing in a puddle of some poor sap's soldiers who had gone on a death march. That was it, wasn't it? The Devil's Den represented the massive birth control cesspool that the Catholic

Church had been condemning the practice of for over a thousand years. The Fallen One hadn't changed his strategy; he'd just become a sly entrepreneur.

Central to the theme of the place was a short staircase built with forced-perspective. It withdrew from a curtain-clad backroom down into what was supposed to be emulating a pool of fire and brimstone. A cauldron of synthetic destruction circled the room, and the girls, I use that term loosely because some, I felt, had seen one too many winters to qualify for the "girl" category, but being the gentleman that I thought myself to be, I gave them the benefit of the doubt. That circle of plastic glowed with a fluorescent intensity the likes of which my decaying psyche hadn't been ready for. In fact, Veps had to come and grab hold of me just as I was about to make an attempt at swimming in Kilauea's flow. "Trust me, trust me, Ash, my man," Veps said, his eyes twitching, "that'll get you a one-way ticket to a bouncer beat down." He pointed to the black t-shirt wearing, arms folded, large men of all shades of skin, standing at strategically-located points. "I've seen so many stupid stage-runners try and make for the girls only to have a terrible, well, um, 'accident.'"

"What did you give me?" I asked, starting to grow concerned with the dryness that had been encapsulating my tongue. "I can't feel the inside of my mouth."

"Just means it's doing the trick!" Veps said, smiling like a fool. "I'm heading to the back to chat up Boss Denham and get my ass-chewing. Go and have some fun."

I was left alone in a place where no man who is losing his mental well-being should be left. Veps had exited the main room and now I was to go about occupying myself. I'd never been to a strip club before. Don't think me a prude (I can't see at this point anyway how you might), but the ones back home were populated with girls I'd graduated grade school with, and I don't mean the pretty ones. They had gone and gotten pregnant by their virginity-stealing lovers who left just before potty-training could begin. But this joint was a haven for tuition-earning beauties and experienced pretties looking for much sought after attention. And I was all too happy to give them what they wanted. Okay, maybe I wasn't. I'd be lying if I said all of this had been easy for me. Veps made it look easy. In practice, it wasn't to be.

At the point I had been left to my own devices there were five girls performing with the greatest of ease on those golden poles of corruption. Limber, flexible, and lacking self-esteem, these women put on such a show. Men, wild with thoughts of fornication without questions, threw their hard-earned dollars through the air, only the real greenback flicking aces got them in the girls' G-strings. I was thoroughly impressed.

I sat down around the immoral Round Table when I saw a spot open up. A person could do serious damage to their neck what with having to stare up and over in order to see the spectacle. A waitress, wearing dental floss in substitution of underwear, came over to take my order. "What can I get for you, beautiful?"

"What do you recommend?" I asked, smiling.

"How about a Jack-and-Coke?" She said, her bountiful breasts bouncing to the rhythm of the music playing in the background.

"If that's what you're suggesting then I'm game, sweetheart. Nothing like a gorgeous girl bringing me alcohol to make the night that much nicer."

"Oh, you're a sweet-talker, ain't cha?"

"Only when I'm hammered…or really tired…sometimes I just can't tell difference."

She giggled a giggle like the kind you've heard in a Marilyn Monroe picture, mostly because that blonde bombshell only had that at her disposal. But don't get me wrong, I'd of killed the Yankee Clipper if it meant getting one night with Ms. Baker's little girl. Elton John, I am not. It would've been a filthy candle burning in the wind.

As I waited for my drink one of those nutty little things sauntered over to where I was sitting. She did this carefully, on her hands and knees, almost as if she was moving in for a kill. That's when it all kind of clicked for me. This was the very thing that Herbert Spencer had coined as survival of the fittest. While those other four played firemen, this young capitalist had taken it upon herself to start making money. The tigress, her brown eyes fixated on me, crawled right up to my face. When we were nose-to-nose, she licked the tip of mine. This was different. She was an avant-garde type of working girl. "You wanna dance, baby?" she asked, using one of those voices you know she'd never use at Sunday Dinner at grandma's house. "Only thirty."

"Only, huh?" I asked, fondling the bills Veps had given me in my pocket. I can only imagine what she thought I might have been doing, although, looking back, she probably knew exactly what I was doing. A seasoned expert in any field can tell the subtleties of the job.

"You want more, it's extra. I'm good, baby, real good. I picked you because you look like a real gentleman who will treat me right."

"You might be the only person in the world who would associate me with the word 'gentleman.' And I thought I was the high one."

"Got stuff to share with me, baby? I can get high and take you into outer space."

"Now, now," I said, "let's stick to the shop's theme here. I want to go down into the abyss."

She smiled and grabbed me by the collar of my shirt. When balance was achieved, she climbed down into my lap. Her brown skin was saturated in her own sweat. I think that's what made it all the more pleasurable for me. Like an animal getting the scent of its mate's musk, I was becoming a ravenous beast. When I tried to touch her, she slapped my hands away. "You want more, you pay more, and we go into private room, baby."

Maybe it was that last "baby," or maybe it was knowing that I'd just be spending Veps' money. Either way, I said, "Sure, let's go, but wait, my drink."

I don't remember tipping my waitress when she put the glass in my hand, hell, I'm not exactly certain I paid for it at all, but that wasn't important anymore. Here, in my lap, was a professional in need of showing me her résumé behind closed doors. Far be it for me to deny anyone the chance to show off their CV. We glided together from the seat, past the crowds of salivating hounds, and through a curtain that a nice hulking bouncer held open for us.

There was no continuation of theme in this room, but it didn't really matter. If you got yourself in there it meant that you were no longer wishing to play the part of the damned, descending through the levels. Although, perhaps, having made it into that room, I was sort of shaking hands with Lucifer himself. That was fine with me. I felt that I needed control after having had it stripped from me over Blake. My girl, I never did catch her name, pulled the curtains shut. Out came the orbs of confusion, but her little Hello Kitty stayed hidden from my eyes.

Up against my face went the breasts, nipples harder than I'd expected, and before she continued, her hand went out. "Pay up, baby," she said, no smile.

The exchange was made and back came the breasts. I was allowed to touch. And touch I did. They were the kind of artificial ones you think real, but when the deception is brought to light, it doesn't really matter. I had my fun. I think she did, too. Okay, I had fun while she worked. The stiffness rocking my pants couldn't be contained once the grinding began. I'm not proud of my lack of stamina, however, in my defense, I had downed that drink on the way to the room, and my sense of up-to-down had betrayed me. For all I knew, she was being serviced by me.

Over and over she worked. The friction was incredible. Just when I thought that there could be no more resistance, Veps walked into the room. "Dude!" I said. "Get out, I'm, I'm busy."

"How ya doing there, doll?" Veps said to my girl.

"Better than lately, Veps, sweetie," she said.

"You taking good care of my boy right here?"

"You know it, handsome."

Somewhere between Veps walking in and the small talk, I lost the erection and the blueness set in. "I need to get up," I said.

"Sit back down and finish, Ash," Veps said. "I can wait another few seconds."

"It could take another hour at this point now," I said, trying to lift the girl off me.

When finally I got to my feet, she was dumbfounded. "But I didn't make you...."

"Don't you worry, doll," Veps said. "He's not asking for a refund. You enjoy that cash. Buy yourself a new textbook or something. You still in school?"

"Struggling a little, but ya."

I zipped up my pants, grabbed Veps by the sleeve, and we walked out of the room together. "Why didn't you just wait a few more minutes?" I asked.

"Didn't know you'd have an issue with me being in there, considering the kicks we've been having."

"Something about the sanctity of a closed-off stripper room, I guess."

"Well, don't worry, my boy! Come on, I spoke to the boss and he's anxious to meet ya."

"Really? He's okay with you bringing me in?"

"Just smile and nod when we're in there, and when he continues ripping me a new one, because he probably will, just let it happen. Boss Denham keeps us fed. Don't go rocking the boat."

"A little nervous around the big guy, eh? Never seen you this reserved."

"No need to piss off the man that makes our living possible is all. Besides, he's the reason we're not cuddled up next to prison husbands tonight."

With my marbles aching, I chose to ignore Veps. I followed him back into the thick of things then beyond into the back. All illusions were put to rest once we went through the double-doors. Colored lights gave way to cheap 7-11 substitutes surrounded by walls of concrete slabs. It was almost like what a misplaced child at Disneyland feels like when the cast members bring him behind-the-scenes. Mickey and Pluto getting it on with Donald filming them. A terrible vibe crept up on me when I thought that, so I kept flushing out negative with positive, problem was, however, there wasn't much positive going on.

This Boss Denham was someone I had but a few thoughts about. Veps never really spoke about him all that much. It was probably because this character didn't exactly fit the general description of an employer. Far as I knew, Veps had a lot of freedom with how he conducted business, and if the boss was getting his fair share, well, he let it all slide. This probably enabled Veps all the more to behave the way he did, and while I had been enjoying it, I needed something of my own. I knew we could enjoy the kicks and thrills even more if we did business alongside one another.

Now I'm not saying that William Taft rose from the dead and is living amongst the people of today, but Boss Denham sure would do well in a variety show or two. When I first laid eyes on the man I had to kind of adjust on account of how much there was of him. This was not the man I had been envisioning. I had expected to meet a Fortune 500 sort of guy who could have doubled for the fat pigs of Wall Street. Boss Denham looked as if he had eaten most of those little swine, knuckles and all. His stomach protruded beyond the natural bounds, sinking well below the waist. Here was someone who might be legally allowed to declare his penis dead on account of not having been able to locate it for some time. God help the poor slut who's being paid to make him feel like Fabio, I had thought.

He was the stereotype of posse leaders. Topped off with a large Cohiba hanging from his clenched teeth, Boss Denham must have been playing the part of Prohibition gangster from the time he entered into this world. Tightly packed into a gray suit that did not complement his girth, I half-expected a button to pop just as I went to shake his hand, which, to my horror, was sweating more than I ever thought that particular appendage capable of.

"Very nice to meet you, sir," I said, hoping he'd let go of me as soon as I'd finished.

"So," he said, holding my hand tighter as if almost to hang on despite the secretion, "you're the one Ricky here has been talking up about."

"Yes, sir, Veps is a good guy. Been taking care of me since I got into town."

"Well," he said, letting go of me finally, "I can't say that he's such a great judge of character. Seems to me he's been in more trouble than most of my others. Doesn't feel right that I should have to get him out of trouble at every turn, does it?"

I was careful to not agree or disagree. People like Boss Denham aren't exactly easy to read, but if you pay close attention, you can get a blip of them on the radar. Here was a flab-faced, bald kingpin of junkies and escorts who needed to feel like you were on his side without getting too far up his asshole. "I think Veps just likes to have fun, sir. No harm in that, right?"

"I think I like this boy, Ricky. He just called you a flake without even making it sound like a bad thing."

Veps gave me one of those looks a person gives when they know that's not want you meant at all but that they're going to play along. "Well, Boss, I can tell ya that ole Ash here is a hard-working stiff. Him working for you with me, you'll rake in even more money. You know how hard it is to get through the Towers by myself? With my boy signed on, we could tackle those two in half the time and find even more clientele."

"I like what I'm hearing," Boss Denham said. "Tell me, Ash, it's Ash isn't it? What experience do you have in all of this? I mean, are you going to need some time in order to figure out the right kind of approach or is this something you've done before?"

Even though I knew Veps wanted me to just lie, I thought better of myself. No use telling a man, who could eat me for an appetizer if he so desired, something that was pure manure only to have it come back to bite me. "No," I said. "Never done work like this before. A frequenter of the products you push but never sold any of it."

Boss Denham rose up, glaring at Veps. "Ricky, did you bring me a junkie! Is this the kind of respect I get for giving you such a cushy life? You bring me another spoon-cooker!"

"Now, now, wait, oh wisest, hold up," Veps said, pushing me aside to perform damage control. "He ain't no junkie. He's a recreational type of guy just like me and most of your clock-punchers. Look at his arms, no needles there. He ain't no fall down fuck up."

My right arm was grabbed and inspected. When he let go, I could see the sweaty imprint of a callused hand. Holding back my vomit, I asked, "Do I make the grade, sir?"

"Ricky," Boss Denham said, "leave us alone for a minute, would you, kiddo?"

"Oh, the pleasure is all mine, boss man," Veps said, taking a quick exit, then, sticking his head back in. "Time enough to go back out and play?"

"Always time for fun, Ricky," Boss Denham said, shooing him off.

There I stood, alone with the long-lost Weinstein brother. Without Veps in the room, I suddenly felt nervous. He didn't say anything for a minute or two, just kept taking drags of that cigar. At one point, he started blowing smoke rings. This was the alpha-male establishing dominance. And I was fine with that. "So," Boss Denham said, finally, "what *really* makes you think that you'd do well for me? I know Ricky likes you, but he's brought others into the circle who didn't quite work out the way I had hoped they would. One even had to be sent, um, *away*."

"I got nothing holding me anywhere," I said. "I'm just a piece of trash floating around hoping for someone to throw me a bone. I had a job at this crap hole of a kitchen and I almost lost my mind. You give me this opportunity and I know I'll make you money. Me and Veps come from the same town. We're a lot alike."

"Better watch how you go advertising how much you two are similar. If that boy didn't fetch me such a hefty income every month, his rump roast would be someone's property over at Riker's. Fact is it's because of the money that I can throw Eckstein out to the far corners of the Boroughs to pull Ricky's ass out of the fire. That's the kind of person I am, Ash. I take care of my own."

"When it suits you, right?" I said, almost not believing the words actually having come from my mouth. I thought myself done there on the spot.

"You have a tongue on you, son. That could get you into trouble one day, but not here. You're right. If Ricky's stock goes down lower than I'd like to see, he's out. This is a world of realism. No room for optimistic views. That garbage went out with Nixon's resignation. No trust in a world like this."

"I need money, sir," I said, deciding to lay it all out for him. "I won't screw up, and I won't get into trouble. Can't afford to, literally."

"I had my mind pretty much made up before Ricky left the room. Just don't like being a nice guy in front of people who don't need to see it. You're getting a shot, Ash. Just one. Don't go lousing it up. Go get your buddy, and bring him back in. Close the door behind you."

Veps was balls deep in three girls when I found him. Two massaged his shoulders as the third gave his crotch a rubdown. Music blasted from all directions, and I saw a procession of latex-covered flesh enter into the fray. Suddenly, and quite calculated, dollar bills, some crumbled, some folded, others in the shape of airplanes, went circling about the room. Had I not been so alert, well, okay, semi-alert, I might have lost an eye. But there I was, having to distract Veps from his own privately public romp. "The boss wants you back inside now," I said. "I think he wants to tell you I'm good to go."

"That a fact?" Veps asked, his face firmly planted between two of the biggest breasts I'd ever seen. "Sounds like you impressed the big guy, eh? That a'boy, Ashie!"

"You gonna be done soon?"

"What's your rush?" he asked, mouth now trapped with no hope of a rescue.

"I just want the preliminary bull taken care of, and I'm still feeling whatever that was you gave me."

"You're gonna be feeling that good shit most of the night. No worries though, because it doesn't escalate. You're coming nicely back down to earth."

"I'd feel much better if you took a reprieve for a few minutes. Take'em in the backrooms with ya when you're done. Hell, I'll help, but you need to go talk to Denham."

"Ah, you're all business tonight, eh? Well, that's all right. You'll be back to the kick-seeking kid that I've come to know, love, and corrupt!" He turned to the girls. "Ladies, I'll be expecting you in my usual room. You know, the one with the vibrating, well, everything! Keep yourselves occupied while I see to some occupational-related matters."

There was a three-way snicker amongst them. I figured they'd be doing that soon enough again with a little moaning mixed in for good measure. Veps knew how to have a good time with anyone at any time and place. I envied him. Here was a dude who had it all figured out. Nothing he did was boring. Even going to work for him was a thrill all in its own. But that's something I wanted. I wanted it badly. I wanted to have that kind of job that paid off in bigger ways than I thought any other profession could. Was drug dealing a valid occupation? Fuck if I cared so long as I had a wad of cash rolled up in my pocket at any given time.

I'd been told to stay out of the last say meeting between Boss Denham and Veps. Didn't bother me, so I stayed unassuming outside in the hallway, eventually sitting down on a crate when I realized that Veps never did anything simple and was probably talking up a storm. When the ten minute mark came upon me, I must've slouched back against the wall, invisible to anyone who might have been passing by me. And there she was. Marci. All dolled up, looking like she was ready for one superb night of who-the-hell-cared, because she looked outstanding. I didn't say anything at first, truth be told, because I was too busy staring at her very bare legs. Something about this woman just made my pants shrink via autopilot.

Then it happened. Veps came out. I silently awaited the smart remark. But nothing. Not a sound from him. Was this a sign of the apocalypse? I chose to refrain from that kind of thinking before I got my facts straight. I'd never known him to be quiet around anyone let alone a member of the female persuasion. All he did was nod, throw out an awkward smile, and trade places with her, going in as he came out. He almost went by me when I grabbed his leg. I got a foot in the chest. "Jesus Christ," I said. "It's me, asshole."

"The piss you hiding out for?" Veps asked. "You on some covert affair I ain't been told about?"

"Got bored is all. You were in there for a bit."

"He had to add some more verbal abuse to feel better about sending Jew Boy, the Attorney Avenger, out to get us."

"But it's all squared away then, right?"

"Ya, ya, ya, just like I told you it would be. We're gonna pop yo cherry, Ash my lad!"

A smile arose on my face the likes of which I hadn't really been used to before then. Money was in my future. Then out came Marci. With what Veps had been saying to me, I had forgotten about her being there. As I attempted to call out to her, Boss Denham came up from behind her. Veps, sensing something was in the air that shouldn't have been there whatsoever, covered my mouth with his hand, quickly falling over on me. "Keep quiet for God's sake," he said in a whisper. "I don't know what you were about to say, but for the love of Slurpee just hush."

I watched in utter horror as Boss Denham's fat fingers felt up around Marci's hindquarters, clasping it with all his might. She smiled then welcomed his tongue into her face. Shock. Best word for me to use. Complete shock. From our place behind the corner of the wall, Veps and I observed the two walk out through the building's backdoor. Not until all sound from the hallway had exited did Veps let me back up. The unfortunate realization that came next almost brought up everything attempting to digest within me. I, the newest employee of Boss Denham, had just recently been blown by his girlfriend.

Sleep. Wonderful, self-revitalization. Sleep. Something I wanted so badly to do that night. Sleep. The one thing that never came. Veps snored on and on in his bed like most other nights. I, on the other hand, stared blankly into the ceiling. Beyond the water stains and crummy patchwork, was a vision of the world caving in all around me. My arms, joined at the hands behind my head, held me in position.

Television was on, but I had the volume turned down. Nothing worth watching. So much to whittle through. A lot of compost to shovel my way out of. Veps didn't immediately seem fazed by any of what transpired at the strip joint, because he hadn't understood at first. He'd decided to pop some pills right after he played full-on tackle with me. Maybe he just didn't care. No, he did. He had to. This whole messed-up situation concerned him as much as it did me. After all, he was responsible for all that I did during my time in the high-rise underworld that New York City was becoming to me.

It was right after Boss Denham and Marci left our sight. Veps slowly let go of my mouth. He stood up, searching for anything he might have been carrying. I, however, had started sweating like some type of zoo-bred animal in heat as they wheeled in my new mate. "What the fuck," I said, not having the ability to use any other word in my lexicon. "What the fuck?"

"Afraid so, my boy," Veps said. "I don't know what you were gonna say to her, but it's best you didn't say anything."

"How did you know?" I asked.

"Know what? About her? Marci's been with the boss since right after I started up with him. I pointed her out to you our first night together. Remember?"

"Ya, you said she was a hooker."

"Huh? I never said that."

"Yes, dude, you did. You said she enjoyed men with deep pockets or some shit like that."

"Exactly," Veps said. "And Denham's got deeper pockets than most on this island. Marci's enjoying a good time on his American Express."

"That doesn't mean she is a hooker."

"Again, I never said she was a prostitute. So since you thought that's what she was, it's best that I stopped you from saying something you were about to immediately regret."

"Wait, hold up," I said, my hands waving in the air. "You just sacked me because you thought I was gonna make some kind of a whore comment to her? Where does that kind of thinking come from?"

"Because," Veps said, finding what he'd been in search of, "*I'd* of said something. Oh, maybe something like, 'hey, dolly, where's your mattress at?'"

"What's wrong with you, man? Just cause you'd say it doesn't mean I would."

"Says you. But I know, Ash, I know. You were looking for some kicks, weren't ya?"

"I already got my kicks with her," I said, watching as Veps' facial expression sank lower than I had ever seen before.

"You and Marci? Shut up. No way. Not a possibility, my friend. You're lying."

"Why would I lie about this? We hooked up. We got a little nasty with each other."

"You stuck it in her? My God, my God, why has thou forsaken us...."

"Calm down," I said, grabbing at his frantically flaying arms. "We didn't have sex. I...I just...."

"Oh, sweet mother of mine," Veps said, his eyes widening. "Boss Denham is about to kiss the lips of a woman whose had your cock bust a nut through it." He was silent for a moment. "Ha..." he said. "Ha...ha...ha!"

"You think this is funny?"

"Absolutely, I do! Ash, my man, you have successfully, single-handedly, humiliated the big guy first night on the job!"

I could see that Veps was anything but truly laughing about this. There was a certain kind of fear in his cackling. This was him scared. Not out of his mind but nervous and unsure of what to make of the whole thing. I could hear the end of his laugh pass away only to be replaced by the paranoid ramblings of a man under the influence of fine product while riding in the backseat of another yellow box of potential death.

"Couldn't be the first time she ever did this to him," I said.

"Probably not, but for the love of Jesus, why did it have to be *you*," Veps said, trying really hard to not bash his head into the back of the front seat.

"This isn't a big deal, is it?"

"Are you stupid?" Veps asked, his face having just accomplished what it'd been attempting. There was a stitching mark embedded in his forehead for a couple of minutes. "Marci ain't gonna keep her mouth shut. She's gonna blab. Women always blab. She is gonna tell Boss Denham it was all your fault and then we both get two in the chest. Okay, maybe one for me, but definitely two for you."

"What do you think will happen to her if she tells him?" I said, hoping he'd get it. "She tells him and she's just admitted to cheating. Not gonna happen. If Denham is as big a screwball as you're making him out to be then if the boat doesn't get rocked any more than it has, everyone goes untouched."

"Way to be the voice of reason, my boy. You're right. Marci's just as likely to get a slap-around session and kick out the door as we are to be...well no need to bring that nastiness up again. Okay, okay, all right, mhm...." Veps was doing his best to think straight. "Yes, I got it, all right. You keep your distance from her. No reason why you two should ever be made to even be in the same room."

"Agreed," I said.

"How was she?" Veps asked.

"What do you mean?"

"Just what I asked. How was she? Good? Meh?"

"It was probably the best sucking I've ever had."

"So long as it was worth it," Veps said, breathing a sigh of half relief, half jealously.

I got up from the couch once the clock struck five. No use in trying to sleep, I figured, when sunrise was imminent. There was nothing in the fridge. Eventually, Veps or I would have to go shopping again. Not that day, though. That particular day was planned to be one of reflection upon the unknowing sins I'd committed against my new employer. My God, what was I thinking? None of it had been my fault, right? Marci was the instigator. She brought me back to her place. Could William Blake be the one at fault here? Possibly. But a person can't go blaming the past for mistakes made in the present. Only Hitler had that innate ability, and nothing within me wished to be counted among those like him. No, there'd be no funny walking for me.

An escape from Veps' constant symphony of deviance was in order. I had to get my head cleared. Back home it'd be easy to do. Take a walk through the woods by my house or just lay up on the roof of some building. Couldn't be done in this city. No stars in the night sky due to light pollution. See, we even destroyed the beauty of the gods looking down upon us. Terrible acts of deicide were being put into effect. Nothing would stop the process. And there'd be no walk through trees. A park here, a park there, but having to share company with a makeshift village of homeless people was not my idea of the serene. Oh, and that central of all parks, well, I'd rather take my chances with drinking arsenic than attempting survival in that place. Besides, it was too far from where I felt comfortable venturing. I figured maybe another day.

Bagels. The thought entered into my mind almost as if a beautiful, plump little cherub had flown down, sprinkling it into my ear. Instead of dying and giving up my throne to a drunk, I laced my shoes. Down the stairs I went and back out into the dew-covered sidewalks. Okay, mostly condensation-covered because of the constant blowing of steam-filled sewers. You got used to the smell. You had to. A person prayed for a nasal blockage, especially during those hot summer months. I wasn't so lucky.

I thought I knew what bagels were before I left Delaware. Evidently, I didn't know anything. Maybe it had to do with the water. The natives of the New York Tri-state area will tell you that theirs are the greatest in the world. They're not blowing smoke up your ass either. Throw on some cream cheese and you're in a dough-infused dream of comfort food. That's what I needed.

Veps had been taking me to a place a couple of blocks away from the apartment. Unlike most places he enjoyed going to, this one was well-known and often frequented. When I got there around seven, a small crowd had already gathered. This wasn't a rowdy bunch nor was it one of those groups you might find Veps and me a part of. You know, the ones where everyone hasn't seen daylight in a couple of days and the very thought of sleeping through the night brings your blood down a few degrees. None of these folks fit the mold.

It was called Grubb, and if the name of the place sounded bland, you were missing out if you didn't just enter through its doors. The owners had gone for that rustic, pretend-you're-somewhere-in-New England-look. For a few minutes of escape from the asphalt melting underneath your shoes, a person could retreat into this place. Exposed brick patterned the walls while hardwood, cheap imitation really, covered the floor. Some asshole with a funky looking ascot definitely made a bill on decorating that place.

A person like me isn't terribly impressed with stupid-looking "genuine" antiques that have labels saying they were made in China which hang on the walls of these establishments. That being said, when Veps had first taken me there, I thought he was losing his mind. But something about the place made him feel peaceful, at least, that's what he said. Once I was able to get over the whole idea of having to buy into someone's cute vision of a Massachusetts getaway, the food spoke for itself.

What bagels had to do with the Land of the Puritans, I'll never know. A hungry individual needs to allow for the suspension of disbelief when they haven't really had a good night's sleep and they're in desperate need of sustenance. I happened to be one of them and also sixth in line. As I came up to the counter, the fool wearing a plaid apron, and who I wanted so desperately to call Paul Bunyan, asked, "What'll it be, sir?"

Sir? Funny how people respond to certain words which they're not used to being called. I don't think many in my entire life up until then ever called me sir. It's been used sparingly since. I was no "sir," but, I figured I'd let him have the benefit of the doubt. "Bagel with cream cheese, please."

He looked at me like I was a moron. Veps had always ordered as I grabbed a table. "What kind of bagel and what kind of cream cheese?" the guy asked.

Even today, I can't believe I actually responded with what I did. I've always chalked it up to low sugar levels. "One with a hole, preferably."

"Excuse me?"

"Ya, one with a hole and white cream cheese."

We stood there for several agonizing seconds before a voice from behind said, "Two everything's with a scallion spread."

"Yes, ma'am," he said, turning around to fetch the order.

I knew that voice. Not very well, but enough to know that it was the sound of impending doom. My own doom. Veps' potential doom. When I looked to confirm my suspicions, there *she* was. Marci, in tight yoga pants and a red hoodie with no logo. She'd not be anyone's walking billboard. But nonetheless, she was standing right there, smiling. "So you going to pay? I mean, I did kind of make better your awkward situation, didn't I?"

"It wasn't so awkward," I said.

"Oh, please. 'With a hole in it?' Seriously?"

"I had a long night of thinking."

"That's your excuse?"

Before I could come back at her, our order was ready. I paid the tab. Very gentlemanly of me, I thought. We took our food over to a small table in the corner. Everything was making me sweat. If Marci knew what I knew, well, she might go absolutely nuts. But maybe she did know. Maybe Boss Denham had told her? I had to play out this little game before the chance evaded me. I'd have to be ever so careful. This wasn't some dumb little twit. Marci had brains in her head. "So not enough sleep last night?"

"Oh, no less than usual," she said.

"Do anything interesting?" I was trying so desperately to not sound like Columbo. Peter Falk I was not.

"Nothing major." I couldn't tell if she was being coy or it was just because she needed to eat her breakfast in peace.

"Really? Hmm. Oh, ya, I went to this strip club last night. First time there."

Not one tell showed up anywhere on her face. Of course, this having been the Big Apple, she could have assumed that I'd been referring to any one of a hundred such places. "The Devil's Den," I said. "Ever heard of it?"

The bite she was about to take went aborted. Marci looked at me but said nothing. I *had* her. I had to have had her. The mechanisms within her mind were churning. The boy from rural upbringings had brought her to a halt. Could I maintain the hold? "Why so quiet?"

"Do you want to say something to me, Ash?" There was a hint of bitch lingering in her voice.

"I just wanted to know if you've ever heard of that place. I mean, you've been in the city longer than me, so I figured you'd know it."

"Has Veps been talking? What's he been saying to you? Did he tell you I worked there?"

She'd obviously misread my form of questioning. To her, this was an attack upon a misperception on what she might do for a living. "Veps didn't say anything to me. In fact, all he did was show me the way in. It's an interesting club. The owner seems like quite a character."

Her look grew grave. She put down the bagel, pushing it slightly away. Marci had made the connection. Now it was time to watch the attempt to dig out of where I'd just buried her. "I know it. Never been in the actual club. No, I'm more acquainted with the backroom area. Where the business end of it goes down."

"Oh, I've been back there too," I said, with my eyebrow raised like I was some slick stockbroker.

"Recently?"

"Possibly."

"Why don't you just say what you're strongly hinting at."

This was it. Here it came. The bomb of words that I'd been holding back since she ordered the food. "Boss Denham's stuffing you like an oversized turkey on Thanksgiving morning!"

The next few seconds felt like one of those moments in the movies, specifically, *The Matrix*. It's that special effect known as Bullet Time when everything freezes in the frame and the camera pans around before action is restarted. That's what it was like right before Marci stood, reached over, and smacked me square across the face. Me, having not anticipated this move, went down off the chair, spilling poppy seeds and grains of salt all over myself.

There's a certain kind of feeling when you've just been hit by a woman. It's not the same sensation as if you'd just been whacked upside the head by some guy. No, because in a bar fight or back alley brawl, two dudes going at it would represent that ancient, hunter-gatherer mentality. True Darwinism. It'd be a pair of barbarians brandishing their swords, or axes, battling until one went down. And if the defeated lived, well, they'd probably split a keg of ale or some ritualistic bonding ceremony like that. But, no, not at that moment.

A sense of shame, defeated shame, lulled over me. As I came to, I realized that not many people in the place had even bothered to turn an eye to what had just happened. That sort of behavior was standard in the city. I'm surprised that no one ever tried to immortalize it on a t-shirt, or, at the very least, a postcard. The only good thing to come out of it was that the coffee had managed to not strike me anywhere. That could have put me in a bad place.

I shook my head a couple of times to get everything up and working again. The shot had been so unexpected that I finally understood the nature of vertigo. Marci made no attempt to help me up. She just stood there, gazing down upon her crushed opponent. I might have held a hand up to her, and she might have slapped it away, or not even bothered to make a move at it. Everything took a few minutes to get put back together.

When I finally regained my composure, I stood up, brushed off the garbage adorning my shirt, and asked, "Does *he* pay you to do that to *him*?"

Don't act surprised by the fact that I asked such a question. I'm not the kind of person who is going to go and hit a girl, no, my retaliation is of a more silvery-tongued nature. At least this time, when she swung, I'd be prepared to duck, cover, roll, or whatever it is one does to avoid a collision with a fist of fury. All that I had readied for, however, was for naught. She didn't throw a hook of any kind. What Marci did was, again, an unexpected move on her part. Tears formed. Tears were shed. A look of complete hatred came over her, and the next thing I knew, she was darting for the back, where the bathrooms were.

What to do? Several thoughts crossed my mind as I stood solo in the midst of an abandoned battlefield. One was to get out of there. Another was to quietly sit down, continue eating, just pretend like nothing happened. The third was to go in the back and try talking to Marci. Veps would have ordered another bagel. Veps would have walked on out eating that bagel. Me, well, I wasn't Veps, not yet, as angry as that made me feel, so my guilt-ridden ass headed on towards the toilets.

No boys/girls doors to differentiate from. Unisex all the way. Never made much sense to me in separating them. We're all God's creatures, right? Okay, maybe I'm just trying to sound like a deep individual. Keep them all one room so that when the hot broads feel the need, you can mosey right on in after them. Perverted? Maybe, just a tad, but, you can't expect much more than that from someone who spent very little time straight-laced.

"Marci," I said, knocking ever so gently, hoping that maybe she'd never hear it, and I could get off squeaky clean.

"Leave me alone," she said, but, of course, I knew that was female-speak for no, no, please, keep knocking. Fool that I am, I continued tapping on the door. "I don't want to talk to you."

"Come on. Open up. I'm sorry. I just, well, I don't know why I said those things. I was angry."

"That doesn't give you the right to talk to me that way. You really stepped over the line."

"Why don't you just open the door, and we can talk about this face-to-face, cause I gotta tell ya, chatting you up through solid matter ain't exactly ideal."

There was silence for a moment, a sniffle, then the turning of the knob. She kept it opened just a bit so that I'd be here to see her puffy eyes. Poor thing, I thought, until she opened her mouth. "You know, Ash, it's probably really unwise to go and make your employer's girlfriend cry."

Sweet Mary, mother of God. Nowhere in the deep trenches of my mind did I ever actually consider that before going and blabbing the way I had. It'd been one thing to have had her suck me off. Hell, in that scenario we'd both need to keep our traps shut. But this was a completely different sort of knotted web of guano. I'd gone and insulted Marci, Boss Denham's woman, making her cry with witnesses if such kinds of people were needed, although I'm sure they wouldn't have been. And when she went to tell her main squeeze about all that had gone on, I'd be a dead man standing. Walking would lead one to think I had a chance of making it out of the room.

No, if Marci went and spilled the beans, there'd be no use in telling Boss Denham about the KGB, the cafe, Blake, any of it. To backpedal with my stupidity was the only method of survival at that point. Kiss her ass, "yes" her to death, whatever it would take to keep her from going gabby with the information that would condemn me to a nice long dip in the Hudson, or possibly the East River. I couldn't be sure exactly how the guy dealt with loose pieces of trash.

"Marci," I said, in my most convincingly-sounding voice of please-don't-tell-your-boyfriend,' "can we just talk? I know I was wrong, but maybe we could start the whole convo over? Come on, I'll even buy the bagels and coffee this time. What do you say?"

She said nothing. There were a few sniffles. Then she opened the door enough to let me pass. I walked in, realizing that's what she'd meant for me to do. I figured that this was going to be a verbal lashing mixed with a few more slaps. Not a problem with me so long as what happened in that bathroom stayed there. "You really hurt me, you know that?"

"Yes, and I'm trying to apologize. Can you see it all from my point-of-view, though? I mean, the other night, you, me, we, you know. And then I go and see you with my new boss. It scared the living piss out of me. Veps was a bit hysterical."

"He knows about what happened?" she asked, some more disbelief painted on her face.

"Well, yes, but don't worry about him. He's likely to be blamed for it just as much as I am if Boss Denham ever finds out."

"So it'll stay our little secret then? No one has to know who doesn't already?"

"Exactly," I said, relief coming back into my world. "Not a soul ever has to know beyond you, me, and Veps. No worries, right?"

This is where I was expecting her to agree with me, throw away the clump of snot-ridden tissue in her hand, shake mine, and depart. No such luck. Rather than go along with the play I'd been writing in my head, Marci strode right up to my face. There couldn't have been more than a hair's length distance between us. "Uncomfortable" would have been a good word to use had my dick not already spent time in her mouth. *This* was now awkward country.

"Do you think he deserves me?" she asked.

"I don't think I'm the person who can make that call," I said, trying my best to not crack.

"I'm trapped being with him. Do you know that? I'm his until he's done with me."

"How long have you been with the guy?"

"Much too long. It's well-known that he likes'em younger than himself. I'll always be younger than him, but I'm far from being young anymore. He doesn't look at me the way you do."

It suddenly started to get hot inside that tiny-tiled chamber. I was sure it would become one of horrors if I didn't just get myself out of there. "Marci, I think I should be getting on. Veps will probably be coming out of his coma soon, and, well, I do have a new job to start, right?"

"You going to leave me, Ash? You going to drop me like he'll drop me as soon as he notices my ass isn't as high up as it used to be?"

"Your ass is quite nice," I said, before I quickly covered my mouth, realizing just what she might be trying to do. If attention was what she wanted, Marci was doing a damn good job of getting it. But I couldn't continue catering to her. To let it get any further was to spell certain doom for me. All I needed was for something else to happen and my ending at the hands of Boss Denham would be written in concrete, which might end up matching the new shoes he'd so graciously give to me.

"You're just saying that to make me feel better," Marci said.

"You're right," I said. "Just to do that. Now if you'll excuse me...."

"I think you're a terribly sly cutie," she said, running her pointer up my shirt, towards my neck. "You liked the other night, right? I mean, you didn't have any complaints about it."

"Marci, listen, I know what you're trying to do. It's not going to work. I'm sorry, but even if I do find you attractive, you're just asking for trouble now."

"How do you know I'm asking for anything? Remember, the game. You recall the game, don't you? It's all a game, Ash. You, me, Denham, we're just players in it."

Ah, Christ, the game. I could just imagine her saying it again in her apartment. Those words slipping off her seductive tongue. See, I'm not a push over, but good God, I'm only human. "Well, you gotta put a quarter in to play a game, right?"

"Bit more than twenty-five cents these days. How about we work off another round with credit?"

"Okay, now I'm completely lost. What are you talking about?"

"I'm talking about two people who want to make one another feel good. Don't you want to feel good again? You made me cry, so, you should *really* want to make everything better. I'm thinking you owe me."

"I owed you an apology. I gave you one. It's all squared away now," I said, feeling the sweat start to build heavier on my forehead.

"You look really nervous? Do I make you uneasy?"

"What do you want, Marci?"

"This," she said, taking hold of my hands and clamping them to both her cheeks, and I'm not referring to her face. "*This* is what I want."

Blame it on the hormones. Entirely on them. I couldn't be responsible for what occurred in that lavatory of lust. My fingers gripped her behind as tight as they could. I lifted her up so that her legs wrapped around me. Her hands held my face, and she pulled me in. We kissed. More than kissed. We swapped saliva like two star-crossed lovers sans the Italian setting, although the cheap imitation marble in the room could have been counted as a poor substitute. Regardless, Marci and I were hot for one another. Apology accepted.

It was probably to my advantage that Veps had a busy week. Meant that he wouldn't be crossing paths with me most of the time. That was perfectly okay with yours truly. What had gone on in that bathroom between Marci and me was something I didn't wish to discuss. At least until I figured out a way to just go ahead and say it. Until then, I kept a lid on it, eagerly anticipating when Veps would begin my training period, which I have been told was going to be that Friday night. Veps always said he could rake in a bundle on Fridays. All those TGIFers yearning for a break from the mundane workweek in one glorious snort of satisfaction. Hell if I cared about any of them. I just wanted to start putting money away in the First National Bank of Ash.

A haircut was something I was in desperate need of. I'd been putting it off for some time, but I figured if I was going to start pretending to be highbrow, I might as well look the part so as to not draw the attention of any bacon brigadiers. Veps had that really expensive-looking suit he'd wear on Tuesdays to the Towers, so I knew even he had to play dress up for the customers.

There are two things in this world that I hate more than anything else. They are haircuts and shaving. If I could get away with it, I'd look the part of Hobo King, never having to cut, snip, or rip a single hair from my body. Always imagined myself in old age with a beard down to my ankles, skirting the floor like the best of the boxcar boys. Unfortunately, until I achieved that dream, I'd be living in the world of judgment for anyone who didn't fit a preconditioned mold. So ultimately, I almost always ended up having to do both the cutting and shaving on the same day.

I'm not a crazy picky person when it comes to getting my ears lowered, but speaking from personal experience, I've had some pretty awful cuts in my life. There was this one time back in high school when my usual girl got stuck home, sick. Well, her replacement butchered me. I'm talking uneven with strays lurking about my scalp. It was a rough month, but I managed to avoid going most places with a skullcap on to hide the massacre.

Never does it cease to amaze me how people can screw up a haircut. The ones who tend to chat you up a lot are the ones spelling out doom before your ass is even in the chair. Needless to say, being in a city unknown to me did not help my situation. I needed to find a competent barber who understood the importance of a perfect shaping job.

When I found the ideal locale, the place just sang out to me. Men of all walks lined up against the wall, sitting, eagerly awaiting their moment in the leather-covered stool which would make them presentable once more. I took to my spot in line. This was the kind of shop you saw on television or in the movies: salt of the earth-type gents who still wore the standard white shirt of a true barber without one tiny hint of a trendy hairdresser ready to spring out of their flamingo dance class right into your face and not a single feminine-themed magazine in sight. Relief came over me like you wouldn't believe.

The one negative aspect about it all was noticed a minute into my wait. It started off low, but the sounds grew louder as I got farther down the line. Seems that on the other side of the joint a kiddie cuts kind of operation was going on. Unbelievable. Simply uncanny was my luck then and to some degree even today. Children, whining little brats clawing just to get a bite out of you. Vampires are what they are. Bloodletting little demons sent by God to punish adults and some wayward youths. When they're quiet and well-behaved, heck, even I'd take a turn watching over them, but when it's the opposite, get me out of there with the quickness.

This is where I realized that the next generation of people were going to endure suffering for the better part of their lives. Now, when I was a kid, you sat me down in the chair, pumped it up to eye level, cut my hair, and popped a lollipop in my mouth, booting me out the door for good measure. Stupid me, well, I just assumed that the tots who followed would continue the act. Sure, maybe the confectionary could evolve into grander things, this now being the 21st century, but what I saw made me cringe for the future.

A hefty-sized mother, who definitely should have been on a hunger strike, or at least a Slim Fast diet, unbuckled her semi-quiet son from his stroller. Piece of cake. No trouble there. Well, as this poor former nut stain came to the realization of where he was, a passerby might have thought that Auschwitz had gone back into business. Holy shit, this kid was spouting out shrills of terror. I almost got up, God forgive, and punched the little bugger in the face. But unlike most situations I found myself in, refrain got the better of me. No arrest for the assault of a minor would end up on my record.

The woman stylist led the boy by the hand, placing him inside a fiery red rocket ship. Fine, okay, no problem, we had those kinds of things back in the day. This was perfectly acceptable protocol. Nothing to discuss any further, that is, until the video got popped in. I almost hit the floor from shock. This child, who was carrying on like they were ripping his fingernails out, sat in silence, a dull expression taking over him as Mickey Mouse and his friends sang, danced, and did a whole bunch of other silly stuff.

This summed it all up for me. The children of the day were being prepped for a lifetime of coddling the likes of which no one was ready for. If that had been me, my old man, even my mother, who am I kidding, would have whipped me on the backside. That expression of giving a pintsized pants pisser something to really cry about should be a staple of any civilized country's set of legal codes. No such luck, it would seem, even in the intervening years since I first recognized one of the many problems facing the fate of humanity.

Dumbfounded, I had obviously zoned out of the room. It took three "excuse me's" before the guy next to me said, "Hey, pal, you're up."

My eyes shifted focus. I was back amongst the living again. There it was, the chair, waiting anxiously for my rear to occupy it. Never can be too comfortable in those things. The behinds of so many have warped the cushions so that you'll never truly feel good. Nope, everything continued on the way it always had once I plopped down. The man before me must've had the girth of a rhino. It felt as if I were lost in an empty space of phantom butt. Like any other time, I accepted this. No good reason not to.

All seemed safe until the voice of my barber called off from behind me. It was the softest sounding tone for a man-of-the-scissors. Fear crept over me as if I'd just had my way with the mayor's daughter and daddy dearest was suddenly standing over me. Don't think of me as a believer in stereotypes, but you know, they do come from somewhere. Well, this barber, whose voice was warmer than one could hope to never hear, came off to me almost immediately as…simple, yes, that's the word, simple. "Oh, hello, sir. So nice of you to drop by. What'll it be for you today? Sorry, sorry, I'm Pat. Not Patrick. That was never an option. Always Pat."

I must attract these kinds of people or least these kinds of circumstances. Here I sat, an anally-retentive mess of a man when it came to haircuts and now the guy who was going to perform the surgery just made me a complete a wreck. His hands didn't even grip the razor very tight. Trouble, that's what I felt I was in, trouble. No coming back from this one, but, too late to get up and make a move. I'm not that type of a person. Rolling with the punches is what I learned to do a long time ago. Only choice for me. "Well, I, how about we go short?" I said, trying my best to not squirm.

"Oh, yes, that sounds wonderful," Pat said.

I'm pretty sure this gentle giant of a lummox had been traveling the short bus most of his life. Jesus, why couldn't I have been more like Veps at that moment? He'd of just taken the clippers and styled himself. Could do a woman I hardly knew in a dingy shitter, but God forbid I went about canceling a potentially fatal trim session. "Maybe do a number five all around?" I asked, hoping to the creator on his throne that this dude knew what I meant.

"Hmm, a five, huh? All around? You've got a lot of hair on your head, um, oh, excuse me, what's your name?"

"Ash," I said, feeling the tissue paper collar around my neck start to absorb beads of sweat."

"Lovely to know you, Ash. I'm Pat."

"Yes, you've already said that."

"Dear me, I did, didn't I?" He then went to make sure his tool was plugged in.

I looked around for help. Nobody appeared willing and able to do anything. From what I gathered, the guy who sat next to me in line was thoroughly relieved to not have gotten Pat. Bastards. All of them. Go and sacrifice the new customer to the angry gods of Barbicide. A fitting name for the product as I now saw it. Yes, murder by barber. Who made it so easy for the dimmest of people to get a license granted so they could wield sharp edges at a person's face? The idea of the early ones being the neighborhood surgeons did nothing less than both infuriate and scare me. An odd combination of sensations to say the least.

When "Curly" Pat, the immediate nickname I conjured for him, came back out from under his drawer, he said, "All right, let's see, mhm, you wanted a three, correct?"

"No, no, a five, please," I said, seeing my own horror-stricken expression in the mirror, positive the pricks behind me were laughing at my expense.

Then it came. A simple, subtle click. The standard buzzing followed. It was on. Not just the razor, but the battle between my thick lochs and the Forrest Gump chopping away at them. A soft touch. Even more worry ventured into my already fragile psyche. The only way I can describe the sensation is that it felt like a baby kitten was pawing its way across my scalp. I don't know about other people, but to me, when it feels like the barber isn't putting enough pressure, all signs are pointing to a chop job. This was not what I needed on that day.

Worse still, Pat was a talker. All the elements that could come together to form a jumbled mess of a compound were present. "Wonderful summer we're having," he said.

Everything was falling apart. I was listening, trying not to respond even with facial expressions. There must have been a slight smirk on my face that registered with him that I was listening. Damn it all to the netherworld.

The entire event must have gone on for only about ten minutes, but they were some of the worst ones I'd ever endured. When it was all said and done, I opened my eyes, which had closed due to extreme duress. Flawless. Pat, against all preconceived notions on my part, had fought the good fight and declared himself the unquestioned victor. He'd achieved the perfect cut. Truly remarkable.

"That'll be fifteen, sir," Pat said, his arms locked in an L-position, furthering my beliefs that he belonged to a world of his own.

So I handed him over a twenty, saying, "Keep it, my good man, for you have worked magic, you old Merlin, you." Even I was surprised by how much I'd just sounded like Veps.

"Oh, wow, thank you so much," he said, dropping the change into a little jar atop his work station. "You have a good day."

An uncharacteristic smile crept over me. Something about having a good haircut must've put me in a fine mood. Strange how the little things that almost everyone takes for granted are what end up being what keeps a person going. No complaints here. But even after

Pat had shown dominance, the next sap in line still let out a not-so-subtle gesture of grief over being next in his chair. Hopefully, like me, he'd survive to feel stupid.

My stroll back to the apartment took up a very short amount of time. When I got in, I kind of wished it had taken longer. Veps was high. Higher than usual. Slouched over the couch, upside down, with just his boxers on. It was a sight I'd gotten used to, but no one upon the initial viewing can just wave it off. Had any of him popped out due to the gravitational pull of the globe, well, no, I can't even imagine what I'd of done or said. A tremendous giggle might've been in order. Who knows? I don't.

"Ashie, old bean," he said. "Where you been? I just got in a little while ago, found the homestead empty, got a tad worried. Thought you might have gotten yourself into some more trouble."

"Trying my best to stay clear of that," I said, suddenly feeling every loose hair left on my neck rise.

"Ya, I bet. Is it hot in here or is it just me? I'm not being silly with ya either. Look at me, I'm in my skivvies trying to cool off. Did you notice, eh?"

"How much of what-in-the-name-of-God did you take?"

"That's the beautiful thing. It's just weed! Plain, wholesome pot. Haven't felt like this in a long time on just that. Feels real good to have a moment of nostalgia like this. Woo, buddy, am I feeling it."

"Where'd the stuff come from?" I asked, forgetting the hairs and focusing in on trying to get at the ganja.

"Picked it up this morning. They told me it was fresh off the boat from the land of the Nether People."

I pieced that together to mean it was from the Netherlands. Veps didn't always make sense when he was altered but even I had to chuckle at that last sentence. "What do they call it?"

"Something about Soviets and guns. I don't know. You remember how bad I was at history." He paused. "You remember how bad I was at *any* subject."

"Any of the stuff left?"

"Don't go worrying your pretty baby noggin. Go check the counter. There's another fatty just itching for us to spark it up and have our way with it. In fact, I demand you get it now! Woo, Ash, you're gonna feel like you're floating."

I found it where Veps had said it'd be. He wasn't kidding. This blunt was huge. I could only guess how much he'd gotten for his trial run. If this piece was of any indication, my man must've smoked an entire bud in one sitting. After the *War and Peace* that had been my haircut, I was in need of relaxation. Veps had, like always, provided the right kind of medicine.

We killed it. No other way to describe the mutilation of that stick of heaven's grass. When the taste of it touched my lungs, I knew this was unlike anything else I'd ever taken in. The fact that Veps had shared it with me truly showed just how much our friendship meant to him. I couldn't have been trusted with such an outstanding batch like that. I've always been covetous of stashes that were mine. But having now been with Veps for as long as I had, my tendencies were changed, possibly for the better. Sharing is caring after all, right? Christ, it's grade school philosophy to connect the theories of passing along the Dutchie. It's true when they say everything you needed to know about life you learned in kindergarten. There was more to the ankle-biting world than I'd previously thought. Of course, by that way of thinking, girls were icky with cooties, and, as it's common knowledge, they don't develop bugs until much later on. Oh, me.

As the thick cloud of oblong reality wavered above us, Veps asked, "You getting hot, too? I'm dying of heat stroke. Holy shit, this has gotta be the closest thing to God's breath. Maybe that's what Adam got blown into him. Wouldn't that be something, eh, ole boy?"

"My lungs are on fire but it's all internal. I got this situation under control, man. No need for both of us to be lounging around half-naked. With our luck, we'd forget to put our clothes back on and be well on our way to dinner before noticing the absence of garbs."

"Seems to me that kind of thing would only encourage us to get into a bit of trouble."

"Ya, because we haven't gotten ourselves into all kinds of messes already this summer. Veps, we've had some good times."

"Yessiree, but I gotta tell ya, I'm worried about cha. I mean, well, if Boss Denham ever found out what happened…I'd miss ya, Ash."

Now at this point in the session, all walls that I'd been able to mentally put up from revealing too much information to Veps were now beginning to break down. The very mention of the boss' name was enough to get me going. Never one to be blabby, I felt that I needed to tell somebody what had happened and Veps was right there. What his reaction would be, I hadn't a clue, but this is the guy who bumped uglies with all sorts of vagina-sporting folks. He'd have to understand. If he didn't, who would?

"Wanna know what happened the other day when I went out for bagels?" I asked, my head soaring above the room while my body lay perfectly still on the floor.

"Did you just say you wanted me to make you a bagel?" Veps asked, sounding less coherent than earlier.

"No, ass, do you wanna know what I did the morning I went to eat a bagel?"

"Calm down, you crazy frig, and just let it out. I got no patience for stalled stories."

"Well, I wasn't going to stall it, but you kept on just muttering over yourself."

"I'm about to slap you if this tale of yours doesn't start going."

Maybe my brain was on a subconscious quest to keep my mouth from letting out what I promised myself I'd keep hush-hush, but that stuff circulating through my system ended the journey. What I specifically said to Veps, I don't think can be retold word-for-word based on the fact that, well, my mind felt like a newspaper word jumble. For this, now, I will do my best to retell the story that caused Veps agita almost immediately afterwards.

"Well, you see, my roommate of roommates, I had the girl by her rear end. Both hands buried deep into her under-curve. We were locked in a deep kiss that seemed to go on for days, but all I could think about was what she must feel like on the inside. Did I mention we were in a bathroom? Hell yes, we were! Right there, under those crapified lights that never seem to fully light up, this broad shoves her tongue straight down my throat while I proceed to lift her. Almost instantly, as if by reflex, she wraps her legs around me, locking her ankles together for good measure.

"With nowhere else to set her, I just let that chick rest up on the sink. That's when I let go of the ass and moved up to the breasts. More than enough to satisfy even you. Terrible time getting under her shirt. What with having to balance the weight of both, I nearly sent us crashing to the tiled floor. We'd of cracked that shit to pieces. But with some strategic hip placement, I managed to maneuver up the shirt and grab hold of those bombs. And good Lord, Veps, they were firmer than I'd previously thought. Real to boot!"

This is where his interest took off. It was one thing to him to just mess around with a girl, but when skin on skin action started up,

Veps' curiosity grew. "Come on, Ash, laddie, don't hold it in. Please tell me you didn't hold *it* in."

"You know, for a person who likes to build up the suspense, you're not one to let somebody else perform. But, yes, I didn't hold anything back. She leaned as far back as she could from where she was sitting so that I knew all was being prepared for my arrival. When her tits no longer did it for me, I pulled her pants right off. Took me some extra effort, because I had to kind of hint to her that she needed to undo the cobra clutch settled around me.

"Flexible is a good word to use for her. Took me off my game when it became clear she was capable of performing a full-on spread eagle. With nothing else keeping me from doing the deed, I entered her. People sipping their morning java must have thought a wild animal was being sent to the slaughter. The girl wailed. I don't know how much of that was my doing, because she'd been crying beforehand."

"Crying, eh?" Veps asked, eyebrow raised. "Because of your terrible short comings?"

"You wish, asshole. She wiggled, jiggled, and then exploded juice everywhere. Had I pulled out, it'd been an eruption the likes of which no janitor wants to ever have to deal with. Nope, contained inside and my dick swirled in it. I can't be sure, but I think she wanted to cry some more. Ignoring those signs, I disconnected us and allowed her to get put back together. Poor thing, never expected all of that to happen. Looks like I'm one up in the game on her."

"What game?"

"Oh, never mind, something she came up with and felt it necessary to elaborate on for me."

"Well, Jesus Christ," Veps said, still upside down. "This chick sounds like one dandy of a time. What's her name?"

"Oh, my bad, I thought I told you," I said, not even being able to process that I was about to completely throw myself under the bus. "Marci."

You would have thought the entire world had ended right there. Veps toppled over on himself, falling off the couch, hitting the floor, hard. He scrambled, almost losing possession of his underwear, and stood, right in front of me, heated. "What is wrong with you? Marci? Didn't we just have this conversation? Yes, that's it, you forgot we had this convo already and are just repeating yourself. No flipping way you went and did something else with her…oh, God, no, no…she blew you…this time…Ash, what have you done?"

The high I'd been riding was now gone. I'd dropped from the sky, back into my own personal dungeon of pain. "Oh, come on, man," I said. "You can't freak out on me. She is the one who made it all happen. This isn't my fault."

"Ash, I want you to stop and think about what you did. Boss Denham is a fucked-in-the-head crazy bastard with a lot of people answering to him. He will find out about this. Somehow, he will. Maybe not from Marci, slut, but somehow…we're gonna be dead."

"We have already talked about this. We're not in trouble."

"No, son-of-a-bitch, no," Veps said, surprisingly stern. "You gotta keep your dick in check. This whole Marci thing is horseshit and will only lead to a bad end for you and me. Can't go having any of this. From now on, she is off limits or I'm not gonna help you out in any way shape or form. I'm serious now. For the first time with you, I'm putting my foot down. Ash, my boy, you are out of control."

For some reason, when Veps said that, I realized that it was true. My entire existence got put into perspective. Mary's little boy now had to come to the conclusion that he was a transformed individual. I'm still at a loss as to why it took my buddy to wake me up to the facts. I couldn't deny them after that. Something had changed inside of me. There were no more hesitations to hold me back from what society deemed as inappropriateness. I stood there, silent, trying not to laugh at the cartoon balloons on Veps' boxers. See, I didn't even have the ability to maintain a serious composure any longer.

The phone rang, and Veps walked over to answer. Suddenly, I was alone. In a city of millions, there'd be no one to encircle me. I, the isolated idiot, didn't know the next step in my adventure. That mode of thinking ended when Veps came back. "Why do you look so pale?" I asked.

"That was Eckstein," he said, looking ready to vomit everywhere. "Boss Denham wants to see us…tonight…."

Sometimes I imagine what it must have been like for Perseus once he entered King Minos' labyrinth. Often, there are moments when I'm the poor sap sporting a toga and ball of yarn. Yes, putting myself into the myth. Dark, damp, and smelling of death, my sandals scrape the blood-soaked floor underneath. These are the visions that I experience up in my brain when outside actions cause me to retreat.

Whether or not a gargantuan bull-man awaited me, I couldn't be sure. However, after the phone call Veps got, a sinking feeling set in. Sick. That's the word for it. Sickened with no chance of getting any better. Boss Denham had called us for an audience. He certainly would be playing the part of the Cretan monarch. Who or what would portray the raging minotaur, uncertainty clouded over that. Fear, dreaded terror, hung over me like it had never done before. I almost wished Veps had gotten us locked up after the fight in the bar. Prison never looked so appealing.

Veps hadn't taken the call very well. He paced up and down the apartment, still half-naked. "What are we gonna do, Ash? He knows. The boss knows. No question about it. And who knows what he knows, right? The blowjob, the sex, you really did it. *You* really did it to *us*."

"Maybe," I said, trying my best to find logic in the whole mess, "he doesn't know anything. Remember, Marci would get in trouble, too."

"Ugh, that name. Just the sound of it kicks me in the bootnicks. Christ, all three of us might meet an untimely end before the night's over. Ash, if I'm gonna die, I wanna be partly responsible for it. Like driving a runaway bus through a wall of flaming television sets. Ya, that's how I'd want it all to end, just like that nutty wallaby's appendix. But Denham, he'll make it hurt real bad. I've heard things, man."

"This isn't the kind of stuff you need to be telling me right now, dude. We could have just gone there, seen what he wanted, and if the axe was coming down, deny every single accusation, but now you're telling me he really does dispose of assholes like us."

"Assholes like *you*," Veps said. "I'm a bastard. There's a difference."

"Now I know you're losing it," I said, walking over to him, trying to get the pacing to cease. "Stop moving. You're making us both dizzy. Tell me, what can we do to make him disgustingly happy that has the possibility of reducing our death sentence to just a beat down?"

Catatonia set in. Veps, still as Bambi's mother before the lead pierced her heart, stared blankly out of the window. If it'd been opened, he might have attempted a Golden Gate plunge, straight down. Not the case. Now I'd have to be the one to come up with a plan. It seemed more and more responsibility kept getting placed on my shoulders. This is nothing I welcomed at all. Never the leader, my existence as a follower made me happy. Veps would have to take back the reins very quickly. "Hey," I said. "What about money?"

"Huh?" he said, coming back to the land of the living. "The hell you talking about? What money?"

"How much cocaine do you have on you?"

"Enough for the next half week. Why?"

"How quickly can you sell it?"

"All right, son, I'm not eating what you're forking to me. Speak the Queen's before I have an episode."

"Boss Denham gets his payments from you once a month, right? When was the last time you slid him the cash?"

"We settled up at The Devil's Den. Ash, speakie the English!"

"He won't be expecting another payment for a while then. Sell it all tonight. Get as much for the shit as you can then give it all to him, free of your cut."

"Hmm…yes…yes…yes! Fantastic! Ash, you are a genius. Good, sweet, baby Jesus, I could sell it all in the blink of an eye. Okay, okay, first thing's first…I need pants."

Veps readied himself in record time, and we were out the door, carrying the briefcase he kept the coke in. We did a line together before we left. Sure, maybe it wasn't the most productive thing we could have done, but this was a desperate time, and we needed to take measures just as equal. It was here that I relinquished control of the situation back to him. He was in command again. Better this way. So much rode on if he could make a bundle before our meeting with Boss Denham. My hopes of impressing him with mucho dinero might have been a long shot, but it was the only plan drafted.

No cabs, buses, or trains were needed for this. By foot made for the best travel arrangement. It wasn't a very far walk, or, in our case, dash. We passed a cop car or two, but my mind didn't dwell on any possible arrests. No, we had to concentrate. This would be my apprenticeship with Veps. He had to teach me at some point. This was as good a time as any. I wouldn't speak, no, I'd be the silent partner in all of this. God, where he was leading me to, I only had far off theories on, but behind him I went, right on his heels.

Not yet come to the endless maze, I at least had already arrived at Knossos but as a slave. I was the sacrificial lamb being led to the slaughter so that the gods might be happy. The instrument, the weapon, the hulking shadowy mass of bovine flesh and muscle must have been chomping away at the bit for a piece of me. I had no sword, not yet, but, I had my wits about me. Who Veps was in this odyssey I couldn't say. Perhaps he represented the Wise Old Man? The Shadow? So many archetypes to shift through that it made my head spin. All would have to wait to be revealed when, really, *if*, this leg was survived.

Veps always rambled on about his clients and what they did for a living. To be honest, I only paid him half of my attention. You hear one session of jabbering, you've heard them all. With Veps, well, it was like listening to Speedy Gonzalez muttering off a grocery list. Okay, maybe not him, but definitely like the Micro-Machines dude from the old commercials. Yes, absolutely like that.

Surprised is not the right word for what I experienced when Veps stopped in his tracks, with me bumping into him, almost sending the both of us toppling to the ground. It was a bakery. Nothing fancy, but nothing that would make a person feel as if cockroaches were occupying the place like Nazis in France. No, this was an unassuming business, with Veps indicating that we belonged there. I began to suspect another tornado of a time.

"Okay, see," Veps said, holding tight to his briefcase, "follow me through the place, and don't look at anybody. I ain't exactly dressed for the occasion. Someone may think we don't belong."

"What do you normally wear when you come here?" I asked.

"Overalls covered in powdered sugar."

"Why?"

"Gotta look like you belong here, Ash my lad."

"You're like an even crazier version of Peter Sellers," I said, trying to laugh through my hyperventilating lungs.

"One of the nicest things you've ever said to me."

The inside of the place was sterile. No flashy signs anywhere to be seen. I'd been inside my fair share of bakeries, especially after having spent time in the city. Up to that point, I had experienced them all: Spanish, Italian, Jewish, German, all the nations of the world were represented. None would be outdone by the other. Over and over again, I would observe the out-of-this-world advertising gimmicks to get people in. Sometimes, more often than not, I wanted to ask the owners if they even knew how to bake the authentic pastries of their homelands, but, why ask a "real" Italian that question when their ancestral stomping grounds were more likely to be located in Brooklyn than Calabria.

There were no flags representing any ethnic group in this place. Veps had somehow managed to stumble upon the only neutral bakery on the island. Nothing really surprised me anymore about his ability to find the oddest of oddities in a sea of crazy. That was Veps, and I greatly admired him for his innate skills of people finding. No one else like him in the world. But all those types of instances came with a price. And this wasn't any different.

A couple of customers waited in line with numbers in their hands. Mindless zombies waiting for a fix that wouldn't be coming from Veps' stash. Theirs was a more acute kind of need. That sugary confectionary substance pumped into the bloodstream that would eventually lead them to a life of overindulgence and diabetes. Those poor fools. Later on, when the kids were graduated and the grandchildren stopped visiting, they'd end up on the floor, unable to feel a heartbeat, and then come to the realization that it was because they chose to take the cannoli rather than the gun. Could've ended it all that much sooner.

"We're going through those doubles," Veps said, pointing towards the doors.

"Who the hell are you planning on pushing the stuff on?" I asked, finally voicing the slow-building concerns I'd allowed to boil up.

"Less talk, more walk," Veps said as if he'd just invented the phrase. "You set this all in motion, Ash, my friend, so keep up."

We walked into the back. Machines lined the place from wall to wall. Quite a fascinating experience to observe the inner-machinations of the culinary-inclined. It doesn't destroy the illusion for me. I was never one of those people who walked in, saw the miracle that was a carrot cake, and not want to know how a vegetable's root could be transformed into sweet goodness. But there are those who would never question the genius of a baker. Those are the types of people who veer away from seeing satellite images of Walt Disney World so they won't ever have to see what is hidden behind the façade of the Magic Kingdom. I mean, who would want to believe that behind The Haunted Mansion there's nothing more than a gray warehouse of gears and gyros?

Veps approached a rather big-boned, oh, the hell with it, a big fat hog of a woman, who probably pilfered cookies on a consistent basis. More rolls in her midsection than in the glass cases out front. But her several dozen chins were what kept hold of my short attention span. Remarkable, the things we choose to pay extra special care to. "Hey there, Mona," Veps said. "How you doing this fine day, lovely?"

She'd been sitting on an old folding chair whose legs looked like they were ready to give way at any moment. A part of me wished for her to take in a breath to speak only to have that be the extra bit of added heavy that would send her plummeting to the ground. God, I am such a terrible person, but funny is funny, and that could have given me a lifetime of retellings before it lost any of its humor.

I was to be denied, however. Chalk it all to the fine metal workers who smelted that chair into existence. Mona, sweating from the combination of mechanized-produced heat and the flaps of extra skin hanging from her overworked skeleton, looked up at Veps with a cracked smile that said to me she'd been sweet-talked by him many a time before. "Hey, baby, missed ya here last time. Wasn't feeling too good so I took off the day. Back's been killing me. Sciatica. Don't know what could be causing it."

Veps must have really liked this woman, because she'd left herself wide open for that one. But this was a business call. We had no time for any sort of delay. Even though it was blatantly obvious that this woman would lead herself to an early grave after her overexerted heart gave her a big fuck you, Veps had chosen to withdraw all applications to announcing it. Maybe he saw a crazy aunt kindred in her? "Mona, my lovely, where is Tuck? I need to see him about a very urgent matter."

"Oh, well, last I saw him, he was at his machine, mixing some kind of garbage into a new dough recipe."

"So fuck if you know?" Veps said, smiling.

"You're a miserable cuss of a punk," she said, slapping his ass playfully for good measure.

"At the mixing machine. Got it. Thank ya kindly, Mona, my sweet." He then turned to me. "Stay here un momento," he said, leaving me with the beached whale.

It quickly became one of those awkward moments where you're just standing there with a total stranger who you have absolutely nothing to say to, so you say the very first ridiculous thing that comes to your mind. In my case, it had to do with her weight, albeit, backhandedly delivered. "A lot of lunch breaks?" I asked, realizing at the halfway point of the sentence that maybe I wasn't being so subtle.

Mona looked at me, gave me a stare that only a fat angry woman can give, then let out a sigh, saying, "Not like it used to be, I'll tell you that. Sometimes, I get so hungry that I think I'm going to start eating myself."

This was one of those instances a person waits for. The victim of verbal abuse has allowed the dealt hand to be continued, only upping the ante. While I could have played this game with her all day long, I chose to venture in another direction because of the limited time we had. God only knows what Veps was up to across the room, but I didn't want to be in the middle of a sarcasm-fest only to be called away at the drop of a hat. So refraining from pushing the Moby Dick of a female any further, I simply asked, "Known Veps a long time?"

"Mhm, known him since he's been coming 'round. Nice boy. Too bad what happened to Ray-Ray, though. I liked that kid."

"I'm sorry, who?" I was somewhat jostled by the lack of knowledge of anyone who went by that double name.

"Ya," Mona said, scratching a now fully visible mole under her jowl, standard single black hair poking out of it included. "Ray-Ray was good when he worked with Veps over there. Those two were hooked up for a while. A shame what goes on with what they do."

"Oh," I said, "so you're aware of what it is Veps does for a living?"

"Sweetheart, how do you think I'm able to work? Those painkillers he sells me work wonders. No health insurance is a bitch of a way to live."

"Yes, I'm sure. Now who exactly was Ray-Ray?" I have to admit that at that point my curiosity was at an all-time high. Even with all that was going on around the two of us, I had an opportunity to learn about someone Veps had failed to ramble on about. Strange, at least to me and those who knew him best, because Veps rambled on about everyone and everything.

"He was his buddy, his partner. Two of them worked together. I think they bunked with one another. Poor kid, didn't think something bad would ever happen to him," Mona said, beginning to lose some interest in me.

"What exactly went on? What happened to Ray-Ray?"

"Can't say that I know all too well about the whole thing. Veps is the guy you need to ask. One day, Ray-Ray was here, the next, he was gone. Never was one to remember people all too well, but that boy was a sweetie."

"How long ago was this?"

"A year maybe, or a little more. Why? You suddenly become Briscoe?"

"Who?" My missing of that pop culture comment still bothers me.

"Nothing important. But ask Veps. I'm barely able to remember how much I got in my purse let alone what went on over a year ago."

That's sort of where big Mona started ignoring me, going back to her work that didn't exactly seem all that difficult. Maybe, just maybe, if the fat ones were given more manual labor to do, they wouldn't be so huge. Never made sense to me as to how a person could let themselves gorge and become the child of a Hutt. Disgusting how the human skeleton was being abused, and it only got worse over the following decade. Supersize us up, Ronald.

I decided to leave the shipwreck of a seafaring mammal to herself, venturing through the room in order to find Veps and make sure our quest wasn't being derailed. A part of me pretty much expected to find him nose deep in his own product, eventually spazzing out on the floor to the point where I would have to join in because facing the ultimate reality of the situation alone would have been such an overwhelming sensation that being half-retarded was the only outlet to survive. Much to my surprise, however, I found him quite lucid, dare I say, very professional.

I've never been to Morocco. I've never seen its bazaars filled up with shrewd merchants who would sell their own daughters in a deal just to say they were offering up a bargain. Nor do I ever have plans to see such a place. But I don't think I would have to. Just watching Veps was enough. This guy, had he not been so reliant on the drugs and booze to maintain, could have had one hell of a career in the used car game. Man had all the ability to sell a six-slice toaster to a one man family, no questions asked. Quite remarkable a talent for someone who barely made it out of high school alive. That's just it though, isn't it? The ones we think are going to fall flat on their asses end up succeeding, because they possess something a textbook can't teach you: streetwise commonsense. I had some of that, but not enough. Veps had it coming out of his pores in such abundance that a person might drown in it if they weren't careful.

The guy Veps was talking to represented the stereotypical baker a person expected to find pulling dough. Sporting a flour-covered apron, and one of those ridiculous hats that signified he had the talent to make a better grilled cheese sandwich than me, he stood silent, his eyes fixated on me as I approached the two. Veps saw me, then said, "Ah, Ash, my good man. This here is Tuck, the finest fudge-packer to ever fill up a pastry." Even in times of duress, he still managed a slur against one he deemed inferior.

"Nice to meet you," I said, my hand not extended due to the desire to not have it covered in bakery jism.

"This guy with you?" Tuck asked in one of those heavy New York screen accents John Travolta made famous. Mr. Hubbard, give us back our Vinnie Barbarino.

"This guy with me?" Veps asked, seeming to channel De Niro. "Of course he is. He's new to the whole shebang, so I'm making sure everything is copasetic for when he starts putting it out there solo."

"Then let's get on with what you were pitching," Tuck said, almost not even trying to show his impatient attitude. Trouble a brewing, I thought. Veps took care of it.

"Okay, okay, yes, now, well, you see, Tuck, this product I got here, yes, this fine merchandise, it can be yours. All of it. The whole kit and caboodle can be yours for such a price that you'll never trust me again for selling it so reasonably marked."

"It's a heck of a lot more than I usually am taking. Tell you the truth, I don't feel comfortable holding onto so much of it. *My* customers tend to not buy up as much as *yours* apparently do."

"Oh, come on, now, Tucky baby," Veps said, speaking with his freehand, "this is one of those rare occurrences where I am borderline taking a loss just because you're one of my finest consumers. It's like I said, needing to get rid of this stuff and I immediately thought of you. Now how can you let something like this just slip on by? It's not like what I'm offering up has an expiration date anytime soon."

"No, but what I offer does," Tuck said, showing signs of disinterest in the whole thing.

"Who said it all had to go in at once?" Veps asked.

At this point, I was completely in the dark on what the two of them were actually talking about. Had I known at the time, I might have been able to help accordingly, but, with our meeting with Boss Denham not too long from then, I felt it necessary to speak up right off the cuff. "Listen, Tuck," I said, probably leaving a surprised reaction etched onto Veps' face, but I wasn't paying attention, "you've been offered the good stuff at such a low cost, the two of us are going to be eating Spam burgers for the next couple of weeks. Have you ever tasted that stuff? Dogs wouldn't even go near it. That's that nasty old leftover crapola the butcher won't even feed his ungrateful little bastards." I know what you're thinking: I'm nuts. In my defense, I never have said otherwise.

"I'm sorry," Tuck said, "but who are you to talk to me like I owe *you* anything? In fact, you're lucky I just didn't punch you right in the mouth. Veps," he said, turning to him, "where'd you find this guy?"

Veps hesitated a moment then cracked one of those smiles a person makes when they realize they need to change up their game. "Hey, Tuck," he said, "if I have to go about eating leftover pig dung, I'd be okay with that, ya understand?"

"Oh, fantastic," Tuck said. "Now you too? I told you, I don't need this much product right now."

"And I'm telling you that if you don't go and buy this up, I'm not coming back here."

"Ya," I said, trying so hard to sound like I knew what I was talking about, "we got a million other people out there ready to snort this snow up." I'm not sure why I said that. "So figure out what your best interests are or you can say so long to the good deals Veps here makes."

"I got this, Ash," Veps said, finally pulling the reins back over. "I'm walking, Tuck, and not just for today, but for good. I do you solids all the time. Now it's time for you to do one for me, and take this fine powder for cheap. Such a hard decision," he said, sarcasm riddled over it.

Tuck said nothing for a few seconds. He had to be thinking about what to do if Veps was being serious. Poor bastard would have to find a new dealer and suffer the costs of being taken the first couple of times or more. Nothing sadder than a dope fiend in need of a new drug nanny to rub their tummy for them.

"Fine," Tuck said, finally coming to grips with the reality of the situation presented to him. "I'll take the stuff but don't go doing this to me ever again. I'm a good customer. Once is enough."

"Everybody gets one," Veps said, his finger shaped like a gun, firing.

The product was handed over to Tuck who, although had made it clear how close he and Veps had become in their professional dealings, went about making sure that we hadn't slipped him any fake shit. Literally, horse fecal matter. Seems there were one or two well-known dealers out their making the rounds with turds rolled up in substitution for proper merchandise. A part of me really would love to have seen some poor sap pay top dollar only to later find out that they were left holding the droppings of some Kentucky Derby reject only fit to carry the weight of an overpaid law enforcement yutz.

When Tuck had deemed everything A-Okay, he dug out the requested fee, handed it over to Veps, who, much like his customer, didn't trust a soul on the planet, counted it, twice. "A pleasure, sincerest pleasure, my good Friar Tuck, doing business with ya," Veps said, bowing as if Richard the Lionheart himself were present for the event.

"Just don't come peddling your wares until I call you to say it's all used up," Tuck said, turning away to signify the audience was over and done with.

Veps, aware of the body language, said no more, and the two of us shuffled gracefully out of the place. What fascinated me most about the entire endeavor was that we'd just successfully sold off enough cocaine that could easily get any one person off the street a near life sentence just for carrying it, never mind using it. It was a dangerous occupation to be involved in, but that very idea, for me at least, made it that much more inviting. The money didn't hurt either, however, this particular time wasn't about pocketing anything. We had to do all we could to keep Boss Denham from erupting because of my dick's terrible habit of finding its way into his girlfriend.

When we got back outside, I felt I had to finally ask the question. "Veps, what is Tuck going to do with all of that?"

"He's got a loyal group of cake-eaters unable to resist the taste of his baked delights. Nobody can say no to a Tuck-made pastry, cake, or whatever it is he is making on any given day."

"I wasn't talking about the bakery," I said, almost smacking him in the back of the head. "I was talking about…you know…the coke." It was whispered right towards the end.

"Was never confusing to me as to what you were talking about," Veps said, straight-faced.

"Wait, what are you saying?"

"Thinking it's pretty obvious what I'm saying, Ash my boy."

"He puts it into the cakes!" I said, surprised by my own raised voice.

"Like I said, the finest confections in the city," Veps said, smiling.

"I didn't see one junkie in there. Not one. How can this place be where it is and not attract attention for the, uh, questionable characters hanging around?"

"Cause the people you're thinking of wouldn't think twice of coming 'round here looking for an angry fix. Tuck's peeps are high-end suits and skirts hoping to score for their end of the week shindigs."

"You gotta be kidding me."

"You gonna meet a ton of oddballs, my lad. Never a dull moment with us, eh? Come on, now, it's time to go see the boss man and, well, meet the Mets."

What I'll never understand about sports fans is the unending love they have for their favorite team. Doesn't matter how often they lose or disappoint, you can bet your ass that when the next season rolls around, the same people will be lined up for the games. I could have been one of those people, but like most other things in my life, I didn't have the drive to work at it. And who could blame me?

New York was a different kind of venue for the National Pastime. Baseball to this place was like heroin to a funky junky. There was a rich history of the game in this city the likes of which an outsider could never truly comprehend until they were deep in it themselves. I, grouping myself in with those just described, was just as blind to the whole experience. To me, it was a game that you played as a child but now got millions of dollars to do it as an adult. You can't beat that. It only justified what Veps did and what I wanted to do. Instead of passing out joints and baggies, these mammoths of the diamond were feeding their worshipping fans with a different kind of drug. I call it nostalgia. Those asses in the seats were there for the reminiscing of lost childhood dreams.

Veps and I were on our way towards a realm of orange and royal blue. The mixing of two loser teams who decided that a change of venue meant going to California. Remember the saying: Go West, Young Man! Well, they did, and, they were better off having done it. National League Baseball in New York meant a balance for the Big Apple. A balance needed, because the Yankees just happened to be the best team in Major League history. For where there is untouchable godliness, there must also be the plebs who have to suffer under such harsh conditions.

Shea Stadium doesn't stand any longer, but in my opinion it lasted beyond its prime if it ever truly had one. When I saw the place for the first time that night on the train, I couldn't help but notice the not-so-subtle markings of it being, uh, unfinished. "Why couldn't they just finish the circle?" I asked, pointing out how the stadium didn't come all the way around. "Looks pretty stupid. They run out of money or something?"

Veps, who was quiet, which was out of character for him, simply said, "Ya, money."

I knew he hadn't really been paying any attention to me. That much was obvious. He was worried. And he had all the right in the world to be. We'd gotten ourselves into this ridiculously dangerous situation, well, okay, I got us into it, and now we were on the verge of seeing if redemption could be ours.

A sudden sense of Sunday Mass entered into my mind. Shea Stadium represented the rotted old churches from back home where my grandmother used to try and drag me to every week. I wanted no part of that, but at that moment in time I wish I had had more experience in the art of seeking forgiveness. With us well-raised Catholics, forgiveness was an everyday thing in our lives. Only half the Bible referenced the act. And that was something Veps and I so desperately needed. Boss Denham needed to look unto us and say he forgave the injustice we'd, I'd, committed against him. Hopefully, the penance wouldn't be a swift kick to the jaw or a bullet in the back of the head. Ideally, it'd be some warped version of the "Lord's Prayer" or the "Hail Mary." Poor Mary, all but fifteen and pregnant, and not even by the guy she was about to be wed to. Back then you got stoned for such atrocities. We call it a welfare lifestyle today. So it goes…I think.

The train came to its stop, and the two of us shuffled on out. There was a second or two right before I stepped fully off onto the platform that I thought I might just hop backwards, sit down, get my ass out of the city, and hope for the best. Then came the images of Veps having to explain himself without me. Boss Denham wouldn't buy any of it. He'd be fuming, pissed, ready to rip a head off, and no, I don't mean a skull-covered lump. Veps needed me to take all of the heat. It'd be terribly wrong for me to not be there in that moment right before the executioner's axe came plunging downward. No, we were in this together. Me, because I'd allowed my semen to entered into my employer's girlfriend, and Veps, because he had enabled me to do so. At least that's how he saw it, so far be it for me to deny him to feel some sort of guilt. Didn't matter how misplaced it might have been. Friends until the hearse comes a driving you away.

"So," I said, walking down the station's steps, "how we getting into the place? Not like we have tickets in pocket."

"Eckstein said there was gonna be two waiting for us. Ash, my boy, I think my palms are sweating."

"Do you have anything for that?" I asked, hoping he would, and, as always, be willing to share.

"Everything I had in stock just went out to the bakery, man."

I stopped in my tracks. Dead in my tracks. It made Veps halt in his slow stride as well. I looked him straight in the eyes. A sudden rush of terror ran across me, but before it had the opportunity to fully overcome my already fragile-self, I pushed all of it down. Deep down. So far down that any kind of repressed memories would shudder with its arrival. "Are you telling me that you aren't high?" I asked, not feeling it could ever possibly be true.

"I'm feeding off of whatever is left in me. That sale took a ton out of me, and it's just not sitting right."

"Are you gonna be all right to go through with this?"

"I don't got much of a choice in the matter, do I?" Veps said, a subtle tone of sobriety entering into his speech.

"Dude, I don't think I've ever seen you like this before. Not even back home. What are we gonna do? You can't speak to the boss this way."

"Alcohol," he said. "Gotta get some beer inside. Let the liver remember I love her."

"Then let's get the tickets and remind her about that long affair you two have had since you came off the sippy cup."

"More like the teat," he said, a bit of the standard Veps still lurking within that less-than-usual smoke-filled body. "Where is the ticket booth?" I asked.

We eventually came upon the thing. Here came one of the many moments to help continue fueling my disdain for people. There, on a little stool which somehow manages to convince the occupant they are Harvard-smart, sat a little old bat of ancient origin. And, of course, to communicate with this individual, speaking through a Plexiglas window was required. I'd rather attempt conversation with the person at a drive-thru window, at least they recognize their station in life. But this was going to be a difficult one. Veps had to repeat his name three times before she even looked up. It's probably for the best that she'd been separated from us, because I'd of slugged her. Yes, I don't care what you or anyone else might think about me now if you even have a decent opinion still, but that lady needed a backhand across the mouth. Didn't a famous woman once write that if someone had had a person to shoot her every minute of every day, she'd of been all right? Why couldn't that have been me? Probably because I didn't have a weird peacock fetish. Sick southern authors and their desire for the grotesque. See, told ya I was up to par. At least, that's what some tell me. Others tend to ignore. Lucky.

"Here you are, fellas," the old bat said as she handed the tickets over to us. "Enjoy the game. Next."

Just like that the two of us were back on track to find our seats, alcohol for Veps, and me (might as well, right?), and butter Boss Denham's biscuit to save our asses. It felt like one of those really frustrating cliffhangers to a show you don't care much for but you happened to catch the season finale and you're completely enamored by the main character. Now you're hooked, watching previous seasons, hoping to God that nothing drastic will be done to the one you love. Maybe that wasn't the best comparison, but at the time my nerves were rattling, and Veps needed a little something-something to start feeling like himself again. His vocal prowess would play an important part in the schmoozing, so to not have it up and running was dangerous.

Through the turnstile, into the massive blue cookie-cutter structure we went. Pat downs would not be necessary, not at that point in time. The smells originating from the bowels of the stadium were enough to make even the strongest stomach feel queasy. They were the types of smells you kind of get wafted into your nostrils when you walk the back alleys of a restaurant district. At one point they might have been integral pieces of culinary delicacies, but after their inability to be chosen, the trash.

In order to escape the rising stench, which I chalked up to it being summer, the heat is never kind to such things, I dragged Veps up the devilishly-constructed ramps. I never bothered to work out a day in my life, so even going up just two levels in that place caused my quad muscles to betray me. I probably deserved it. Not sure how Veps did it, but that couldn't be on my mind. Everything in me pushed to find the first vendor with some suds.

"Tell me again why we're here?" Veps asked.

"You're losing it, dude," I said, holding his arm tight, knowing that he was fading fast. "Don't get all normal on me."

And there it was. Like a godsend descending from heaven just for us. An ugly counter-boy with acne the size of golf balls, anxiously awaiting to serve a customer so he wouldn't have to contemplate his useless role in life. We were just the two he needed. "Beer," I said. "Large."

"Can I see some ID, sir?" he asked, his voice squeaking with each pronouncement.

"You just called me sir," I said. "Doesn't that automatically make us all good?"

"I, uh, what?"

"Well," I said, not being able to resist, "you've established that I am a 'sir,' ergo, I am a man. A man wouldn't be in need of ID, right?"

As one or two of his zits spontaneously popped, his brain obviously working overtime, Veps staggered. "I don't wanna be here!"

I took my ID out of my pocket, threw it at the counter-boy, and shoved the money into his shirt pocket. "Check it, pour it, serve it," I said, knowing that Veps had all the potential to be an angry sober.

"If I can just find the date of birth...."

"Asshole, it's a Delaware Driver's License, not a cuneiform-ridden document. I'm twenty-one. See!" I said, jamming my pointer finger onto the appropriate part of the plastic tag.

After that fun bit of tension, the beer was poured, the change was made, and down Veps' hatch it went. Not enough. Another. Child's play. A third. I'm pretty sure he burped out a curse against Budweiser's weakness. Three more, and a college semester's worth of tuition later, and Veps was looking like his true self. "How are you feeling, champ?" I asked, eyeing his mouth in case vomiting ensued.

A larger belch than before rang out from him. "I'm feeling pretty good, Ash, my lad. Woo! No flipping way I was gonna make it through the National Anthem, man. All this is taking years off my already shortened life."

"We gotta go and talk to the boss man," I said, having to be the one to turn the tide of celebration to utter terror.

"Lawyer Boy, the Jew Wonder," Veps said, obviously referencing Eckstein, "said for us to meet him during the 7th Inning Stretch."

"Christ, you didn't tell me that. We have to wait now for the noose to slowly wrap around our necks?"

"Ours? Remember, killer, you're the one on trial. I'm the not-so-innocent bystander."

"Don't get silly with me, ass clown," I said, my awkward way of challenging Veps, "there are plenty of bystanders serving life sentences for just hanging around the action."

"You're not allowed to watch Sipowicz anymore," Veps said, putting his arm around me, leading us to the right section to sit.

The usher who sat us said his name was Bops. At any given moment I felt like he could fall, break in half, and we'd be going to jail for manslaughter because we were the ones in need of finding our seats. He was a short man, probably lost a foot in the intervening years between his middle-aged crisis and joining up with the AARP. Said he'd even worked at the old Polo Grounds when the Mets played there back in 1962 and '63. Why do these people insist on telling stories nobody wants to hear? I tried being silent. It worked. Veps, on the other hand, decided it'd be time for him to practice his sarcasm. "They played a lot of good ole fashion polo at them grounds, eh?" he asked, imitating a gray-bearded hillbilly for obviously no other reason than to amuse himself.

"You're a fucked-in-the-head kind of fella, ain't cha?" Bops said, much to *my* amusement.

Our seats were quite good for two guys who probably wouldn't have paid for bleacher seats to watch this team. Sure, the Mets had been in the World Series, and lost, the year before, but if you knew what they were to become the following season, a diehard fan might've taken their own life before Opening Day. Truth be told, I don't know how they had filled the stadium that night. Veps tried telling me that it was because the Atlanta Braves were in town. He then had to explain to me what a Brave was, and, to my surprise, there's yet to be any kind of litigation against them for using such a name. Of course, we Americans like our caricatures.

What stills confuses me is the fact that it would seem that every other team in the league uses the color red in their design. You'd think that they'd eventually try for something different, but, I guess I'm wrong. Doesn't make much sense to me, but I've been told that what I don't know could fill the Grand Canyon twice over. Sometimes I miss my grandfather.

As the overpriced Mike Piazza came to the plate, the crowd went gaga. This, to me, felt kind of ridiculous. Here was a normal dude who'd gone from mullet to frosted-tips in the blink of an eye, not doing much of anything for his team that was paying him more money than he'd ever know what to do with. Good thing he went and married himself a Playboy cover girl. She'd help him spend it all, I'm sure.

What I remembered from the previous October was this guy's inability to man it up when faced with an outright attack. When that hulking, steroid-charged Roger Clemens hurled a piece of shattered bat in the guy's way, Piazza made a cute little Italian snarl, taking his sweet time to walk towards the pitcher's mound. I saw it as one of those moments when you're at a bar with friends and some douchebag starts it up with you. When you let it be known to him that you're down for a fist-to-fist session, he waits patiently, or, maybe not so much, for buddies of his to hold him back so he can struggle with them, putting on a nice show for everyone, hoping to God you don't actually try to get to him. That was my take on the pizza-man. Because, well, you have to figure a shot in the mouth from a guy like Clemens could have come at your face going about ninety-nine miles an hour. No thanks, Rocket Man.

Right before the final out of the top of the 7th, Eckstein came down to us. "Hello, boys," he said, acknowledging us begrudgingly.

"Salutations, my good man," Veps said. "Must really wax your ass to have to be nice to us, me especially, eh?"

"One day, pally boy, I'm going to watch you head on off to prison, smiling all the way."

"One day, dear Ju Ju Bean, I'm going to whack you across the mouth, just to see if you've got any gold fillings already a tad loose."

"Easy to talk to me like that when you aren't in police custody."

"Just easy talk to you like that in general," Veps said, smiling like the biggest jerkoff in the world. To be fair, he at least was a contender for the title.

We were led by Eckstein up through the innards of Shea, past the elevators, the press, even the overly expensive restaurant that no one actually realized served anything good, and into a corridor the likes of which no ordinary pion of a fan could ever hope to see. These were the Diamond Club Suites. The places only the rich and powerful were allowed to inhabit. Here was where the New York Mets organization separated the train riders from the limousine ones. Little did they know that sometimes they were deceived and some crazy parent would go and spend a month's salary for one game of sitting in an air-conditioned room where you had the shittiest view of the field.

Truth of it was, if you opted to occupy one of these boxes, you weren't really going to watch the game. Too much distraction all around you. From the fancy-looking food to the fully-stocked bar, you ended up lounging on the comfy couches, watching the game on a television. That's where the world had gotten to, and we'd only just entered the 21st century. But here we were, Veps and I, standing in the middle of one of those suites, with all the possibility of it being the last thing we saw before being blindfolded and escorted to the backseat of a black town car. With our luck though, it'd probably be the trunk.

Boss Denham, we were told, was in the bathroom. Something about the shrimp cocktail not fully agreeing with him. Fantastic, right? Not only did the two of us need to impress this guy, but his internal organs were betraying him at the same time. Nothing ever seems to go right when you desperately need it to. Eckstein told us to go out to the seats. He'd grab us when we the boss man was ready.

Of course, right there, like nothing in the world had happened, was Marci. Veps took one look at her, and her at him, before he said, "I'm gonna go get a drink and proceed to vomit it up."

That left me to sit down next to the very reason why tomorrow might never come. "You really screwed me, you know that?"

"I thought you were the one who did the screwing?"

"Jesus Christ, will you please keep your goddamn voice down?"

"What do you care? We're the only ones here. Eckstein has the other drones eating Mrs. Fields cookies and worrying about the day's take. That's what my man loves to do, spend money on a suite for twenty and populate it with five. Never could figure him out."

"Well, he's got us figured out," I said, trying not to be shrill.

"You know that there is no 'us,' right?"

"You need to stop picking apart my words, and you might as well stop pretending like you don't like me."

"Just cause we have a little fun doesn't mean anything."

"Go ahead, wiseass, be smug about it all. You're not the one whose getting the hammer brought down on you."

"What the hell are you talking about?"

"He knows. Denham knows. There's no question about it. He's brought Veps and me here to punish us."

"You're out of your smoke-filled mind," she said. "I haven't said anything to him, nor will I. I've got more to lose than you two."

"Maybe you didn't have to say anything. Maybe he had someone watching you."

"You're being completely paranoid," she said, taking a sip from her glass. "I know why you guys were called to come here. In fact, I'm partly responsible for it."

"What are you talking about?" I asked, puzzled now more than ever.

"He needs something done and after a round when he still didn't know who to go to, I casually suggested Veps in my oh-so-subtle way."

"Why would you do that?"

"Because I knew if it involved Veps, it would include you. I guess I wanted to help you get a leg up. I mean, I gave you two in the bagel shop."

"You're killing me," I said, hoping to God that nobody else could hear the words coming out of her mouth.

"You're perfectly safe. Fact is, Ash, you can't be a lackey forever. That's what you are right now. I'd be interested to see you rise up to the challenge."

"Are you telling me that all of the crap I've had to endure today was for nothing? Veps and I were ready to shit twice, die, resurrect, and do it all over again!"

"You'd better keep *your* voice down. Don't get too animated. Denham's going to think something is up with us."

"Is there *something* up with us?" I asked, almost immediately regretting the very soft tone having been used.

"You're a fun guy, Ash, and a good..." she lowered her voice then said, "you're a good fuck, but in the end, it just wouldn't work."

I guess I had to accept that answer from her for the time being. There was something about Marci that I couldn't resist wanting. Maybe it was because this had been the one girl I'd come across since getting into the city who didn't turn out to be whacked out of her mind. She may have marched to the beat of her own drummer, but at least she was genuine. She had her quirks, no questioning that, but I felt something between us that made sense until you dissected it. Once you did that, it stopped working, but there could be a spark, even if it were just a small one, between us. What did I know, though? I was just some burnout with nothing going for him. Marci, even if she wanted to admit that there was something, couldn't in good conscience say it.

And that was the sad truth of the matter. Here she was, an obviously educated woman who somehow ended up getting a bad deal along the highway that is life. One thing had led to another, and any dreams she might've been harboring within her were dashed against the deadly rocks of reality. In Boss Denham, she saw a life that wasn't necessarily a fulfilling one, but a life of financial stability. Why they weren't married was beyond me, but I could only assume it was because he knew better. "Cheaper to keep her" was a saying men used when contemplating divorce, but if you never got hitched to the broad, you wouldn't have to even mull over the phrase. No need to cut the leg off if gangrene never materialized. But that's not to say that I wanted to marry Marci, but guys are guys, and we don't like to share even if we say we're okay with it. It's a form of jealously we hate to confess being victims of. It happens more than we'd care to say. We're all creatures of habit. Each and every one of us. Evolution hasn't really taken us that far up the line of commonsense.

"What's the job?" I asked, finally burying away the feelings I had for her.

"I don't really know the particulars, but it looks like Veps is getting the rundown right now," she said, excusing herself to the restroom.

When she was up and out of sight, my attention veered over to Boss Denham, arm around Veps, holding in his hand the cash we'd scored, and looking positively delighted by the initiative his boys had shown. So for the moment, it looked as if we'd been spared a most unpleasant penalty for my crimes. Veps smiled, big, proud, and when the two of us made eye contact, he mouthed a sentence that I read as, "Holy fucking shit!" The exclamation had been long and drawn out. Something was transpiring in that temperature-controlled haven of escape from Doubleday's baby. It wouldn't be until we were out of the ballpark that the whole assignment got laid out to me. But when Veps spelled it all out, I could only stare off into the distance, not even able to figure out if the Mets had won or not. The sensation of being completely stupefied had taken over. We were being asked to handle, with gentle care, one of Boss Denham's big projects. We were being asked to go to the true Promised Land. It'd be a most holy pilgrimage. We were going to Amsterdam.

It was a quiet train ride. One of those times when all you can do is sit in a near-coma state of mind, hoping to the great creator of the Universe that nothing else would jump up and surprise you. The lights were dimmer than usual, and the place smelled of cooked onions. We had probably plunked right where some back alley dumpster diver just got done sitting. Can't afford a cheap hotel to shower, but has all the ability to take the subway. The hypocrisy of the homeless astounded me.

Not much talking had gone on after the big news got delivered, but I knew it was coming. Veps, beside himself with endless joy, continued rubbing his palms together like a pedophile who just got a lifetime pass to the circus. "It was Marci who got us this," I said.

"Ash," Veps said, finally verbalizing again, "that chick is dangerous. I'd rather you went out and played with lit dynamite."

"I know," I said, feeling like I was being chastised by my old man again. "There's just something about her that I can't seem to get over."

"I could get you any broad in this city of any size, shape, or whatever, but this one, the one who happens to be with Boss Denham, that's the one you want? I'm gonna go ahead and give you some valuable advice: get her out of your mind."

"It's not that easy."

"The hell it isn't. Come'on, let's get you some place where the females are frolicking; I'll strike up the conversation for you. We'll get you bumping uglies with someone soon enough. You can even provide your own special sauce!"

This wasn't just a simple suggestion that he was making. Veps had a plan, but it didn't center on me. He was using me to get us where he wanted to go. "What do we have to do tonight?" I asked. "What haven't you told me?"

"Denham wants us over to one of the clubs he does business out of. Wants us to get a sampling of the product we're gonna be moving for him."

"That's what we're gonna do?"

"Yep, he says that it's one heck of a quality product. Won't take up too much space either. Told me he wanted what we bring over to serve as the appetizer. If it tests well, we're gonna be doing more business with those Dutchie folks across the Atlantic."

"You do realize what they're doing over there in that city, right?"

"My boy, my boy, my boy!" Veps said, nearly jumping out of his seat. "What they are doing over there in that beautifully red-lit metropolis brings tears of joy to my eyes. We won't be there long, but from what I gather, there's gonna be plenty of time to enjoy the fruits of their government's liberalism. It's a great time to be alive."

"What's the product?" I asked. "What are we moving?"

"The boss said we'd get some of it tonight."

"Why are we supposed to try it?"

"You got a problem with that? Of all the stuff I've been handing over to you, I assumed you wouldn't get prude on me like this."

"No, man, not at all. Just wondering."

"Questioning existence is dangerous, Ash, my lad. Socrates drank the hemlock because of it," Veps said, strangely out of character. I wrote it off, considering he was still reeling from the news of our impending trip.

"All right, but, you still haven't answered."

"Sigh, and you were the one who I had such high hopes for. President Grishin, ladies and gentlemen," Veps said, giving a wink before standing in salute. "We have to try out the product in order to be able to make sure that what they give us over in El Dorado is the real deal."

"Oh, well, ya, that makes sense. I was just a little off on the idea of being guinea pigs."

"Ash, you have to be less stressed, brother. It ain't good for your oh-so-special complexion."

"Me? The stressed one? I'm pretty sure you're the one who was pacing back at the apartment. *I* was the one who had to pull it all together."

"Well, now the inmate is back running the asylum," Veps said, doing his best to impersonate a lunatic in a straightjacket.

"And what does that make me?" I asked, slightly dreading the allusion he was about to come up with.

"Just think of yourself as the underpaid doctor who makes sure I get just enough meds to not swallow my own tongue. Ya, that'll work just fine. All we need now is one of those nurses with the short skirt and red stilettos."

"I'm almost certain they don't actually exist in real life."

"Ah, Ash, since when did you and I start to live in the real world? Much rather remain in the Eden of our design."

"Now you're getting religious? How much did Boss Denham give you to drink once he told you what he wanted from us?"

"I lost track after the first bottle of Bourbon dried up. My God, my liver is going to one day just give out on me, but it's better to burn out than to fade away. The Kurgan said that, you know."

"Pretty sure he didn't make that up all by himself."

"Says you! Now about that slut of a nurse we're on the lookout for. Gonna get me a lick or two of that candy-striper!"

"They are two separate things," I said, starting to become annoyed at him, but not being able to hold in the laughter. Veps, when he was this way, could make a hospice resident giggle.

"Fine," he said. "You get the nurse. I'll take my chances with the candy cane. I wonder if she'll taste like peppermint."

"We aren't going to a hospital!"

"No, even better," Veps said. "We're going to a place to pick up some medicine without having to wear a gown with no back flap."

And just when I thought that New York City couldn't surprise me any longer, Veps showed me that I knew nothing. He'd brought me from an athletic cathedral to an actual house of worship. Well, yes, it had been deconsecrated, but that isn't the point. There I was, finding myself staring at the outside of what used to be some standard Episcopalian church in the middle of the city, which, having been spared the wrecking ball, now had been wrecked in a whole different way.

The Limelight happened to be one of those strange places you went to when you wanted to forget the worries of the humdrum life of reality, entering a house of God that He no longer dwelled within. What has always fascinated me about such places is how ridiculous some people can be. Here it was, a church, a place where services had been held year after year, yet nothing could save it. You had Jesus and then, the next moment, you didn't. A standard in the Christian faith, this building where the Lord was supposed to be, an axis mundi to Him, now stood as a testament to the true nature of all Holy Scriptures.

Sodom hadn't really been wiped off the face of the earth; in fact, it seemed to be doing quite well. All inside the place were enjoying the fruits of their sinful, lustful, prideful partying ways that made me wish I'd read the Bible more closely in order to fully appreciate the failure of the day up on Golgotha. Veps had yet to take me to such a place as this, and I couldn't understand how anyone conducted business there. It went on though, the business, because that building of preaching had seen the terrible death of its very own Angel not too long before I crossed its threshold. Horrible, dreadful, uncontrollable vibrations rattled me to my core upon stepping into the structure. No turning back. Veps had made it clear that we were to be partaking in a tasting. One of those instances where human testing was no longer frowned upon, but instead, treated as a necessary evil.

There were two accessible floors to the place. The first was an unholy gathering of flesh into one cohesive unit of glow sticks and body paint. Yes, the raving sensation continued crawling on despite the hard evidence that such things were on the out. Far be it for me to have told all of those people, because they probably weren't about to start listening. Veps seemed to know some of them, and I suddenly had a vision of him in a desert poncho, proselytizing the Word of Boss Denham. In a voice to match all those really odd Sword & Sandal Epics of the 50s and 60s, Veps' voice sounded off in my head. "Ye shall listen, boy oh boy, to the Word for it is good, clean, and ready to inhale. In the Garden did ye lose yourself, but redemption shall cometh again, my lads, my ladies." Then he would show them how to roll up dollar bills and perform a new form of prayer.

Despite my worries that Veps might have indeed been the Antichrist, I followed him through the crowd. The music, if you want to call it that, blasted from the speakers which were positioned on almost every bit of wall space. So many, in fact, that a person might actually consider for a second that the sounds were coming from the trumpets of heaven. But again, angels weren't exactly welcomed in the Limelight anymore.

Even though the servants of the Lord were no longer granted easy access, the place certainly was full of celestial bodies of the female persuasion. Only good thing about clubs like the one we were in was the fact that women who went felt that it would be in everybody's best interest if they wore as little as possible. Tight pants, short skirts, skin showing, and, if you were lucky, a cleavage that almost spoke to you, saying, "Come on, sweetheart, dive right in, and stay a while."

Up to the second floor we went, accessing a rickety iron stairway that probably should never have passed a safety inspection. On our way through a mass of some important looking individuals, I saw Veps tap some guy on his shoulder. "Hey, G-man," he said.

"Veps," he said, "how's ole Denham doing?"

"Can't complain for him, so I won't," Veps said, smiling as if any breach of this odd protocol I'd started to notice might ruin our night. "Looking for Kiki."

"Ah, okay, yes, she's over in the VIP area. Tell Tyrese you need to speak to her."

"Well, all right, G-man," Veps said, slapping on a handshake with him.

"Whose your friend?" the guy asked, looking at me.

"Newest recruit in the war against oppression!" Veps said, his voiced raised, sounding more a militant than holy man now. Not much of a difference when you really sit and think hard about it.

"Good to meet you, 'officer.' Glad to have you on the team," G-man said, turning away, back to his group.

Following Veps, consistently and always it seemed, I watched him go up to a very large black man whose arms were probably bigger than my own body. He definitely looked like someone who would be named Tyrese. Unlike the, um, gentlemen at The Devil's Den, this guy wore a suit, tie and all. Very professional looking and I knew, deep down, anyone who would feel his wrath might be compelled to comment on how lovely his attire looked. Of course, a person would say just about anything if it meant not getting a beating from this hulking bulk of nasty.

He smiled, listening to Veps. Not a sure way of assessing a situation, because my old pal had all the ability to make a person giggle as he insulted them. But I didn't think Veps capable of such idiocy. Then again, I was in a structure built of faith which no longer existed within its walls. By that logic, all types of insanity were possible. And after the kind of day I'd been going through, I wasn't entirely sure if I'd be able to survive.

"Ty, my black brother from another mother, how you be?" Veps asked, shadow boxing the gargantuan.

"I be good, my brother," he said, surprising me for not showing any signs of wanting to squash Veps.

"Ash here and I need to go in and speak with the mistress of the house."

"Ah, no problem, brother, my brother. Kiki is inside doing her thing."

He let us into the VIP area where things were happening that I could never have imagined. This is where all those viral videos from the Internet that showcase girls in microskirts must originate from. Men, women, of questionable backgrounds, were humping, grinding, caressing one another, and some even were making love to the brass poles descending from the ceiling. The messengers of the Lord wouldn't have found one single soul alive in that place who could redeem the rest of them. Veps and I were now one with this group of hedonists, and I knew nothing could be said to alter the situation. This was one of those times when I had no doubt in my mind that some sort of awful event loomed on the verge of happening. I did nothing to stall nor stop it. The light, colored with the twinkle of lime, called me home.

After passing a young girl, who couldn't have been more than a few days over her eighteenth birthday, wearing nothing under her skirt accept a lack of morality, I saw *her*. There she was. This Kiki that Veps had identified as the one we were in search of. She sat upon one of those rounded booth couches where the one in the center was always designated as most important. Sporting a tight, very short, black dress with a red belt tied around her waist, Kiki's long brown hair spoke to me. The image of Marci left me, and all I could think about was this chick. Why, well, maybe because she represented no imminent death for just looking at her.

When she stood up to greet Veps, I saw her in all that she was. Tall, curvy, with breasts a man could play with all day and never get bored of. Kiki was the kind of girl the average guy would never be able to have but could masturbate to for years without becoming tired of it. Yes, she was Prime-A jerkoff imagery come to life. One could only hope to have her crash and burn with porn being the only way to make a living. So many dreams of the average man unrealized.

"Veps, baby, how you doing?" she asked, with a voice that had an odd combination of Brooklyn and Bronx. She could no doubt be the result of some forbidden inter-borough romance.

"I'm fine, just fine, you lovely thing," Veps said, kissing her on the mouth. "This here is Ash. Best buddy in the world. If World War III went off tonight, I'd want him in the trenches with me. He's good people."

"As good as you?" she asked, smiling with her lips pouting. I wanted to rape her, or, at least, possibly sniff her panties. Either way, her vagina needed to be close to me somehow.

"Not yet," Veps said, answering her. "But he's got the potential to be just as amazing as me."

"Well, Ash," she said, leaning in and kissing me right on the mouth, "it's nice to meet you."

So many things within me were pushing to blurt out how badly her hips needed my hands grasped around them. But I fought my ancestors back into Tartarus. There could be no more vulgarity instigated by me. Veps would have to play lead fiddle on that one. I resolved to return as a not-so-innocent bystander for the time being. Safer for everyone involved in the deal.

We all sat down to discuss business. Kiki brought her right leg over her left and all I could do was quietly drool over the muscular thigh of this living goddess. Marci, oh Marci, why didn't I just tell you to run away with me? I am a man with desires, testosterone-driven yearnings for the female body. Damn women, all of them. Marci wanted to play games. I would need to decide if I wanted to continue with that. But at that moment, Kiki existed. The Limelight existed. Nothing outside of our sphere had any sense of reality. We were now enclosed in a bubble of seductive divinity run amuck.

Veps, who hadn't stopped blabbing since the salutations, spoke up, over the music. "We need to test out the product before Amsterdam."

"You have no idea how jealous I am that you're going there," Kiki said, her voice equally raised. "Ash," she said, turning towards me, "are you excited?"

"Oh," I said, stumbling over my words after being caught off guard. She had to have seen me peering deep down into the crevice of her cleavage. Women need to understand that we aren't all being perverts. Some of us, like me for instance, are simply admiring the view. So many similarities between a nice space between two tits and, oh, let's say Mt. Rushmore. Difference being you can take pictures of the latter without getting sued. Although, touching both would pretty much get you penalized.

"Is that it?" Kiki asked, bringing me back from my thoughts only to realize I'd lost track of the moment.

"No, I, yes, very excited. Never been there before. Never really been anywhere before. Enjoying all of it."

"Well, that's wonderful to hear," she said, doing some kind of too cute nose curl that made me want to bone her in the face. Yes, that had to have been it. This girl was the Devil! The Satan of the Christian underworld called hell! Sent to test me. Oh, please, oh please, test me baby was all I kept repeating inside my head.

"So," Veps said, "Kiki, beautiful, darling, and all those other pet names I, and many others, call you."

"Yes, Veps my dearest handler?" she asked, continuing the agonizing foreplay I wished had been directed towards me.

"We need to know what we're acquiring from the Land of the Dutch and need to sample it to make sure what we're getting is on the level."

"Of course, dear," she said. "Scootch on out so I can go get it."

Veps leaned back with a smile and Kiki crawl over him, pausing for a second upon his lap only to grind in a little as she laughed. When she was off and out of sight, Veps shifted over to me. "Whatcha think of her?"

"I think she's a bombshell."

"See, my boy, you don't need Marci. You can have Kiki."

"I keep thinking about Marci. I'm not sure why. And there's no shot I could ever get Kiki. Besides, she seems entirely into you. How many times have you slipped that girl the trouser snake?"

"Not a single time. She, unlike so many other dumb broads, seems to know, or at least assume, where my dick's been. That being said, well, she's playing it safe. But there are ways to make the impossible quite the opposite."

"What are you talking about?" I asked, thinking back to my thoughts about rape, fearing Veps would actually act upon them. Could he read minds? I never did bother to ask him.

"I am proposing the two of us work together. Think of it as a comic book superhero team up. I'm Superman. You're Batman. Come'on, we got this down. Kiki won't know what hit her. And I do mean, what *hit* her. Ha, ha! Ash, my lad, we could have one heck of a good kick tonight if you follow my lead. I've missed you, man. It's time you came back to the School of Veps!"

"More like the Church of You," I said, using my hand to draw the uppercase "Y."

"Then let us share in the Eucharist," he said, taking out some coke. "G-Man slipped it to me. You ready to go back to the land of the living?"

I wanted to. I needed to. There could be no mistaking me for a straight-laced human being. I'd been corrupted early and turning back wasn't an option. We shared in the Body and Blood of Ricky "Veps" Donnardo. "I love the trickle," I said. He chuckled and moved back to his original spot when Kiki returned.

"Here it is, boys," she said placing a small baggie onto the table.

Veps took hold of it, sliding it over to me. I looked at the white circular tablets inside of the clear plastic, noticing the sign for pi etched on all of them. "What is it?" I asked.

"Ecstasy," Veps said, raising it up to the light. "I don't remember seeing this mark before, though. New stuff?"

"The latest," Kiki said. "That symbol is supposed to stand for infinity or something like that."

"It's pi," I said, leaning over to get their attention. "It's from math. An infinite decimal number."

"Since when did you become Einstein?" Veps asked, laughing over himself.

"He wasn't very good at math," I said, smiling at Kiki who didn't seem very interested in what I had to say. I couldn't blame her. Here she was trying to explain to us the purpose of our overseas trip and I was trying to impress with my limited knowledge of what anyone can look up on one of those really expensive scientific calculators. You know, the ones that cost hundreds of dollars but you end up just playing pong on them. Never did understand the concept of spending all that moolah just to play a game that pretty much climaxed before the 80s got rolling.

"Veps, my lovey," Kiki said, opening her mouth and sticking out her tongue. "How's about you give that stuff a whirl with me?"

I thought his eyes were going to bulge and pop right there. Quickly, although with a slight hint of flirtatious play, Veps placed the ecstasy on her tongue, and we watched her retract it, ingesting that bad boy. She fed him his. I was left to feed myself. That was okay, I guess. Veps seemed to get all the fancy treatment. Maybe that was why Marci appealed to me. She didn't want anything to do with Veps. Making me feel special the way she did kind of felt nice. I had to be careful of that. Could I have been looking for a mother-figure in some crazy ass Oedipal-type of way? Sophocles, save my soul.

The effects were slow in the building stage. I remember some of the experience of that night, but it all sort of combines into one long orgasm of discomfort. The kind you get when you're doing a girl raw, hard, and she sticks her finger in your asshole. The forbidden pleasure of the moment overtakes you, and, all of a sudden, you're coming, but there is no good explanation for such intensity. That was the best way I could describe the sensation. Music. I could see it. That house beating sound of a DJ doing nothing but mixing random bits together in order to form a more perfect union. My head rocked back and forth to it. Haze came over my eyes. There was this sudden sense of being in the right place at the right time. I knew Kiki and Veps were still next to me. I knew there were more people in the room. But for the life of me, I couldn't see beyond my own nose. Reality began to alter.

Kiki had started to straddle Veps. He grabbed onto her thighs, hiking up the skirt in the process. There was a healthy amount of meat on that girl. Their tongues joined together in his mouth, then hers. They were meeting in that in between where neither of their facial orifices played home but centered in midair. I watched. I ached. When Veps pulled her skirt up higher, revealing a black thong that Sisqó had once been singing songs about, I lost it. From my spot on that couch, I leapt over towards them, knocking all of us over. I half-expected Kiki to smack me and storm off, but before I knew it, her tongue had entered into my mouth. Veps cackled the way the Wicked Witch of the West might have had she been able to slit that country girl's throat. "Ash, my boy of boys! That's the spirit!" Veps said, lifting me off of Kiki to look me straight in the eyes. "I feel that it's time for a change of venue."

I didn't know what he was talking about. Kiki writhed on the velvet. Squirmed is a better word. Veps leaned down to her and I could hear him say, "Let's get into the private chamber."

She smiled, kissed him after biting his lip, got up, not bothering to fix her dress, and dragged the both of us by our hands to this small room with a mattress laid out on the floor. No sheets, one pillow, and a crappy bulb dangling from the ceiling. "Fuck me, Veps," Kiki said.

"Well," Veps said, "I could very well be obliged to do that, but what about Ash? He can't just watch. I mean, you brought him in here with us."

"Is he big?" she asked, laying down on the mattress and spreading her legs.

"Ash," Veps said, "show the lady what she wants to see."

There didn't seem to be a moment's hesitation on my part. That goddamn infinite decimal of a drug had grabbed hold of me like a Siren to her sailor. My pants were down before Kiki could even start to finger herself, which she did once my dick was in full view. Veps slapped me on the ass. "See, sweetheart, all ready for you!"

"You first," she said, kicking off her red high heels. "Then him."

Veps, like the lion onto his prey, pounced as I stood there, my eyes fixated on the transpiring sex. He hooked her thong with his right pointer, ripping it off her. His hands gripped tight the top of her dress, and before she knew what hit her, he'd successfully ripped it straight down the middle. "Veps," I said, "you all right?"

"Not now!" he said, showing just how much the ecstasy-coke concoction was affecting him.

I kept quiet. There had been a slight hint of rage within his voice. Better to remain silent than to interrupt his, um, feeding. His face got imbedded in her pussy. She'd left no hair upon it. Looked smoother than newly laid asphalt and came off just as hot. Kiki held tight his head, staring up at the ceiling, moaning like I'd never heard a girl do before. This turned me on to the point where I'd started stroking and didn't even realize it until my own pre-cum trickled down onto my hand. I knew music still played on outside of the room, but all I could feel were the seismic vibrations.

Then he did it. Veps tore off his own clothes and proceeded to hump the living shit out of Kiki. There was no slow start. He simply couldn't control himself. Me, standing there, observing the ritualistic sexual exploits of how our ancestors might have committed themselves to the fertility goddesses of old, watched in awe of this man. He rose up onto his knees, took hold of her rear, cupping his hands to both cheeks, and pounded her into what seemed like erupting unconsciousness. She screamed, she cried, she accepted her role in the ceremony of the ancient ones. We'd gone from mystical cactus juice to the refined chemical compounds of MDMA. This couldn't be normal; I knew it, deep down. This pi variant represented a whole new generation of drug-crazed lunatics looking for a fix. Heaven was actually becoming a place on Earth. Belinda was right.

I awoke from a daze of a dream. The left side of my face burned. A bruise, I could feel it, had formed there. There were others with me. Veps and Kiki. All three of us lay on the mattress. We were all naked. The room smelled of sweat and sex. My senses were slow in coming back to me. How had all of this happened? What, in fact, was "all of this," anyhow? Unsure of even what time it was, I looked for my pants, finding them stained in semen. I hoped to God it was at least my own. I'd grown close to Veps in the months with him, but two heterosexual men shouldn't share *everything*.

Kiki, her marvelous breasts out for the world to view them, slept soundly on her back. Veps, on his stomach, ass hanging out in space, stirred but only for a moment. I wasn't entirely sure what to make of all of it. My mind tried to find the last couple of hours, even the last couple of minutes, before the obvious blackout which had afflicted me occurred. There had been no telling of what had gone on in that chamber within a godless church. Putting my hands up, I rubbed my sore face, and realized it wasn't the only tender part of me. My legs, arms, and crotch were killing me.

I sat down against the door. I didn't want to open it. I didn't want to do anything. Relax. Yes, that was what I needed to do. Figure out the play-by-play of what the three of us might have been doing. Mr. Smith, if ever I needed a hand in grokking on a situation, right there would have been an opportune time for you to appear.

What in God's name could have happened? It hurt to think. Flashes of what seemed like memories kept passing through me. The bodies of my two companions were proof that whatever I felt weren't just made up sensations. Focus. That's what I needed. Focus all of my energy on putting back together the fragmented visions from the previous hours. Needed to stay on task. None of that shiny object syndrome crud I'd been susceptible to for the better part of my life. Okay, now, first things first, what could I recall without question?

Veps, yes, he was doing Kiki like a jack rabbit in perpetual heat. Both were naked. My pants were down. There might have come a moment when Kiki experienced a flood of vaginal juices. Could that be the smells emanating from my lips? Quite possible. The scent was mild. It'd had time to ferment upon my skin. Yes, okay, there was some sort of piecing together going on. Veps was deep into her when he must've remembered I'd been in the room with them. Walked over to me. He pulled out of her, walked over to me, and said, "Come on, Ash, my dearest of dears. Time for the Jeopardy! First round."

What had I said to him? I couldn't recall. I was crouched down in that little chamber of secrets, sans a giant snake, well, yes, because in all honesty Veps at that point had gone fully flaccid. I'd said something. Something he didn't want to hear. All right, got it. "Nah, bro, I can wait until you're finished. I may not even want any of this." Yes, that is what I had said to him.

"Don't be such a bitch," Veps said. "It's time for choosing a category, and, hey, you know what? I won't even ask you to phrase it in the form of a question."

No sense. He'd been losing his marbles with each passing moment. The ecstasy. It'd had a more-than-interesting effect on him after mixing with the cocaine. Endless pi. Remembering more. Not enough to figure it all out, but more was coming back. There'd been a tremendous amount of growing fear within me up to that point. Ever so casually, I stretched out my neck, ensuring that Kiki had actually been breathing. Success. No fatalities at least. But wait, what had I said to Veps in response? "No, really, dude, you go and have your fun. I'm going to watch and see if I can build myself up to trying her out."

Evidently, this had evoked a terrible anger within him. My throat hurt like a motherfucker. Then there was a sensation of Veps' hand grabbing the back of my head. Hair in hand, he brought me up to his face. "Get on her, now, Ash, my lad. Time for the Jeopardy."

There had been no humor in him. Whatever the chemical reaction happening inside of him was doing, I could never be certain of the science, but Veps was losing it. His natural, or at least, hard-practiced keeping-it-cool attitude was failing on him. An animalistic side to the boy began emerging. Fear swept over me like the locusts descending upon those poor Egyptians. Let my people go, Pharaoh, before the death fog comes a calling. No such luck, it would have seemed.

"We're gonna show her what it means to be Eifel-Towered," Veps said, no explanation following. It couldn't be a good sign if he began to hold back tricks of the trade.

"I...I..." I forced myself to remember my words. "I don't know about this, Veps. I mean, look at her."

Kiki had started to convulse. There was no question as to what just started. An overdose. Mild compared to others. But her body was surely attempting to reject the abuse she'd exposed it to. Veps let go of me to tend to her. He wouldn't have done well as a doctor. Without a good bedside manner, he'd of been tossed out to some Third World country where you just need a pocketknife to practice medicine.

Flipping her over, Kiki proceeded to gag. Something tried working its way out of her. "What the hell is happening?" I asked, scared for my own skin more than hers. "Should I get Tyrese?"

"You do," Veps said, "and I'll brain you myself. Just shut up and let me handle this." He turned his attention to her. "Kiki, it's your honey bunny of the night. I'm gonna help you get what you need. Come on, that's it," he said, placing his right hand under her, positioning it against her stomach."

"*Is* it an overdose?" I asked.

"Didn't I tell you to shut up!" Veps said, looking back at me in a way he'd never done before. My friend was lost in that more than drugged-out screwball.

Then, looking to the side of the mattress, and trying to keep remembering, I saw a pile of puke. By that point it started to congeal, but there was this pushed down recollection of its fresh smell. He'd made her vomit up whatever had been causing her to lose it. Shaking ensued, and so did Veps. Now with Kiki turned over and facing away from him, Veps drilled her like a bull to its matador, only he wished there'd been two horns accessible. And, unfortunately, as I felt the soreness of my dick, there might have been.

"Ash," he said, "get over here now and help me. Come on, she won't bite. She probably doesn't even know what's happening to her right now. Ain't that right, sweetie pie?" Kiki provided no reply indicating higher brain functions. Only thing out of her mouth were the sunken sounds of pleasure-induced moaning. No one was behind her wheel at that point. I can't even be certain cruise control was functioning at one-hundred percent.

My face burned more than ever then. I could remember the cause. Me, dazed, standing there, not wanting to join in Veps' holocaust of Kiki's genitals, said, "I'm gonna leave I think."

He pulled out, dropping her body to ground level, and punched me in the face. "If you interrupt my good time once more, I'll kill you!"

"Veps," I said, trying hard to not cry from the perceived rejection of my only friend, "don't hit me again, please."

There seemed to be specks of orange in his eyes. What that meant, the moment couldn't explain to me. "Ash," he said, "just do what I tell you to do. Come on, up and at'em. Time to forget Marci."

Rubbing my bruise, I realized that the physical reaction I'd elicited from him was his way of trying to help me and feeling rebuffed. Could a person be mad at a compadre if they were only doing their very best, in their own personal capacity, to aid? That black and blue I was sure to be sporting was proof that Veps had my best intentions in mind. Heart like a reformed Grinch, that kid had.

When we were both standing above Kiki, Veps kicked her legs apart. She had her arms raised, fingers calling out. Finally, she spoke through a series of moans. "Baby, baby, more, I need to *feel* it."

"Ya, ya," Veps said. "Dr. V has the medicine you need."

He dropped to his knees, lifting up her lower half, plugged in, and began charging her for some atom smashing. I remember looking at him, thinking about when my turn would come if I could perform the way he did. My face didn't hurt as much, I guess a hit never does until it's had time to form a mark. I felt dizzy, but I wasn't sure if it'd been the hit or the pi. Kiki groaned. We'd moved beyond the standard sounds of sensuous arousal. When Veps flipped her over, him on the bottom now, my immediate reaction had been to back away. This, evidently, would not be part of the plan.

He'd said something to me then. I know he did. Veps was speaking over the resonances of sheer enjoyment spouting from Kiki. What had he said? I tried my hardest to think. There were words. Not sentences. Words lingering out there in the infinite void of space where nothing really forms in whole but you hope to God or Brahma a formation of one thing or another occurs. "Go for it." Could that have been it? "Go for *it*." Yes, that was closer to what he'd said. There'd been an emphasis, devilishly, place on the "it," which, without mistake, had not been Kiki, per say. Oh, he referred to her but not her. It didn't make much sense to me either then or even sitting in the aftermath. But living inside my head, I saw what "it" was and what I was supposed to be going for.

There'd never been a time in my short young life where I remember having licked the asshole of another human being. My natural instinct, and preference, would have been, obviously, that of a female's. There's just something one-sided in regards to the way men and women maintain their assholes. Guys, well, we're given the unfortunate curse of having hairy butts, however, the ladies, at least the ones worth masturbating to, they get gifted with smooth, rounded derrieres.

It was far from open. Kiki's brown hole of darkness that is. I could see Veps' dick plowing her from underneath. The gods truly had blessed him, no question about that. What could I do? Yes, that'd been the million dollar conundrum I found myself facing. Wait, exactly what did I do? Shit, that Swiss-cheesed brain of mine wouldn't work properly.

Licking. I'd licked it. As she took all that Veps was, I knelt down, my nose touching just the rim of her, er, rim, and, with a moment of hesitation mostly due to the fact that I still had to come to grips about what was about to happen, I gave Kiki one long wet tonguing around that oh so forbidden opening. Jesus could have heard her after that. She'd hadn't been a virgin to it, no doubt about it. This broad definitely, at one time or another, enjoyed the gentle salivation of a hormone-raging person's talking muscle around the tip of her anus. "Get her ready."

I looked up. They were still asleep. Recuperating might have been a better word to use at that point, though. Veps had wanted me to get her ready. Ready for what? Exactly what had I ended up participating in with him? Forcing myself into the depths of the hollowed out cavern that was, and to some degree still is, my mind, I pushed through the years of substance abuse in order to locate the shattered visuals that were my memories. I needed to know what had been done to Kiki by me and Veps. For better, or for worse.

Deeper. Penetrating. That's what had come next. Kiki, getting filled by Veps, was now getting a tongue massage by yours truly. Good. She tasted good. Are assholes supposed to taste good or does it depend upon the tastes of the person doing the nasty? Regardless, she opened up for me. That tight little muscle just relaxed and became a gaping black hole, waiting for Kirk to fly his *Enterprise* into it at warp speed. Then it hit me. Veps, the admiral that he was, had intended just that the entire time.

I had to unzip my pants to inspect my penis. No visible residue, but when I touched it and held my fingers to my nose, well, you guessed it, Kiki's scent all over. The aroma of tainted ass brought everything back to me. Like a soldier coming home from overseas after having successfully killed his share of women and children, my PTSD subsided long enough to grasp the tremendously wrong that had been committed against that poor girl just hours beforehand.

"Get 'er in, Ash, my boy," Veps had said. "Time for Double Jeopardy!"

Finding myself without the urge to stop, I took hold of my cock, and not ever so gently inserted it into Kiki. "Oh, oh, oh!" she said, screaming into Veps. "Yes, hit me harder. I want more."

"You heard her, brother! Give her the overdrive!"

Slamming into her, my balls slapping against her Veps-filled pussy, I got pretty deep inside. Feeling her flinch, tighten, I knew that this was something she welcomed even if she probably didn't realize it at the time. Amazing. That's the best way to have described it. Simply amazing. Kiki took me and Veps all at once. There was no stopping us. All would have to be accomplished first, our goals achieved, before this girl could experience any relief from our double-teaming efforts.

"Time for the Eifel Tower, Ashie, ole bean," Veps said, sending his arms out, reaching for me. "Just like playing mercy back on the blacktop. Take hold."

Without hesitating, which might say something about me as a decent human being, but, let's be honest, at what point have I even resembled one, I took hold of my friend's hands, interlocking our fingers. "Pull," he said. "Pull like you've never pulled before."

And just like that, I did. We'd let go our firm grips upon Kiki's flesh and jammed ourselves farther into her soaked-with-pleasure body. "Veps, Ricky, please, don't stop," Kiki said, completely disregarding my presence, which I could have found insulting, but who was inside of who, right?

"Don't worry, honey, we's taking care of you," Veps said, motioning to me to work even harder on her.

She started lighting up like a pinball machine. There'd be no tilt penalty for this one. Kiki came, long, hard, soaking everything beneath her. I thought her anus was going to cut my dick in half. Veps basked in all his triumphant glory, came, then shouted at me to bring it all on home. Complying, my load busted into her ass and she lost all muscle control, falling over, semen bursting out of her undercarriage tenfold. Kiki had been conquered. And France still could boast its monument to steel manipulation.

So there I sat, in the filth-ridden aftershock of a threesome. Saying that I was light-headed would have been an understatement. My mind raced, stalled, puttered, then raced on again. It felt like an old dial-up connection, oh, Christ, maybe even worse. But nothing could be changed. What had happened had happened without any serious, or rather, obvious, repercussions. The girl had initiated it all. Sure, Veps might have taken it to a whole new level but when you begin to mess around with that kind of electrically-charged basket of Tasers, well, don't pretend like you aren't prepared to get *it* beyond your once thought of limits.

Veps stirred. Consciousness was beginning to resume. The behemoth's massive appetite for sexual exploits over and above the average mean awoke. I couldn't entirely see his eyes. There was a moment where I shuddered, thinking it quite possible he might still be held by the grip of endless pi and coke. I didn't say anything. All I could do was watch him rise, the conqueror cometh back to survey the aftermath of furious war. He glanced at me, fully aware of the situation we'd awoken into. There seemed to be a sense of slight surprise in him when he took notice of Kiki's enduring nakedness. "Morning, sunshine," he said to me, his own body out for the world to see.

I didn't respond. I didn't know how to. Nothing could be formulated in me. Then, as if what transpired hadn't been enough to ensure continued dominance over the female population, Veps did something not even I thought him capable of. Okay, scratch that. Even though there still lay inside of me an odd bit of hero-worship for him, Veps might well have been both God and the Devil simultaneously. So when he spread his legs as he stood over Kiki's body, I anticipated nothing less from him than utter crudeness.

As the steady stream of dark yellow urine shot out of him, I watched as it struck Kiki. It started on her generously-sized breasts, working its way up until her face got fully glazed. To this day, I have no true opinion because I am not entirely sure what I saw can be either damned or justified. Was Veps doing this heinous act in order to warn Kiki of the dangers of hooking up while under the influence or had he done this out of it being some strange afterhours ritual he knew this girl enjoyed? Good questions, but, alas, not an answer to either in sight.

After the customary shaking of excess, Veps turned around, giving me a still sleepy-looking smile. "I'm hungry," he said. "How about you?"

As if I no longer had full control of my thoughts, I innocently said, "Hot dogs might be nice."

"That a boy, Ash," Veps said, getting himself clothed.

When the door to the room opened, I took one final look at Kiki. There she lay. One of *His* finest works of art. But she would never be meant to hang in places like the Louvre or the Sofia. No, this masterpiece had always been destined to be displayed on soiled mattresses behind closed doors in places no sane person should ever want to venture. She, like so many others belonging to her erotic breed of style, would forever be expected to be exhibited for those who could never go a night without a fix in one form or another. Kiki's purpose was to be the Mona Lisa of party girl sluts who yearned to be loved for what they truly were, but when you got right down to it, *this* is what they were: sperm-covered, and filled, skanks who would wake to find themselves the victims of golden showers. I hoped, for her sake, she'd gain weight, get a breast reduction, and go unshaven for the rest of her life. No need to repeat the vicious, endless cycle that undoubtedly was her existence.

But no matter how dark it must have seemed inside that building of glow-in-the-dark confessions of adulterous covetousness, outside, back in the sunlit streets of the endless city, things were normal as ever. Normal, of course, being that murder, rape, and unchecked alcoholism went on as usual. Veps had ideas for us. There was nothing in my mind to doubt that. The night before had been simply the beginning of what he considered my rehabilitation, or, rather, my being weaned off of one older woman of the cougar persuasion. He could keep trying, I told myself then, but I was unsure of the possible success rate.

We stepped out into sunshine. Summer continued on around us. Through that entire ordeal with Kiki, I kept on forgetting the season, the month, the day. Everything with Veps seemed to simply combine into one long night of enormous potential to fall apart at any given moment. But we kept on surviving. All of the ridiculous things that we seemed to get into had consistently failed to entrap us. So there we were, the master and his apprentice, the way things should always be, I assumed. At that point in the game of life, I'd of followed Veps anywhere. He knew, or at least appeared to know, just which road in the wood to take. His choices, however, continued to be the ones that constantly bent in the undergrowth. Again, I'd follow.

He found a vendor putting out franks. In my daze I had mentioned eating them for breakfast. Veps obviously had no problem with that. I'm sure he'd partaken in an early morning water dog more often than not in his time. They didn't bother me. A hot dog was a hot dog and anyone who says otherwise is a picky eater. Gourmet? Please. No one should be able, no, allowed, to tout that meat product with such a tag. Nathan's could do as they pleased, but no one else. Just make sure mine are covered in mustard and sauerkraut. Hot, too. Sans the berserker lesbian, trying to tear us apart, of course.

Veps paid the man his wares, and we took to a bench in one of those random parks the city had deemed necessary to set up in order to maintain the status quo. People needed their delusional sense of natural freedom in an artificial world. So long as the hobos came in when the children were gone, well, everyone needs a place in life. This was theirs. But for that moment, it was ours. And the hot dogs were good, well, as good as one could be after the eater has been drinking, popping pills, and fucking a poor girl into orgasmic oblivion.

"Who was Ray-Ray?" I asked, finally getting a chance and not caring whether it had come out of leftfield or not.

"Now where did you hear such a funky little name like that?" Veps asked, shoving another frank down his throat.

"Don't play around," I said. "You know who I'm talking about."

"Can't say that I need to answer these types of questions."

"Come on now, dude. Since when are there secrets between us?"

"Ray-Ray ain't around no more, so it would do nothing to talk about him. But who *did* you hear about him from?"

"That whale of a woman you flirted with at the bakery."

"She's a miserable fatty," Veps said, tossing his trash out in the bin next to us. "What else she say?"

"Just that Ray-Ray was a sweet kid who was here one day and gone the next."

"So you know everything there is to know."

"Never seen you so reluctant to talk about something. Going soft on me, eh?"

I got a dead-arm for that last remark before Veps said, "There are people in this world who belong for a bit then don't belong after. Simple as that."

"Was that a parable?"

"No, what we did to Kiki was a parable."

"You have no idea what a parable is, do you?"

"Careful, that kind of talk will get you a one-way ticket to another stiff hit."

"Did you do that kind of stuff with Ray-Ray?"

"Listen, Ash, that kid was a nice one. Real nice. A roommate, a chum, whatever. But he isn't around anymore. There isn't any reason to talk about him. One day here, the next day gone. Nobody stays around in one place forever."

"They do back home."

"You didn't."

"That's cause there wasn't anything left keeping me."

"Never was."

"My mom."

"She had the *law* on her side."

That last remark took me by surprise. He'd insulted my mother. He'd basically called her a whore without saying it. But he was right. I ignored it. Only thing I could do under the circumstances. "Why'd you pee on her?" I asked, trying to move the conversation elsewhere.

"On who?"

"Who else have you pissed all over today?"

"Ah, well, Kiki was in need of a reminder that such things in life are possible."

"Man, you're getting vaguer, and more vulgar, by the minute."

"Ash, my lad of lads, I had to use the bathroom and not a urinal was in sight. Kiki lay right there so, hey, might as well take care of business right there and then. Besides, it's sterile. That chick probably gave us more of something than we to her. Ha! Imagine that!"

"I'm trying really hard not to."

"Don't worry. We'll be out of this festoon of a place soon enough. The land of plenty awaits us," he said, before adding, "How'd you get that bruise?"

We'd left JFK on a Thursday night. If you ever want to experience a cattle drive with humans, just book a trip out of that clusterfuck of an airport. I mean, Jesus, I felt like one of those worker-ants in their glass, or, for the working man's child, plastic-encased farms where you simply get herded from one point to another. That's what I got to live through as Veps and I were escorted, closely, by Eckstein. Never crossed my mind once to question why he was with us. He'd been sent with one mission: to ensure that Veps didn't screw the whole operation up. A lot rode on what we were being asked to bring back, and I guess Boss Denham needed to make certain everything went off without issue.

"Now listen," Eckstein said, "don't go and mess this up. If you do, it's not just your ass. Wait, scratch that, it is *your* ass. You hearing me?"

"Ah, for the love of dreidel, calm your ass-loving-self down," Veps said.

"I can't wait until you fuck up royally, Ricky."

"Trust in Veps, my good Jew, for I shall bring back the good product from its bondage. See, I'm just like Moses!"

"Keep your voice down. Are you crazy or something?"

"Or something," I said, getting a chuckle out of Veps.

"Don't even start, kid," Eckstein said, his finger pointed straight at me. "I don't even know why you were brought in on something like this. I'm not even sure why this jackass was either," he said, now pointing at Veps. "I swear to God, if you do anything to ruin this...."

"We're not gonna...."

"Don't you mean Y-H-W-H?"

"Shut up!" This last outburst from our lawyer drew attention all around.

"Now who's drawing attention to themselves?" Veps asked, smiling proudly.

Eckstein wiped his sweat-beaded forehead with the back of his suit sleeve. "Take these passports, and get on that plane before I make you for what you're probably carrying on you right now."

He handed over the USA-issued booklets that would both signify our love of the Stars and Stripes as well as Bugs Bunny and Mickey Mouse. "You wish I were holding," Veps said, looking his over. "Ash and I already took care of business." It was true. We'd taken enough to last, I had hoped, the duration of the anxiety-ridden flight.

"Get going," Eckstein said, unable to add anything more.

"I'll miss you, Super Jew," Veps said, suddenly grabbing hold of the guy and laying a big wet kiss on his lips. This, not surprisingly, got the attention of mostly everyone around us. Eckstein stood there, stunned, infuriated, looking ready to either cry or punch Veps' lights out. "I love this man," he said, putting his arm around him. "He's my hubby-wubby and I'll never, and I mean *never*, cheat on him."

I nearly pissed my pants at that display. Classic Veps. But Eckstein, well, I don't think he felt the same way. It would have appeared that his sense of humor did not cohabit upon the same plain of existence that ours did. People are far too uptight in my opinion. "Come on," I finally said, taking Veps by the arm. "We're not getting on that plane if we don't head through now."

The actual process of moving from metal detector through terminal went relatively routine, much to my surprise. Veps behaved himself quite well actually. Eckstein would have been proud. But into the plane we went, Veps eyeing every female flight attendant, and swearing the one male did the same to him, sat down, after enjoying a fun game of fight for overhead compartment space, and prepared for the takeoff. We survived. I was still unsure. After all, that had only been one-third of the process completed successfully.

As we flew somewhere over the middle of the Atlantic, and the same episode of *Mad About You* played for the third time, I took out the passport I'd been given. I couldn't tell if it had been one heck of a forgery or just a rush job Boss Denham had managed to arrange. Not having taken a photo for it, my driver's license one had been used. None of it, regardless of its origin, could have really been legal, but, we'd gotten out of the country with what had been issued, so there didn't stand to be anything keeping us from getting off the plane when it landed. That was my mantra the entire eight or so hours. Kept my mind off of the idea of being locked up abroad. A lot of seething nuts hungering for some top choice American ass.

Veps slept quietly. It didn't surprise me. Somehow, like with everything else, he was fine beyond all means. Made me sick, thinking how he had no issue with being thirty-thousand feet in the air with nothing to truly hold onto. I felt that I needed to take my mind off of it all. So I started looking over the one flight attendant whose skirt happened, for one reason or another, to be shorter than the rules might've allowed.

She was ebony, beautiful, and even though I'd never been attracted to any girl of her persuasion, I found myself wanting more than anything to know what her pussy might have been like. Sure, I'd seen my fair share of black porn before, but obviously not live and up close. I wish she'd of seen me looking at her, pining over the idea of spreading my not-so-pale white ass over her. The analogy of butter over pumpernickel popped into my head once or twice. Could we have been two members of the Mile High Club? Perhaps, but, in another life. I didn't have the skills Veps had. There was no doubt in my mind that had I brought the subject up to him that he couldn't have somehow gotten her into the bathroom. How had I gotten Marci? I don't think I even tried. No, she'd pounced on me. Always seemed to be like that. Never anticipate, because you'll be let down in the end. That seemed to be the story of my life. So when she came over and asked if I'd like anything to drink, I said, "No, thank you." Her tag read out her name to be Shantay. I'd never get to know the pleasure of her company.

I fell asleep sometime after that. Off I went into the land of slumber to dream terrible dreams of apocalyptic themes. Okay, maybe they weren't exactly like that, but when you're under the influence, soaring at high speeds in the air, and ready to let your insides spew forth at any given moment, your dreams would be of an odd nature as well. You'd see your father. That's who I saw. It wasn't a replay of a memory. Or, maybe, it was. I think that it could have been one of those things where several memories mishmash together in order to form one semi-cohesive set of events. There was happiness, very little to be honest, where he played with me.

Of course, he had a beer in his hand the entire time. Finally, the can got imbedded in my skull. The next second, he was gone, just like in life. I realized then that I had made very little effort to find him. Didn't really bother me all that much. Who needed him? That bullshit about sons needing their fathers is just that, a steaming pile of excrement. If I did go looking, maybe I wouldn't be exactly thrilled by what I might have found. The dream concluded with me kicking him in the groin, but then I instantly became him and ended up holding my crotch, doubled-over, and woke up to Veps nudging me. "We landed, my boy."

"Really? I didn't feel a thing."

"You sure looked like you were in a world of hurt inside that pretty little head of yours."

"What time is it here?"

"Something like nine in the morning. I can't wait to get off this tin can and experience this city."

"You realize this is actually a country and we're simply visiting a city within it, right?"

"Don't go getting all geographical with me, brother. This is one of those times where I'll be damned to be upstaged by some intellectual such as yourself."

"I'm pretty sure you're the only person in the world that thinks I am a smart person. You do realize I have just about as much of an education as you?"

"We're a different breed, you and I. You've got that smart thing down, but just don't realize it. You should've read more books, Ash, my lad."

"Do comic books count?"

"I ain't no judge on what's literature or what's crap. All the same to me. But, now, well, it's time to put all learning levels aside and enjoy ourselves until the moment of business presents itself."

We waited for the cabin lights to illuminate, and all I could think of was how Veps thought I was intelligent. I didn't think I could receive that as a compliment, having considered the source of it. But he was a man of brains in regards to his position in the world. Life would never be hard for Veps so long as he was able to maintain his strategic center deep inside. Expose him, however, and you could very well lose him altogether.

With our bags in hand, we strolled through the sliding doors of the airport, out into the fresh air of the Netherlands. This was the good stuff. Not like the garbage we breathe back in the States. One good whiff of New York oxygen and you're liable to contract some random form of cancer.

I knew we had a contact, but Eckstein had given the paper to Veps and he hadn't bothered opening it. "Think it's time to go and look at that name, eh?" I said, elbowing him as he drifted off into his own special world.

"What? Oh, ya. The guy's supposed to be here to get us. Taking us over to the hotel or wherever I'm gonna ditch my stuff and possibly pass out."

"We're only here for two full days, pal. Probably want to not lose track of your stuff, especially your passport."

"That thing ain't worth the counterfeit paper it's printed on," he said, possibly confirming my own suspicions, but with Veps, you could never really be sure.

He finally looked at the paper with our contact's name on it, but before the name could be read aloud, a man with an Irish accent approached us. "Hullo there," he said. "Ash and Ricky is it?"

"Veps, please."

"Oy, that's right. Meant to remember that one, I did. My apologies."

"Quite all right, gov'na," Veps said, performing a really bad bow.

"You're a funny one," the man said. "Good to meet both of you. My name is Finnegan Beubu."

"Shut the fuck up," Veps said, smiling with his mouth agape. "Is it *really*?"

"It's the name me mum and pap gave me. Not exactly a traditional name on Eire, but I've made due."

"Have you ever told Yogi that the Ranger wouldn't like something?" Veps asked, with me almost choking on a laugh.

Finnegan smiled. "That kind of questioning, me boy-o, will only get you a puck in the gob. Catch the drift?"

"You're speaking English, right?" I asked.

"Oh, you Americans are a load of fun, you know that? Makes me never want to travel across the Pond. But we've shot the breeze enough here. Time I be getting you both into the city. We've got work to do."

"It's a little early to be so serious," I said.

"I concur with Watson," Veps said.

"I didn't say we were jumping right into the work, boy-o. We've gotta get you both settled first. Then, if you stop with the mouth pissing, we might be able to let ye get a little fun in first."

"Liking the way you handle things, Finn, my boy," Veps said. "Lead the way."

We loaded up into a two-door car, and Finnegan took to the wheel. He reminded me of Veps in a way, but with some weird European elegance, if such a thing were possible. Not even off the proverbial boat for an hour and the pot was in stirring mode. No, literally, the pot was preparing itself for us. As much as Veps and I knew we had to settle up and do what we came to do, the city of Amsterdam called out to us, beckoning its two lost sons to come home. We were ready for it. At least, we thought so.

The hotel was nothing special. One step up from a hostel, which made me feel better, because now I wouldn't have to worry about hiding my valuables inside my asshole in order to secure their safety. No, I swear, I think I watched a documentary once where it said that was what people had to do. Anyway, its name was something like hemp, but I can't be sure as to exactly what. That probably just means we did everything the right way those two days and could never be told otherwise.

    Its location lay just outside the old part of the city. I figured Boss Denham was just being cheap until Veps and Finnegan clued me in. "Gotta keep yourselves on the edge in case of any nasty play."

    "Exactly right," Veps said, agreeing out of character. "Just gotta make sure there's a straight line to the airport."

    "How serious is this going to be?" I asked, finally realizing this wasn't going to be some kids' game of ring-around-the-rosy.

    "No need to worry, lad," Finnegan said, handing over our room keys.

    "Why are they attached to a big keychain?" Veps asked. "I'm gonna have too much good shit in my pockets for this. It's liable to get treated like a female midget."

    "Sorry," Finnegan said, "I didn't catch that one."

    "Like a second-class citizen," I said, helping to make sense of our crude American humor.

    "You Yanks are an odd match."

    "I take that as a compliment," Veps said.

    "Just leave the keys with the front desk when we leave. Show them your identification to get them back. Someone will be there all day and night."

    "Nice little system they got here," Veps said. "Americans might be too stupid to allow that to work."

    "Among other things you'll experience here," Finnegan said, smiling. "But if you two aren't in need of diddling here anymore, I can show you bucks the city. Ready for a trip?"

    "And by trip you mean…."

"Boy-o," Finnegan said, putting his arm around Veps, "you're not gonna know what to think once I get you out there."

And it was true. Veps had been calm up until this point. But when we stepped onto the transit train to get inside the canal-dominated world of the Dutch, he became something else. If you could imagine a dog who has contracted rabies, and who has been denied food for a week, well, that was how Veps appeared when Finnegan brought us up to the first coffee shop on the trail. I don't mean anything remotely resembling a Starbucks. No, this was a different kind of java hut where very little coffee actually got consumed. In fact, I'm not even sure this particular establishment even had it on the menu. Oh, the menu. Dear blue sky, *the menu*. "Is this for real?" I asked.

"What do you mean?" the gentleman behind the counter asked back. He was an old soul-looking kind of guy who you knew had never spent a second desiring to leave his European home.

"The entire menu is just pot," I said.

Veps pushed me aside. The dog's leash had been cut by its captive's own teeth. "My God," he said. "Purple Haze, Super Silver Haze…AK-47!"

"In the arms business now, are you, Johan?" Finnegan asked, sarcasm drench all over.

"Can't says that I am," Johan said. "But if you boys would like to partake in our little treasure trove here, well, I'll roll you a fatter joint than your tiny lungs can handle."

"Impossible," Veps said, grabbing hold of me. "We're heavyweight champs of the world. Ain't nothing you got that we can't handle."

"Poor dumb bastards," Johan said. "It was nice knowing ya."

We sat at a small table, the three of us passing that magic stick around. It was *good*. It was probably some of the most amazing marijuana I'd ever taken in. So good, so fantastic, in fact, that it could make the most dedicated pothead in the world choose a straight-edge lifestyle when they weren't in windmill country. I could feel it burn my innards in a way I never thought possible. AK-47, the gem we had experienced, stale it would seem, back home, was more like the breath of some demonic deity of our primitive ancestors than Veps' original theory. Holding it in as long as I did could very possibly have scarred the tissue for good. But the sensation afterwards could not be compared to anything else upon this planet of ours. "How you feeling over there, Ash?" Finnegan asked me.

"What…" I said, not being able to do much else.

"Veps just went up for another order."
"I don't know...."
"Don't know what, laddie?"
"How he...does *it*...."
"You're in a good place, ain't ya?"
"How many of these places exist?" I asked, only because I knew I should be polite and continue the conversation, and at the same time fully aware I might be making very little sense.

"Over fifty," Veps said, sitting back down. "Got us a full-on bud from old Johan up there. Jamaican. Untouched by the likes of Boss Denham's dirty dealings."

We probably spent another hour in that place. A cloud of cannabis resin hovered over our table. When my mouth went completely and utterly cotton-like, Finnegan ordered me a Coke Light, which I was thoroughly confused about until I realized it's just their name for Diet Coca-Cola. Crazy Europeans. Crazy me.

"And we're not even in the Central District, boy-o's," Finnegan said.

"You mean there's *more*?" Veps asked, an eerie child-like innocence shining over him as if he'd been seven again and found out he had more Christmas presents to open.

"You got no idea what lies ahead, do you?"

"Can't says we do," Veps said, pushing me over and laughing.

I didn't want to move. So they moved me. Something about red lights and a district. The weird thing about Amsterdam is that it's the kind of place that could very well have been set up to entertain the worst victims of ADHD. From one moment to the next, a person is tossed around in a mentally unbalanced frenzy of food, bars, coffee shops, and people going this way and that way. Veps and I were *home*. No questioning it. Somehow, we'd ended up being born into the wrong lives. We should have been Dutch. Maybe we were. Perhaps, like so many other things, we just didn't know the truth.

We came to it. The Red Light District. De Wallen to the natives and those who wished to pretend being them. Possibly the most important spot in the civilized world. Windows. Countless windows. In each and every one of them stood an almost naked woman. "Prostitution's legal," Finnegan had whispered to us. No cops to interfere. No dirty back alleys. We were in the center of a society who pushed for humanity's oldest profession to continue on strong. I thought Veps was going to rocket off into the stratosphere and straight on towards the moon. Finnegan put his arms around us. "Your employer took the liberty of forwarding cash over in case you needed anything last minute. I've got your euros right here."

"I don't know if you handing that over to us is such a good idea," I said. Veps slapped me in the back of head. "I mean, we might lose it."

"He gets weird when he's high," Veps said, pointing at me.

"Not true. I'm just a little...okay...weird."

"That's right, Ash, old bean. Time to enjoy a ride...or three...ha!"

"I'd wait on that, gents," Finnegan said.

"What in the bloody hell are you talking about?" Veps asked, almost crying over the idea of being denied access to the buffet of female flesh selling their wares.

"These girls belong to what I call the day shift crowd."

"And I'd like to shift a few of them myself," Veps said.

"Keep your dicks in your pants, fellows. Wait until the lights really come on. Don't you boy-o's say something about the freaks coming out at night? Well, it's true."

"Don't toy with my emotions, Finn," Veps said. "Are you telling me there are hotties to be had here in a couple of hours?"

"My job is to keep you two out of trouble and to see to it you make your scheduled meeting on time. That's tomorrow afternoon. Until then, I'm simply a mate, traveling on the road of life with two likable Yanks."

"You're a beautiful human being," I said, realizing just how messed up I was.

"What do you suggest we do between now and fun?" Veps asked.

"You two ever eat Tibetan?"

"I once did a Korean."

"No, Veps, I meant actual food."

Beyond the he-she windows, through the endless stretch of what I came to call munchies-stations, which we ended up at eventually, and after several stops at cutely-themed coffee shops, we found the restaurant. I remember noodles. I recall veggies. I don't think there had been alcohol. I'm sure Veps partook. Only interesting thing that stayed with me was the fact that our food had been prepared down in the place's basement and sent up via a dumbwaiter. Funny what a person retains when they have most of what would amount to the state of California's yearly amount of illegally grown pot in their body. All the while the very thought of where I was still threw me for a whirl. Of all the places I could have imagined myself in before I left home, this would never have been on the list. The uncanny summer I'd been living through just made me realize how lucky of a person I was because I knew Veps, and he liked me. That man could do no wrong that registered as such with me. Ridiculous, idiotic things, but never wrong. Not in my book.

Finnegan brought us to the original Bulldog. The one, the only. This had been the reason Amsterdam changed its policies regarding the distribution and sale of pot. Local officials got tired of arresting the same schmucks, heroes now, over and over again, so they finally just decided to ignore them. I was fascinated by the place. Nothing special. Crazy drawings all over, and had I'd been off my cloud, I might have been scared of the whole thing. In this instance, no. Upstairs was small. Juice bar and tables. Space cakes at a reasonable price. Downstairs was where the magician worked his wonderful tricks. A light-up menu at the push of a button illuminated the flavors of the shop.

As we smoked our after-dinner joints, I took notice of an open slot just above Veps' head. The alleyway directly adjacent to us had exposed one of the infamous windows. There, a thick blonde in a tight white bikini stood proudly in red stilettos. Her face wouldn't have won her any sort of beauty award, but I'm pretty sure that didn't matter to the average guy looking for a good time. I watched, Veps joined in, and Finnegan, who grew more amused by our amusement, this hardworking girl peddle her assets to no less than five men within the forty-five minutes we sat for. A machine. A regular vaginal Terminatrix of unquestionable ability. To take in that many dicks in that amount of time showed just how serious these women took their jobs. You don't get that kind of work ethic in America. Even our hookers are lazy.

"So," Finnegan said, "you boy-o's ready to partake in a bit of the ole in-an-out?"

Veps, who'd finished his third joint in that session, wiping his hands upon his pants, stood up. "I was born ready for this, brother."

"I don't get it," I said. "Why should we have to pay for sex? We get the pussy for free back home."

"Well," Finnegan said, leaning in, "think about it, me lad. You've been to a strip club, I take it, eh?" The sudden image of Satan and his slutty mistresses flashed through my mind. "Consider this: you got a ten dollar cover charge, right? Possibly a two drink minimum after that. Think about the price of just one lap dance and what do you really get except some clothed grinding. Do you have any idea what goes on when those girls out there close their curtains?

"You get the fifty euro special, oh ye of little faith. A suck and a fuck. Fifty minutes. Whatever comes first: you or the fifty minutes. No poor fool who ever entered into one of those windows ever came out without a smile. Dear son of the West, go and sip the nectar bestowed upon us mere mortals." By the time he'd finished, I realized Veps had crawled out of the window. The beast was loose.

I knew that if Veps could buy into the whole concept then I had no choice but to follow. I didn't take his exit, however. Better not take any chances in the state I was in. The odds of hurting myself grew with each pit-stop in a coffee shop. Such is the way in which all things adhere to the cycle of the machine that we are a part of. Simple cogs, some greased, some dried up and ready to snap. A person had to be careful.

For someone not used to actually being able to hand pick the girl he is about to have sex with, the process of choosing a prostitute in the Red Light District can be daunting. First off, you have to accept the fact that rejection doesn't exist anymore. The one whose glass you decide to tap on will almost never turn you away. I'm sure there are snobbish whores out there who are only out working to enjoy themselves, but they are more than likely few and far between the good ones who behave and allow the dicks of strange men to explode inside of them.

There is a science to this whole thing. You assume, at least I did, that you'd walk down the first street, do your window shopping, and decide right there and then. This is incorrect. Wrong to the very core. It's like watching porn on the Internet. There's an abundance of sites dedicated to the idea that women should be allowed to show off their naked bodies, but when you do a search, you tend to keep searching until you find the one who you deem worthy enough to masturbate to. The same can be said about the process in De Wallen.

I didn't know what to do. There were so many women just looking me up and down. Couldn't let a personal connection happen. When you think they like you that only means a not-so stellar time. No, a person needs to fully enjoy it all. But it literally was a cascade of flesh tones, faces, and breasts. I saw Asians, ebony princesses, Europeans with endless legs. Some with meat, others with asses that could make Jesus' Second Coming finally happen if only they would call themselves Magdalene.

Finnegan had informed me to just not be awkward. Like all females, these enjoyed a confident man. One who appeared like he knew what he was doing. So naturally, because I'd been smoking all day, for the first time in a legal setting, my mind wandered from thought to thought as if Woody the Woodpecker was darting in and out of my brain, splattering all my attention across the streets. That annoying laugh became even more irritating as time went by. I tried to largely ignore it.

I rounded the same block for the fourth time before I noticed a short set of stairs, leading down to four windows. This could either be the hidden treasure Captain Silver had sought all his life or the final nail in my libido's coffin. My mind can't recall the first two but the third had been dirty blonde. A red bikini. Little maple leaves adorning the space in front of her nipples. Canadian? Very doubtful. Young, though. Probably around my age. She looked at me, and I felt disdain. It was almost as if she'd been saying to herself how loathsome it might be if this loser made the attempt for a business transaction. So rather than ruin both my high and night, I decided I'd take the next window, regardless of who might be there. This was a matter of principle. I had to push forward and do what any hot-blooded male in my position would do. Veps was probably, no, most definitely, out having a hell of a time. Now it was going to be my turn.

She was a tan woman. Older. Possibly, even older than Marci. Yes, I thought of Marci. I imagined just for a moment what she might be having to do back in New York in order to please that hog of a man she forced herself to stay with. Well, if she could lower herself to such standards then so could I. Here was a hot little number, in black lingerie and heels. When I tapped on the glass, she made a motion with her hand as if to say, yes, sure, come on in and slam my pussy for me. Those were enjoyable vibes. In I went. She locked the door behind me, drawing back the curtain. Now it'd be business. *All business.*

The room was chilled. Tiled. A bed and a sink with a chair set off to the side. Dim lighting, which probably accounted for these girls' ability to get it on with less-than-good-looking dudes. Mirrors were on the sides and ceiling. Veps must've been turning one trick after another. "You got what I want, baby?" she asked.

"Fifty sound good?" I asked, holding up a bunch of Monopoly-looking money that the Europeans considered legal tender.

"Oh, yes, that is what I like. Maybe you give me a little tip, too?"

"Tip? Um, well, don't you have to earn that first?"

"But, baby," she said, sitting down on the edge of the bed, crossing her legs in defiance, "you give me special gift in American dollars, and I make sure you get to touch everything you want, yes?"

It hadn't occurred to me that rules such as those could be set like that. Finnegan hadn't warned me about this. Was I about to be taken? How many times in a person's life could they say that they were in a situation like this where the sex was legal and attachment didn't exist? I took a twenty from my wallet, added it to the euros, and handed it over to her. She smiled, put it away, then proceeded to unzip my pants where I stood. "Mmm," she said, "you get nice and hard for me."

I hadn't realized it until she said something. My cock was rock solid, but she didn't immediately go for it. Instead, my balls found themselves in one of the best massages ever. I found myself moaning in pleasure. "Ah, you a little fucked up, yes?"

"Been enjoying myself outside."

"I see. Oh, baby, you getting so big for me. I like."

"What's your name?"

"Katia," she said, obviously lying. Sure, you be Katia and I'll be Captain Nemo. No skin off my ass, which, by the by, is what she started touching next. "Oh, baby, it's so tight. Will you open for me?"

"I…I don't know…what are you gonna do for me?" I asked, trying my best not to ejaculate right there. The cannabis had brought my senses of touch and feeling to a whole new level.

"Maybe you just lie down and let Katia love you?"

In thirty seconds, I was naked, socks on, back first on the bed. Katia stripped, kept on her heels, applied a condom with her mouth, and proceeded to suck me like the pro she was. In my daze, I looked up to see the image of her head in my crotch, bobbing up and down, with the feeling of her tongue wrapped around me. Pre-cum surely trickled out of me, but the poor thing would never know my taste. Marci knew it. She'd even said I'd been yummy. But, no, this was Katia.

"You want to try the fuck now, baby?"

"What, um, sure, okay."

She mounted me. I was in her. We rocked back and forth on the bed. I started rubbing her nipples. "Please, baby," she said, "don't bite them. They so sensitive." That, I took to mean, please do so, and, I did. "Oh, baby, your mouth so warm."

"Can I get you from behind?"

We switched positions. I held onto her hips. She sported a butt-plug. No unwelcomed visitors there. Smart lady. "Can you flip over?"

She was under me. Looking into my eyes. Suddenly, and unexpectedly, I came. It was all over. Katia, bless her soul, gave me a wonderful performance of a fake orgasm as if to say, "Hey, kid, I hoped you enjoyed yourself, now, time to clean up." She took my condom off, wiped my dick clean, let me kiss her on the cheek, and said, "Good night, baby, you so great, yes?"

"Sure," I said, realizing I'd just spent the equivalent of a hundred American dollars on a higher form of jerking off.

I searched for my two amigos among the red-tinted streets, finally finding Finnegan sitting in front of The Bulldog. When I sat down, he handed over his joint. Gladly accepting it, I took a couple of hits. Two cops passed us by. They tipped their hats to me. My life was complete. A dream had just become reality. Veps joined us shortly after, sitting down to my right. Finnegan got up. "I'm gonna get a drink next door. Don't go wandering. We need to get some rest."

When he was gone, I turned to Veps, who had been oddly quiet. "How many did you do?"

"None."

"Wait, what?"

"I didn't find any that I wanted."

"Who are you, and what have you done with my friend?" I received a shrug in place of a real response.

Something about that attitude he was exhibiting just didn't sit right with me. Here was a guy who couldn't wait to get it in wherever he could. How had I been able to achieve this and him not to? I realized it then that Veps needed that sense of control, of power. Somewhere in that mind of his, he'd been unable to successfully concede to the fact that the girls in those windows were no more interested in him than he'd been to the Queen of the Trailer Parks, or that crazy gargoyle-loving chick.

I woke the next day to the sound of Finnegan's voice talking inside my head about pancakes. We'd made our way back to the hotel the night before, Veps quiet at first but back in character once we'd visited our last coffee shop of the night. Afterwards, we'd gone to one of those munchies-stations. They seem to be located on every other street corner in De Wallen and for good reason. Once a couple of fools like us ingest that much cannabis, you bet your sweet rump we're going to be hungry enough to chew our own feet off. Well, it turned out to not be necessary. The one we stopped at took care of us.

There was a glass case filled with pizzas, hot dogs, pastries, but none appealed to me. What I cast my eyes upon were these thick Belgian waffles with melted vanilla frosting all over them. I'd of been quite content to enjoy it right off the shelf, but that damnable Dutch hospitality insisted the baked beauty be heated up first. I did not complain upon consumption.

But that morning, waking up, my stomach yearned for more fuel. Veps, positioned on the windowsill, smoking, looked over to me. "There she is," he said, trying to be funny. "Ash, my boy, how you feeling?"

"Feeling just fine there, killer. Where's Finnegan?"

"Our Irish escort called up a couple of minutes ago. Said to be down in about twenty for breakfast."

"When are we going to make the exchange?"

"Sometime this afternoon I'm guessing." He took a long last drag, inhaling every bit of it. "You have fun last night?"

Not knowing for sure if that was a true question or an attempt to create an argument situation, I shrugged and said, "Good times as always, bro."

"Just couldn't find that right one," he said, closing the window and lacing up his shoes. "Maybe tonight."

I knew better than to get into it with him. Veps, for whatever the reason, couldn't do what I had done. To think, me, the "quiet" one, would end up being the guy who solicited a prostitute. Could I even brag about it? I mean, it was legal, right, so by that reasoning how could one boast about it? When you're a kid and buy cigarettes, you tell anyone who will listen, but when you're actually of age, well, who cares? That might have been the reality of the whole thing, but hunger outweighed all other thoughts. One needs a full stomach when dealing in hard drugs, at least that's what Veps had once said to me.

Before we headed down, I smoked. There was just no stopping it. Both of us knew better than to not take full advantage of the local laws. When we got downstairs, Finnegan sat in the lobby, sipping a coffee. "Morning, mates," he said, standing. "Glad to see you're both up and alive."

"As opposed to up and dead?" Veps asked.

"Does he ever just accept a word from anyone without a smart remark?" he asked, looking at me.

"I've never known him to be of the silent persuasion."

"Sure was last night after not tapping any arse, eh, boy-o?" Finnegan said, slapping Veps on the back. He was a stranger and could say those things. I owed Veps. My mouth never opened.

"Keep it up, ginger," Veps said, playful as he could, "and I'll make sure that really big tranny gets its hands on ya."

"Now that's a threat never worth testing." He tossed his empty cup in the trash. "Ready for some grub, gentlemen?"

"Ya," I said. "You kept talking about pancakes. You guys got an IHOP or something around here?"

"I can't even snark ya for that one. If we didn't have McDonalds, Burger King, and KFC here, I'd of had fun with ya. But no, IHOP probably would never be allowed anywhere near a Dutchman's stomach. And, my lads, you'll understand why in just a few short stops on the tram."

"Well, whatever you're talking about," Veps said, "it's not getting into my tummy any quicker while we stand and dance around."

"Then," Finnegan said, "by all means, your majesty, follow me if you please."

"See that, Ash, I've already got him treating me like royalty!"

After that enjoyable display of schoolyard antics, we hopped a ride to this mini-park on the water. When we approached it, I smirked at the style in which it had been built. Somewhere, the Brothers Grimm were missing a small little sugar-shack. This tiny restaurant looked like it had been baked, frosted, and seasoned with cinnamon. A real-life gingerbread house stood there right before my eyes, but I knew better than to take a bite out of it. Although, after a few stops at the various coffee shops, the possibility could arise.

"Gonna be sitting outside today, friends," Finnegan said. "Nice ripe day in the sun, but we got us a fine bit of proper shade to cool the meal down with."

"If you keep talking like the Lucky Charms dude, I'm gonna imitate, gov'na," Veps said, loudly, for most everyone around us to hear.

"He doesn't mean half of what comes out of that gaping hole of a mouth," I said to Finnegan, who, unaffected by Veps' ignorant comments, simply sat himself down, and ordered another coffee.

We joined him right after and proceeded to also place in a request for some hot java. There were a few others sitting outside along with us, but they seemed content to keep to themselves. I glanced inside the place only to see one man, the cook, surrounded by a giant sheet of metal. One big stove, the likes of which you'd think only to see inside one of those crazy Japanese-themed Hibachi steakhouses. But considering the fact that this was supposed to be breakfast, I doubted very much if we were going to be seeing some funky onion volcano anytime soon.

The menu fascinated me. Some standard morning meal choices of eggs, bacon, the usual, but what caught me off guard was the amount of pancake variations available. Finnegan had ranted about them, so it only stood to reason that we'd been brought to partake in these hotcakes. "Best in the city," Finnegan said, sipping his just brought over coffee while perusing his choices. "I'm here at least once a week. Twice if I'm trying to impress a girl who spent the night with me."

"So usually once a week?" Veps said, smiling without looking up from the print.

"You certainly know how to make a man feel inadequate, ya know that, boy-o?"

"All in good fun, my dear companion. Besides, if anyone else had come a calling to ya other than me and Ash, you'd be one bored mick."

"Careful now," Finnegan said, dropping the playful attitude for a moment, "you go too far and the fun has to end. Ya catch me?"

"Boundaries, boundaries, boundaries," Veps said, moving his right hand in acknowledgment. "I get ya, boy-o, ha, ha!"

"So what am I supposed to order?" I asked, not really caring either way if the two wanted to continue their pissing contest.

"I'm a firm believer in picking something ya like and sticking with it," Finnegan said. "I'm quite partial to the ones with fresh strawberries," he said, referring to the pancakes.

"Is this for real?" Veps asked, flipping the menu around. "Cheese & Bacon Pancake?"

"That's right," the waitress said, having walked over to us. "Can I put that in the order for you, dear?"

"Shit," Veps said, "oh, sorry, I mean, yes, sure."

"My usual, please."

"Sure thing, Mr. Beubu. And you?" she asked, turning to look at me.

"Well, okay, I guess I will go for the ones with bananas?"

"Was that a question, dear, or a statement?"

"Oh, um, statement, sorry."

"Very good. More coffee?"

We shook our heads in unison. Sitting there, awaiting the food, Finnegan leaned in towards us. "Now, boy-o's, listen, and listen very carefully. Today is a very important day indeed. There's very little give to what we're about to participate in. The money your boss man over in the States deposited is cleared and ready to be used. He lost a tad bit in transfer, but them's the breaks for working on an international level."

"All right," Veps said, "but, what is up with you? You're acting more nervous than a virgin girl's father on prom night."

"He means...."

"I caught the gag, Ash," Finnegan said. "You had yesterday to have a little fun. Your boss knew you'd be in some need of it. I guess he knows you all too well, eh? But it's time to work and work we shall. I don't have a true dog in this fight, lads. I'm here as a potential translator but mostly middleman. My pay came half before you got here, and I'd appreciate the opportunity to receive the rest in a timely fashion."

"So just tell the Dutchies we're dealing with to behave themselves, and we won't have an issue," Veps said. "Besides, I thought this was going to be a cut-and-dry show?"

"The people you're meeting today don't have a reputation for playing by the unwritten rules," Finnegan said. "They've been known to peddle poor product and even jack up the price at the last minute."

"I don't think Boss Denham would be happy with that," I said, looking at Veps who waved a hand in my face. "But it's true."

"I'm the one who's gonna be doing the talking, right?" Veps asked.

"Can you control yourself long enough? Put enough of your ego aside if they get a bit nasty with you?"

"All depends on whether they need to get the professional me or the not-so-professional me."

"Veps," I said, "we're in a foreign country. Do we really wanna chance this?"

"You'll have to excuse him," Veps said, pointing at me. "He's fairly new to the whole thing."

"I kinda figured that," Finnegan said.

"Hey, ya know, I'm not an infant," I said, slightly raising my voice. "Ya, I mean, I may not be a veteran like the two of you, but I'm also not a complete moron."

"No," Veps said, "you're right, Ash. You're not a complete moron. In fact, why don't you do all the talking?"

"Hey, now," Finnegan said, "what's your game here?"

"No game, just like I said, let Ash handle it."

"I'm good, man," I said. "I just don't like being talked down to like a child."

"Fine," Veps said, "but don't think you know more about it than I do, all right?"

I shook my head, realizing that Veps had probably been correct in his handling of the situation. A large part of me kept forgetting that even though he was a bit of a degenerate, Veps had been dealing in and with the stuff for a lot longer than I had even been out of my home state. I'd be quiet in the deal, I decided right there. Shake my head, smile, sometimes nod, nothing that would screw it up. Boss Denham must've had a reason to send me along and the thought crossed my mind that it had been to make sure Veps stayed alive and out of jail in order to secure the cargo.

When the food was brought to our table, my world became a better place. I had ordered pancakes with bananas and assumed they'd be somewhat similar to the banana-nut kind I'd known for the better part of my life. Very pleasantly, I was surprised to see how wrong I had been. There were no stacks. None tall nor short. Buttermilk, I believe, was nowhere to be found in this recipe. There, sitting in front of me, anxiously awaiting for me to devour it, was a thin, crispy pancake that took up the entire plate. Atop this beautifully flattened sphere of goodness were whole pieces of bananas, baked. Imagine the insides of a warm apple pie then switch the two fruits. That is what I had. Veps' looked like a pizza and he had been taken aback for a moment.

All of the hesitation subsided once Finnegan began eating his beautiful doughy concoction. So there we sat, three of the most unlikely of people to call themselves acquaintances, in the middle of a small restaurant in Amsterdam, enjoying Dutch pancakes. Who could have predicted this sudden burst of luck when the year had been rung in over seven months ago? Not me. I had been the poor scrub watching his mother fade into nothingness. All I thought I could have amounted to was the best waste of life my small town had ever seen. But there I sat, enjoying my breakfast, taking a moment to smell the coffee, and preparing myself to do some serious work.

As Finnegan paid the check, Veps and I smoked a cigarette. "How you feeling about all of this?" he asked me.

"What do you mean?"

"Well, we're about to enter into a deal the likes of which you've never seen before. I've never fronted something like this, but Denham obviously thinks me capable."

"Maybe I should be asking you if you feel a little nervous?"

"Me? Nah. But I also think we need to put a little less trust in Finn over there."

"Why's that?"

"He's a nice guy, don't get me wrong. But he ain't one of us. Know what I mean? He's getting paid to do us this solid. It ain't like that money he's settling up with is his. Picking any of this up?"

"Ya, I hear you. He's the only guy we can really trust though, right?"

"What other choice do we have, eh? Just pay attention when we get into the lion's den, all right, Ash my lad?"

"I always got your back, bro. Wouldn't be here right now without ya."

"That a boy," Veps said, dropping and stomping out his cigarette. "We gotta get to a shop and take in a joint or two before the whole business transaction. You suggest it to Finn. Don't want him to think I have an addiction or something," he said, winking.

After a short jam session, Finnegan led us out of an oddly comfortable Rastafarian-themed coffee shop and back into Central. He'd said to simply follow, ask no questions, and, like the night before, if any dealers on the street offered something, say no thanks, and move on. He'd told us that while cannabis was a no holds barred type of thing, if the authorities found anything hard on you, well, that was essentially a one-way trip to being a human crepe inside a true-to-life Dutch oven.

Feeling good, feeling energized, I can't deny that there was a small pit inside my stomach just waiting for my guard to go down so it could expand and take over. But I wouldn't let it. I couldn't. This was serious stuff. I couldn't let Veps down. And he'd been right about Finnegan. The guy might have been nice to us, but he was being paid to be. While he would help us and do his job well in order to get the rest of his cut, unless he got extra, we were on our own. I never once thought, however, that there was a malicious nature to him. I don't know that the Irish have that. That is, unless they've spent the better part of a night swimming in whiskey.

We were led to a window with a tall brunette, tanned, sporting a tight, very tight, Catholic schoolgirl outfit. No knee socks. I remember that for some reason. Very hot. Very used, more than likely. Finnegan tapped on the glass. She smiled and opened. "How you doing, Finn, baby?"

"Doing just dandy, but not too dandy, eh?"

"You coming in with your friends?"

"It'd be nice, darling."

The idea of a foursome definitely danced through my mind and Veps' as well by the fact that he held up four digits with a wide-opened stare at me. This wouldn't be the case. The girl let us in, closed the curtain, then Finnegan opened up the back door where a bathroom probably should have been. Instead, a staircase appeared, leading up. "Keep the shop closed until we leave, all right?"

"Sure thing, Finn, baby," she said, laying back down onto her bed, exposed calves making me want to hump her like an unfixed puppy.

As Veps closed the stairway door behind us, he whispered to me. "She could have taught us a few things." I had no argument against that belief.

Each step creaked a little more than the last until we came to another door. Finnegan knocked, it opened, and we walked through. The room was small. It was also very simple. Bare bones. I knew this could not be a place of anything but transactional business. The intense work went on elsewhere. More than likely it didn't even happen within the city limits. No, this was a sensitive commercial endeavor, and one would need a place disassociated from the factory.

There were three of them. Three to match us. One had a gun. A plain little handgun that couldn't have been packing much punch but probably enough to put any one of us down for the count. He proudly displayed it upon the end table next to him. I never caught any of their names, because they never offered them up. But for the sake of narrative, I'll assign my own pet monikers to each. The one with the gun was Popples; he had acne scars all over his face. The other one who was sitting down, I called him Shady; he was darker than the others. Whether he was of African descent I couldn't be sure nor did I care enough to ask. But the one who spoke, I called him Regal. This guy was the epitome of the Aryan race. He'd of done well within the confines of the Reich and probably would've been smart enough to run off to Brazil or Argentina. A piece of coal among diamonds, Mossad would've brought him back to the land of Jehovah for a legal lynching. Take that, Mr. Eichmann.

But Regal had a nicer voice than any of his German cousins. His English wasn't as terrible as it could have been. Finnegan made the introductions and after Veps shook hands with him, I knew to be cordial and unassuming towards Regal. "Good day for some good business," he said, his voice taking on an elegant depth as if to intentionally make us feel better about being in a closed-in box of an apartment building in the middle of a foreign country where if anything serious went down, the only thing we'd be able to do would be to pray and die, hoping for purgatory at bare minimum.

"Any day is a good day," Veps said, stepping forward, indicating to Finnegan that he didn't have to participate unless language barriers popped up.

"Would you fellows like drink of something, maybe?"

"We've had our fill, thanks."

"Excellent. Then time for business, eh?"

"Time now is good as any, right, my friend?"

"You are a funny one, Mr. Veps."

"No need for titles. We're all good here."

"You make things very comfortable for first time."

"It's what I do, sir."

Regal motioned to Shady, who, getting up and revealing a small duffle bag, brought himself with it over to Veps. "Take look here," Regal said. "Inspect merchandise before money comes out. Sound good?"

"Sounds very good," Veps said, raising his hand up for me to come over. "Take a look at the pills, Ash. Let me know what you think."

Surprised by the request, I unzipped the bag, which still rested in Shady's hands. There were the pills. Each one, like at the Limelight, engraved with the sign of pi. "They look the part," I said, eyeing Veps. "But how do we know it's the real stuff?"

This, evidently, was an improper breach of etiquette. Shady withdrew the holdings, Popples rose, and Regal's eyes widened. With voice raised, he said, "You think I give you fake? Is that it?"

"Now, now," Veps said, seeing Popples begin reaching for his piece, "no need to get all excited, gentlemen. Ash here is a little new at this." Veps stared not just at me but into my very soul, eating away the refuse that obviously had clumped up my proper thinking channels. "He didn't mean anything by it. Just a little kaka like old Dr. Beckett."

Popples muttered something inaudible and Regal waved a hand. "My associate wishes to know who Dr. Beckett is and what the hell is kaka."

Veps, realizing there was the potential for disaster brewing, spun his head towards Finnegan, who, having remained silent up to that point, stepped forward, pushing me to his previous position. "Let me talk over this whole thing," he said to Regal. "I'm sure there's an explanation. No insult intended, of course."

Regal nodded and Finnegan pulled Veps aside. A moment later, Finnegan returned to address our hosts. He tried his best to explain the pop culture reference Veps had made that I understood but which had somehow insulted Regal and his pals for lack of comprehension. Uneasily accepting the clarification, Regal signaled to Shady that all had been settled. "Money now," he said, looking at Veps.

"I have it here, boy-o," Finnegan said, reaching into his pocket and pulling out an envelope of euros. "It's all there."

"Forgive if I don't trust," Regal said, handing it to Popples for an official counting of the paperbacks.

When the pockmarked-faced one finished, Regal allowed for the duffle bag to be given to us. Veps took it into his hands. "Much obliged to be doing business with you."

"Maybe next time you tell him to keep mouth shut," Regal said, pointing at, and giving me a look of a high school jock who just caught the class nerd drooling over his girlfriend. Yep, that was me at that moment.

We exited the upstairs room without having received the Holy Spirit. Or, maybe, we had, but I'd ended up being the doubting Thomas. Stupid? You bet I was. I felt like the biggest boob on the planet right there and then. As we walked out of the curvy schoolgirl's room, and I did have the chance to brush up against her, wishing I could enjoy her wares to feel better for a second or two. Finnegan was quiet. Veps, on the other hand, well, I'd managed to piss him off. He threw the duffle bag into my hands. "We don't even know if it's real now because of you."

"But that's what I was trying to say up there," I said, confused.

"You weren't supposed to speak more than, 'yep, it looks like the right ones'. No, you kept talking."

"I didn't know I wasn't supposed to stop speaking."

"Because of you, those pills in there might not be worth more than a Mentos."

"So you were going to ask them if they were genuine?"

"There's a right way, and a wrong way, to handle people like that. You have to ease into questions like that without risking insulting them. Now, Ash, Boss Denham might be getting clunkers."

"It's a risky thing," Finnegan said, interjecting. "They probably had a way to prove if those little darlings were real."

"Oh," Veps said, "don't worry. We're going to test these babies for legitimacy." He unzipped the bag, reached in, pulled out a random pi pill and stuck it in my mouth, forcing me to swallow. "And don't you dare throw it back up."

I didn't say anything. I simply allowed the breaking down of the potential ecstasy to begin. My blood system would tell us the truth about the drugs. Still, I just wish Veps hadn't done it the way he had, but I understood the ramifications if the boss man back home were to receive silly sugar pills. Yes, this had been the only way to do a proper test. If the tripping started and resembled the last round, Veps would be able to determine the truth. Just call me the lab rat.

It felt different than from the first time. That previous experience had been laced with a fine line of cocaine. This one had saddled me up with pure pi and no outside influence. There was a build. I didn't freak. There'd be no bad trip. A feeling of smooth sailing washed over me. We hadn't even made it to where Finnegan had been leading us before my eyes began to bug out. I enjoyed it. It felt calm. At that point in the trip, I welcomed the calmness. However, knowing who I was with, I knew this could only be a temporary reprieve from malevolent playtime. One in my position could only sit back and allow Veps to observe me for any signs of tampering by our compatriots from the upstairs room.

A neon-lit sign caught my attention. I gazed into it. Imagining just jumping into that aura of artificial light and heat made me fall that much more into the abyss I'd been sent to explore. But it's when I started to lag behind when Veps came back for me. "How you feeling there, champ?" he asked, seeming somewhat concerned for my well-being, but, in the same instant, angered by me still, after all, if the ecstasy proved to be faked product, we'd all be fucked three ways from Christmas Eve with no hope of Santa Claus bringing his fat ass down the chimney in order to save our collective asses from the fires of Boss Denham's temper.

"Feeling fine," I said.

"Not what I want to hear," he said, staring into my eyes. "Pupils are dilated, good."

Finnegan had realized our delay and came back over. "Come on, boy-o," he said, pulling on my other sleeve. "We're gonna get you to a fine place of refuge for the time being." He looked at Veps. "It's also gonna help determine if what you gave him is legit."

"Get us there, my Irish-born bro."

Beyond the windows and coffee shops of Amsterdam lies another aspect to the city's life that a person unprepared could lose their mind to. Finnegan brought us to a line. Yes, a line. One made up of people. All peoples were represented. We had blacks, whites, Asians; there were couples, singles, even doubles, but what they were lining up for didn't register with me immediately. Whether it had been what my body was digesting at the moment or my own oblivious nature to my surroundings, I can't be sure. But when we started to get let in, I took notice of a large pink elephant of massive proportions. Had a little tie on too. Everyone was on their best behavior here in paradise. I should have taken notice of the three little x's that were imbedded on its tie. You can't blame me for simply following Finnegan in with Veps behind me.

Walking had evidently kept the effects under semi-control. When we sat down, the sweat started up. It could have had to do with the amount of people we were sitting with. The layout of the land was like a theater-in-the-round. But something told me that we wouldn't be seeing a performance based off of anything that crazy Willy Shakespeare had put out over the course of his rather short life. No, there'd be no star-crossed lovers on that small plush stage in the middle of the humanity. Nor did I expect to see Lady Macbeth suffer the effects of insanity. I had Veps to watch should I wish to see such a display.

The house lights dimmed and an eerie red glow overcame us. I've always wanted to know just who decided that lust and fornication should be represented by the color red. Why not black? Yes, black. That darkened shade of pigmentation that really stood for sex. Because when the one participant realizes their partner no longer wishes to be involved, that black hole where the heart used to be overcomes all other emotions. Yes, it should have been black, but, if it had been, well, I wouldn't have taken immediate notice of the very naked chick who seemed to appear out of nowhere, laying herself down upon the pillow that was the stage.

When the sounds of techno began, I thought my ears were going to explode. This was followed by a strobe light. If Finnegan had intended to induce a seizure, it could have worked if I wasn't anticipating what I'd be watching so much. Everyone remained silent. I was sweating bullets at that moment. Veps saw this, shook his head in satisfaction, and sat back to enjoy the show.

She used toys on herself. Fingers were dipped in, then an entire fist. The girl must have been set up with a microphone, because all I could hear was her. Music was still playing, but I couldn't make it out. No, all I could focus on was her. My head began to bob back and forth as she moaned louder and louder. Then *he* entered. This would not be a solo performance. He was big. No, I mean *big*. Now I could never be certain if it had been the guy's entrance that kick-started the freak out or the pi had finally gone into overdrive, but, either way, once I began screaming with a unhealthy mixture of laughing, Veps and Finnegan grabbed me by the arms and the next thing I knew, we were sitting in a coffee shop. Time had become something only mere mortals were affected by. The endless number with an inaccurate abbreviation had sent me into another dimension.

"All right," Finnegan said, "are you pleased with the product?"

"Can't say that I'm not," Veps said, rolling a fatty. "Ash here seems to be gone beyond where any normal person could find him. Hopefully, he comes back to us."

I knew they were talking about me. But I didn't have the ability to respond and join them. When I saw the picture of Jim Morrison hanging on the wall beside me, the Lizard King began speaking. No, it was more like crooning. Yes, that shaman of the flower children was trying to tell me something, but he had no naked Indian with him. It was more accurate, my hallucination, than anything Hollywood could ever put out. I began to appreciate the drugs much more just then.

As the crystal ship began to fill, I had visions of Marci giving me a thousand thrills. I missed her. She was simple. Scratch that. She was nothing like simple. So much more to her than that Boss Denham would ever be able to see. I wanted her just then. Maybe, I thought, I could go out and find a window girl who looked like her. Could such a clone exist? No, it was impossible. I knew that. She might look like her, but there was only one Marci. And as whacked out as her priorities might have seemed to me, I realized that it made me want her all the more.

Finnegan suddenly had a bottle from out of the blue. I assume that he left us for a few minutes, but I might have very well have replaced him with a shirtless rock god sporting love beads. The things I had been seeing were beautiful and funky. Made me happy to see that my subconscious had a sense of flair. Too bad my regular thinking didn't match up. But there was Finnegan, our gracious guide, with a bottle of green liquid. Veps seemed pleased, ready to take on the world, but with my vision blurred, the words on the glass weren't able to be read.

"This is to us," Finnegan said, handing out what looked like tiny goblets. "We lived, survived, never died, and now shall celebrate your successful dealings."

"I'll drink to that," Veps said, turning his gaze towards me. "How you feeling, buddy?"

I might have shook my head but not too hard as to spill over with the green drink in my hand. We toasted, clanked the glasses, then drank. It tasted like strong licorice. I hadn't had anything like it ever before. Trying to ask what it was only made odd little noises come from my mouth. Veps laughed. It was good to hear that. I'd been afraid that he would be pissed off at me forever. I didn't need that. He was my friend. A true friend. Hard to come by guys like that.

"I think he wants to know what we're drinking," Finnegan said.

"Ah, well, Ash, my boy, listen up. You're drinking Tinkerbell!"

A vision of Barrie's miniature slut of a fairy popped into my head, and I swear I thought I saw her fly by. "He's wrong," Finnegan said. "Tinkerbell only wore the color. You're drinking the *green fairy*. Absinthe."

Suddenly, I was sitting with Gertrude Stein and Pablo Picasso. It was the 1920s, and we were all a part of that group of talented artists who needed to escape the horrors of war by living in one of the very countries it was fought in, which, never made sense to any of them, but it was trendy and whatever is trendy is never thought of to be that way. That's why it doesn't have to make sense. None of it ever needs to.

With the wormwood mixing in with the pi, my mind became a jumbled mess of fantastical beauty. Not that I can remember any of it in a conventional sense, no, I can only recall what burned itself into my retinas. We left that coffee shop, and The Doors, behind us, but there would be more to our night. Veps needed to make sure we enjoyed ourselves before the trip home. Our short time in the Netherlands was just that: short and nearly sweet. The absinthe had made sure to add a bit of bitter into it all. And even though my recollections of my second night aren't entirely accurate, or even possibly true, I can say that the last thing I am able to bring up from my files is me taking a head-first jump into one of the canals. Everything from there still seems to elude me.

Our farewell to Finnegan didn't produce any tears or soft-spoken whispers of how much we'd enjoyed one another's company. There were several man-hugs, as is of course proper, before Veps and I walked into the airport, ecstasy-filled bag with us, ready to bid Europe adieu. I've yet to ever make it back there. Maybe one day.

Have you ever been in a position where you knew there lay a foul smell in the air and there could be no doubt in your mind that it's of your own making? That was my experience on the plane ride home. My sudden dip into the canal the previous night hadn't done anything to improve nor enhance the pleasant body odor one hopes to achieve. In fact, it will do everything within its powers to ruin your body chemistry for all time.

It would seem that no matter how much I scrubbed the morning we woke to leave, nothing worked. Veps, laughing his ass off in the background, did nada to help me feel better. He was just happy that the pi pills were the real deal and that Boss Denham wouldn't be cutting off his testicles any time soon.

We had done one last walking tour of the coffee shops after killing off a second bottle of absinthe together. Whoever the kind soul was who invented that drink, I hope they're sitting in heaven at the left hand of the Father. That stuff sits inside your throat, burns going down, but makes up for all the unpleasant feelings fairly quickly. Makes a person more jovial and without evil. For one to go and be a prick after trying to embrace the green fairy, well, that individual should never be allowed access to the afterlife. Keep them paying indulgences with the rest of the Catholics.

But we had all met up with some fine soccer hooligans as they watched two random teams in one of the many homily bars in that city. They were singing. I think Veps might have joined in with them, although if memory serves me correctly, and there is no indication that it does, I might have started in as well. The problem with me, however, was that I had become a belligerent American. Looking back, I probably wasn't so different from the average sports fan sitting in a dive somewhere outside a stadium, praying to al Mazda for divine retribution. In laymen's terms, I gurgled through the song they were chanting, and the locals took that as an insult.

"Hell of a time last night," Veps said as the plane reached cruising altitude. "Those fine fellows liked you quite a bit, eh?"

My head ached. My stomach was in knots. But I actually engaged in the conversation with him. "Ya, I mean, if you take me having to escape their rampage by jumping into water not fit for a sewer, well, sure."

"You're just sore because you smell like a vagina that's seen far too many dicks without douching."

"That's disgusting. Why didn't you or Finnegan do anything to help me?"

"There was a bag of very valuable materials in our possession, and it took priority over you. Had to happen that way, Ash. No question there."

You couldn't argue with that kind of reasoning. Veps was right, of course, but I wouldn't admit it to him. Knowing he was right suited him just fine. Didn't change the fact that I still had to go for an impromptu swim. All I could do at that point was grin and bear it, hoping to pass out at any given moment and sleep through the rest of the flight. Well, a person can only hope for such things, right?

Don't go thinking that I awoke to Veps manhandling a passenger in a sadistic airborne rage, or that he had somehow managed to slide it in every flight attendant, male and female, right in front of the first-classers as they ate their ice-cream sundaes. No, nothing like that at all. Now that I think of it, however, it all did sound quite possible, knowing Veps. But, alas, no need to ever write down or talk about what exists only in my mind. What I woke to helped bring me out of my cloud faster than all the cups of coffee Dunkin' Donuts could ever mass produce.

I'm not one for sentiment. Nor am I a person who needs to seek natural beauty in order to appreciate life that much more. My mother didn't raise me that way, and if she had tried without my knowledge, she failed. Not her fault, no, entirely mine. When I saw Greenland outside of my window, I didn't know what to say. Veps had 'assed out, and I didn't bother to wake him. As I stared into that desolate wasteland of ice and snow, I felt small. Smaller than I ever have felt in my life, and you're talking about the guy who participated in drunken sex games in a seedy hotel bathroom.

Looking down into that world where the Vikings had attempted civilization made me come to the conclusion that nothing lasts forever. Why it took a giant glacier in the northern Atlantic to push that thought into my head, I'll never know. But for that brief time as we flew over, Greenland made me ponder my place in the world. As it would continue falling into the sea and retreating so too would I back in New York. All things, good or bad, must come to an end.

The landing at JFK was just as petrifying as the takeoff had been three days prior. Planes and I would continue to not get along. When I die, and have the opportunity to meet the Wright Brothers, I'll tell them that they should have kept humanity's feet planted firmly on the ground. I wonder what it must have been like for the one who didn't die young to be alive and see the atomic bomb drop down upon Hiroshima and then poor Nagasaki. A long, deep bender of a drink fest must've ensued. I mean, how else were we going to do it without an airplane? Poor bastards are just like Nobel. Yes, sure, let's name the most renowned peace prize in the world after the guy who invented dynamite. Makes perfect sense to me.

Customs continued to be a bit of a joke. We walked right through, duffle bag and all, tipping our invisible hats to the security guards. Funny thing is, as much as you might think things have changed, with the crackdowns, it's all bull from what I hear. God, I knew Veps was wishing we'd brought back more. Could have been one hell of a business venture, or, at the least, one shit show of a weekend with a couple of girls who were in need of forgetting about the woes of returning to college in the fall. Yes, we might have been able to help quell their depression. We were those kinds of guys, always willing to help those less fortunate.

No car waited for us. We'd been told about that. Something about drawing attention to ourselves, as if Veps couldn't do that all on his own. It didn't matter. A car is a car, a cab is a cab, and when you know the address to where you're going, you'll get there. And do that we did. We sat in the back of an old taxi that might have very well had the Son of Sam as a passenger at one point in its not-so-illustrious tenure. The adventure had come to an end. A chapter, really. Just another inclusion to the story that Veps and I were carving out.

The sights of our skyscraper-ridden metropolis shot back into our views. Home sweet home, right? But after seeing, albeit for just a short time, a different kind of city where bigger isn't necessarily always better, and older can be beautiful, I wasn't entirely swooned by things like the Chrysler Building. Veps, as I eventually noticed, looked tired. "What's going on with you?" I asked, giving him a nudge.

"Just a little anxious to make the delivery," he said, patting the bag that lay between us as our luggage slammed around in the trunk. "And I'm a little on edge. In need of some stuff."

"Well, I'm sure Boss Denham will have something for you. Are we getting paid for doing this job by the way?"

"What do you mean?"

"We risked our livelihoods to do this."

"Point being?"

"I figured we were going to get paid for doing this."

"We didn't spend any of our own money. No, we won't be paid for the trip. We'll be paid for services rendered just like I get when the month's over. No such thing as a bonus or overtime."

"Seems a little stupid to me."

"Stop talking like that, because, my lad, if that kind of verbiage slips out in a few minutes, I'll have to stand there while the boss man sticks his very expensive Italian shoes up your ass."

"But," I said, realizing I needed to just be cute about it all and bite my tongue on anything serious, "I need my bottom. It keeps me happy and content."

"You're a sick puppy sometimes, you know that?" Veps said, laughing. I'd obviously lightened the mood.

"Learning from the master," I said, poking him.

When we arrived at the restaurant, Eckstein was standing there, ready to pay the fare. "Did you miss me, baby doll?" Veps asked as we got our belongings out of the back.

"I'm surprised you're alive let alone actually having accomplished something," Eckstein said, trying to take hold of the ecstasy-filled bag.

"Nuh-uh," Veps said, slapping his hand away, "I got this just fine."

"You're a child, you know that?"

"Spank me then, or go eat a goddamned pickle or something. Come on, Ash, we have business-related ends to tie up."

It was one of those eating establishments that forced vintage on you, but everything about it was fake. I've never understood the fascination Americans have with nostalgia. What, in God's name, were we trying to hold on to? Didn't people know about our country's past? When you really sit and pay strict attention to it all, you'll quickly realize that nothing is ours in true origin.

The food was going to suck. No place like that could ever employ a true chef, because the budget was spent entirely on old-looking Coca-Cola signs that were younger than the newborns crapping their diapers as they lay in hospitals cribs at that very moment.

We walked through the place, which was fairly filled up with people being pretentious as they drank wines they assumed were so expensive because that's what they were told. In reality, it was all a lie. I'm not a big wine guy, but I know the brands that are on the "Under $10 Shelf" in a liquor store. And that was the thing about people like them, the ones sitting in this unnamed place because it was trendy to not display the name anywhere even on the outside: they never went out to experience anything for themselves. They were given experience in a mocked-up restaurant of false memories and pictures of celebrities on the walls who probably never set eyes upon the place.

Veps and I were better than these people. Better in the sense that we weren't going through our lives with everything spoon fed to us. I don't think Veps could ever exist in that kind of a life. I might have been able to for no other reason than we take reality for granted, but my companion in mischief was more knowledgeable than the average schmuck. No, this man was my yogi, the teacher-sage who was showing me truth. I'll never be able to forget his lessons. They'd been ingrained into my mind that summer.

Boss Denham sat in a corner table at the back end of the place. The fat pig seemed to be perpetually smoking on a stogie. Then I saw her. Marci was with him. When Veps noticed this, he turned to me, not saying anything, but I could hear words in his stare. He was saying, "Ash, behave yourself, don't look at her more than you have to, and if you even dare try to make any kind of physical contact with her, we're all fucked forever. Keep us alive, Ash, my boy."

"I promise," I whispered, but because he hadn't actually said any of the stuff, he just kind of looked at me, slightly confused but slightly aware. He was good that way.

As we all sat down, Eckstein included, Veps kind of made it so that I was farthest away from Marci. God, she looked stunning. Just beautiful. I had missed the sight of her. This woman, who had somehow become the desire of my affections and lust, made me burn inside. She'd cut her hair just a little and wore a tight, almost too tight, black dress. I never got to see her footwear, but knowing her, they definitely had to be fuck-me-shoes. Marci oozed of sex. I would've had her right there on the table if allowed. Unlikely, though that would have been. Had I tried, I'd of been a dead man before my dick reached its fullest extent.

"You can go ahead, Ricky," Boss Denham said, looking at Veps, "and give that bag over to Mr. Eckstein."

"Oh, no problem, sir," Veps said, doing as he was told, and not a minute sooner.

"How's it all look in there?"

"Seems just fine, boss," Eckstein said, zippering it back up.

"You hold on to that for the time being. Now, Ricky, Ash, I have to tell you boys that I'm very proud of you both. Were there any issues overseas?"

Veps would never mention the hiccup I had caused, and I loved him all the more for it. "Just fine, sir," he said. "Ash here helped out in the deal, and our guy over there ain't bad either."

"Well, that is good to hear. Isn't that good to hear, sweetheart?" He'd been referring to Marci, who just smiled at us, and I'd like to think spent just a few extra seconds with her eyes on me. Maybe it had been in my head, but, I didn't care.

"Are the pills going to become part of my regular stash?" Veps asked.

"Not this time, Ricky," Boss Denham said. "In fact, we won't be in possession of them for very long. Mr. Eckstein has arranged for an entire handover tonight. Isn't that right?"

"Yes, boss," Eckstein said, turning to Veps and me. "You boys aren't done working yet."

"Right he is," Boss Denham said. "You two up for the last leg of this deal?"

"Of course," I said, surprising Veps for my abruptness. He had to have known I was trying to show off in front of the woman of my yearning desires. Damn pussies and their ability to hypnotize the blood.

"You're rubbing off on the boy, Ricky," Boss Denham said. "Don't you think, Mr. Eckstein?"

"I'll be quiet on that, boss. No need for my two cents."

"I detect a little frustration there. You're not frustrated with my boy, Ricky, and his friend, are you?"

"Not at all, boss," Eckstein said, swallowing all the crow in the world. "I'll be happy to escort both to the drop as you asked.

"Um, sir," Veps said. "What's he talking about?"

"I want him with you tonight," Boss Denham said. "Problems with that?"

I knew there were problems with that. Veps hated Eckstein. But Veps also hated being homeless and penniless, so he shook his head in complete compliance, and that made our employer a happy son-of-a-bitch. "Well," Marci said, "are we going to eat, darling? I'm sure the boys here could use a little something in their stomachs before you send them off on their errant, right?"

"Isn't she the most?" Boss Denham said, showing his age. "Right, of course too. Mr. Eckstein, get us a waiter. No, wait, get us *my* waiter," he said, enforcing his ability to throw his massive amount of weight around.

My sneaking suspicions in the food were confirmed when my chicken arrived. Undercooked and bland. Veps ate without saying a word, and I followed suit. Eckstein sipped coffee. He'd taken the easy way out. Even Marci showed me subtle signs of dissatisfaction, but Boss Denham slopped away. This was the kind of guy who ordered soup to nuts with everything, and I mean everything, in between. Pompous jerkoff. He didn't deserve what he had. And that, for me, was Marci. I wondered about her. What she thought of me. Truly thought of me. Did she wonder what I thought of her? We'd had some fun, I'd been away for a few days, but now here we were. Things happen for a reason, I knew this.

"Did you boys have fun in Amsterdam?" she asked, we all held our heads up to her.

"Ah, honey, they were working," Boss Denham said. "But did you, Ricky? Ash? Did you have a good time over there? Never been there myself. Too European for me. Like my feet planted firmly on good ole American soil. Ha, if I ever make it over there, I'll fill my shoes with it just for principle."

God, I wanted to throw up. Had he really just said that? Yes, unfortunately, he had. Marci, she made no sign of displeasure, because she had probably gotten used to it over the course of being with him. No fairness in any of it. But with the response having been delayed so long, I spoke up, saying, "Very nice city to be in, and I did have a good time."

"I hear the women who prostitute themselves are quite hideous," Marci said, prying. Yes, she was looking to see what I might have been doing over there. This intrigued me.

"Some are," I said, feeling Veps squirm next to me for his own personal issues. "But there are some lovely, hardworking ladies as well." That pretty much stopped the undercover interrogation in its tracks.

When the check came and Boss Denham dropped down a wad of cash to satisfy his ravenous hunger, we parted ways. It'd been made pretty clear, crystal even, that Eckstein was coming along for the ride. Didn't please Veps all too much, but I think he was just happy to be closing in on the end so he could get back to his daily routine. It was a good routine, and Veps was in need of it back. I'm surprised he'd lasted as long as he did.

Before Marci followed Boss Denham out of the place, a piece of napkin, because this had been the kind of restaurant that couldn't settle for fancy cloth ones, got placed in my hand. She was slick, I'll never take that away from her. Hands that she knew how to work. Nobody saw it. Veps might've, but if he did, nothing was ever said about it. When I had a moment to myself in the car, I opened it. She'd written something down. This isn't what I needed at that point in time. She called me a true-blue, hooker-fucker. Good, right? I wanted her to hate me, because I didn't think myself capable of hating her. This was a suicidal fantasy I had been pursuing, and I suddenly realized that I wanted it more than ever. Story of a guy's love life: if any girl, somewhat attractive, shows a hint of interest, we flock to her without question. So foolish, yet so natural.

We didn't have a driver. Eckstein handled it. Veps sat up front with him. There was a silence until the lawyer man said, "Now listen up, you two, I don't want to deal with any shit tonight. I don't even want to be here, but the boss says otherwise. So listen," he looked at Veps, "I'll make your life a miserable existence if you mishandle this."

Veps, stone-faced, said, "Go to hell...oh...wait...you don't believe in that either. I'm compiling a list by-the-by." And the wonderful ride continued on.

We came to our stop in one of the many sections of the Bronx that time had left forsaken. Of course, that happens to describe most of that borough, so I'm sorry if you can't get a clear picture in your head. Nowhere around the stadium. More outwards, where you don't expect such places to exist, but in reality they've always been there and always will be. The Bronx, to me, was the neglected child of all that made up the greater New York Metropolitan Area. But you have to hand it to the natives, right? Only they, true-blooded Americans, could go ahead and give a quasi-city a definite article, not just in colloquial use, but in legal speak as well.

When Eckstein stopped the car, I thought he was trying to be funny. The outside of the warehouse looked like a fire had raged through the place long ago, and it just ended up being cheaper to leave the structure standing. A lot of those kinds of place existed from what I had learned during my stay. Oddly, Veps didn't seem surprised by the choice of locale for the exchange. We sat for a moment longer before Eckstein shifted in his seat to speak to us. "Okay," he said, "we're going to go through the back entrance. Veps, you know it, don't you?" He'd asked that with a strange look of satisfaction, and Veps seemed somewhat affected by his words.

"What is this place?" I asked.

"Doesn't matter," Veps said. "Come on, let's go get this over with before Cinderella over here turns back into a pumpkin."

"Her carriage turned back into a pumpkin, not her, you idiot," Eckstein said, climbing out of the car.

"You sure that's kosher?" Veps asked, stepping out as well, me following right behind.

"I don't think you even know what that word means," Eckstein said, making sure to lock up.

"Doesn't matter what I think it means so long as someone less-frequented with it laughs as I spout my muck out," Veps said, clinging tightly to the duffle bag of pi.

"You'll get yours one day."

"Ya, but not from you, ass-mouth."

We went to the back of the building and found a ripped out door that had been boarded up. Veps walked up to it, simply sliding the plywood away, revealing that anyone with any small amount of sense could enter into the place. Of course, who in the name of Davy Crockett would want to hang out there on their own accord if they weren't trying to escape something, or themselves?

The place stunk of something I can't even begin to describe, because I don't think enough adjectives have been invented for the task. However, you could say that it was comparable to being in the old high school boys' locker-room the Monday after puberty hit all around and everyone quietly was ashamed for the amount of masturbating that had gone on. Yes, that is fitting for my purposes here.

"What time are these people supposed to show up?" I asked, trying to not throw up from the smell.

"Soon," Eckstein said, reaching into his pocket, pulling out a new cell phone. He handed it to Veps. "Denham just bought up a bunch of these for his street vendors. You being one of them, you get it."

"Well, I'll be a piece of apple strudel," Veps said, holding his new toy. "Ain't had such a beautiful present since my parents bought me the Technodrome one birthday. Ash, you remember that one?"

"Ya," I said, "but the eye never stayed secured on top of the thing when you moved it around."

"Listen to me," Eckstein said, drawing Veps' attention away from the phone and back onto him. "This is not for you to go ordering an infinite amount of take-out, or for you to go calling up all your dirty little sluts. It's a business phone to be used for business. Understand?"

Veps wasn't listening. Oh sure, he was looking at Eckstein, even right in his eye, but, Veps was special that way. He looked at me, smiling as he held his prize. A regular boardwalk pavilion victor who had just conquered the crane-game.

Eckstein checked his watch. "They'll be here in about twenty."

"Glad to be done with this," Veps said, lifting the duffle bag, shaking it.

"I gotta take a piss," I said, completely just throwing it out there. "Any chance there's a broken toilet around here?"

"The whole place is a toilet," Veps said. "Go on, find a nice quiet corner. If there is anyone else in here, ignore them."

"Should I expect to find someone in here?"

"That plywood ain't exactly Fort Knox-issued, my boy."

I took my leave of the two and hoped they wouldn't tongue-lash one another to the point of throwing punches. The banter between them was liable to make the urine crawl back up in me. But I found a place, probably three ripped up rooms away, and proceeded to make water. As I began the shaking process, hoping to God I wouldn't get any on my pants for Veps to claim I'd peed myself, my eyes took notice of a wallet. It just lay there, mostly covered by an old decaying newspaper. Upon zipping up, I knelt down to get a better look. Nothing special about it. Imitation leather, cracked in all the regular spots, empty, of course, but I didn't intend to find money inside. I'm not even sure what it was I intended to find.

There was a driver's license in it. The picture of a young white-looking dude, but Hispanic might've fit him as well. Name on it was Raymond Duluth, which helped none in the race determination game. When I slipped the thing out, a piece of yellowed scrap paper fell into my hand. I unfolded it, and that's when everything just kind of aligned. Jupiter must've come so close to Mars or Saturn or whatever, because on that piece of pulp, the name of one Ricky "Veps" Donnardo had been scrawled down into it. The phone number to the apartment would then show itself on the opposite side. Raymond. That was the name on the driver's license. Ray would have been this guy's nickname. And if Veps had had anything to do with it, that diminutive could have been transformed into Ray-Ray. Here one day, gone the next, right?

I had little chance to continue processing, because by the time it all began clicking, I could hear raised voices, some of them belonging to Veps and Eckstein, but others had mixed in that I didn't recognize. The next sound I heard was that of a gun going off. The echoes of feet shuffling and people scrambling followed immediately after. I didn't freeze. For that, I was proud of myself. However, I didn't rush to see what had happened. I'm a survivor. That's just another word for coward, though. I ran. Sprinted is more like it. Beyond the smoke-filled lungs, I pushed myself forward. Out the back door, through the Bronx, I believe I hailed a cab at one point. Everything moved in slow motion, and I didn't exactly know where to go.

My mind must've been working overtime, or not at all. For reasons above my own thinking, I chose not to go back to Veps' place. Instead, I went a little farther. When I knocked on the door, I half-expected it to be slammed shut on me. But when it creaked opened, well, the smile on the face that greeted me gave me a sensation of warmth. To escape something I wasn't even sure had been something I should try escaping, I'd gone to Marci's. And she invited me in.

I've never experienced that sensation of feeling lost and misplaced from awaking in a strange bed not my own. That didn't change when I opened my eyes to see that I was still in Marci's apartment. It hadn't been a dream. Might have felt like one, but this was reality. She didn't lie next to me. I could hear her off in the distance, in the kitchen maybe. Soft music played in the background. The sun shone through the bedroom window. I felt safe. More than I had felt the night before when I ran like an escaping slave from the Deep South or a Mexican across the Rio Grande.

When Marci opened her door, and saw me, there'd been a smile on her face. A look of surprise as well, but I could detect the subtle grin of happiness. "What are you doing here?" she asked.

"Trouble at the deal spot," I said.

"Bad?"

"Bad."

"Exactly how *bad*."

"I heard a gunshot and nothing more. I don't know what happened. I ran out of there." My feeling of abandonment-ridden guilt took over me. "I was a coward."

She took me inside and sat me down on her couch. A soothing hand began rubbing my head. Believe it or not, I started to cry. Goddamn it, I wish that hadn't been the case. She took her hand and started to rub the back of my neck. "It's all right, Ash. You can't let yourself feel that way. You did exactly what anyone else would have done in that kind of situation."

"But Veps might be dead, and I didn't do anything to help him."

"If you were in the other room when it happened then there isn't anything you could have done. What happened was always going to happen."

"Do you really believe that?" I said, trying my hardest to cease the crying.

"Yes, I really do," she said, bringing my head down to rest upon her chest. She proceeded to rub my back. "I'm so glad nothing happened to you."

This made me sit up and look her in the eyes. "You're happy that I'm okay?"

"Of course I am. How could I ever not be?"

"You confuse me, Marci. We do our thing, you ignore me, you slip me a note to jab at me. What am I supposed to think about all of it?"

This is when she stood, and I noticed for the first time she was wearing a silk red robe over a black little nightie, sporting bare feet. Taking my hand, she pulled me to a standing position, led me into the bedroom, and stripped me naked. Upon my cheeks hitting cool air, she went on to mimic my appearance, resting upon the bed, spreading her legs ever so slightly in order to show me herself. "Make love to me."

"We've already done that."

"No, we haven't. I've sucked you dry, and you've banged me. I want you to climb onto me and show me how you feel about me."

"I don't know if I can do this. My head is pretty messed up right now, Marci."

"Take me, Ash. Show me what you want most. Do anything you want to me. I need you to make love to me."

She'd said it twice. To make *love* to her. I didn't know what that meant. Obviously, this was a request, no, a demand for sex, but she hadn't verbalized it that way. I don't think that I had ever made love to a woman before that night. It'd always been a wham, bam, thank you officer kind of thing with me. I'm not even one-hundred percent positive I'd ever even been in love. Which led me to my internal dilemma: how does one make love to someone when they don't understand what love is?

But Marci was there. She was naked. The wet lips of her seasoned vagina were there for me to stare at and have as my own. I did what anyone else in my position would have done, no, wait, scratch that, because anyone, and I was thinking of Veps, would have mounted her, bent her over, and pounded away until her cervix bled. Not me. Evidently, there were still parts of me unaffected by the summer. So I made love to Marci. I think it was beautiful, but I couldn't be sure until she grabbed tight my waist, squeezing me as hard as she could while we came simultaneously. We kissed. Made out. Tongued one another like there would never be another sunrise and everything we did was going to be one of the last events in recorded human history, left behind long after we were gone for some star-faring peoples to later discover. Yes, Marci and I went the distance several amazing times. It'd been the culmination of everything that had started at that little dive of a bar Veps had brought me to our first night together.

So as my dick lay throbbing from the session of love-making, and Marci lay curled in my arms, the night didn't seem so bleak. I hoped that Veps was okay. I could care less about Eckstein. Marci, sweating to match me, asked, "Are going to be here in the morning?"

"Do you want me to be?"

"Kind of."

"That wasn't a 'yes.'"

"I don't know if I can bring myself to say that to you."

"Why do you think that is?"

"Maybe because I'm scared about how I feel."

"I can understand that. Maybe you don't have to ask. Maybe I can just invite myself to stay and save you the internal struggle?"

"That would be so chivalrous of you."

"See," I said, "I'm not entirely like Veps."

"Thank God for that, but I think you're more like him than you realize. Do you think he's all right?"

"I hope he is. I'll go looking for him after I leave."

She held me tight. "But not now, right?"

"No, not right now." A thought suddenly crept to my mind. "Why aren't you with Boss Denham tonight?"

"Really, Ash?" She pushed off of me and rolled over, clutching her pillow. "Why would you even bring that name up right now?"

"Hey, I'm sorry, it was just a thought that passed through my head. Please, come back over to me."

"I'd rather not. Maybe you should go now." I could hear in her voice that I'd hurt her feelings, and for that, I felt like a jackass. "I don't think it's good for you to be here."

I reached over to her, spooning her, touching her, making her feel my presence so that she knew there were still yearnings that only she could satisfy. We kissed, her head turned into my mine to make the connection. It felt right. All of it felt right. No one could ever tell me otherwise. When we were done, and I'd regained her affections, Marci, snuggling back into me, asked, "Have you ever loved somebody?"

"Maybe," I said. "I've never been sure of those kinds of feelings."

"I remember the first guy I ever loved. I think you remind me of him. Which could explain a lot."

"This is that moment where if I don't let you get your feminine ponderings out, I'm in trouble, eh?"

"See, sweetheart, you're learning so fast," she said, kissing my chest to show me her approval.

And she spoke her peace. It was one of those stories where she loved the guy more than life itself, but he could never fully commit to her for one reason or another. Essentially, he was like every other guy out there. This is what I have never understood when it comes to women, that idea that they think all men are able to enter into a committed relationship and never want out of it. I don't know how the female mind works, but I know how the male's does. We are never happy with what we have. No matter how hot the girl, we always have it in our heads that there is one better than what we've got. A lot of the misery that men experience is caused by their own inability to accept the truth of it all: that the grass really isn't greener on the other side. In fact, the grass tends to be browned and in a state of utter decay.

Marci seemed to have been the one left behind for greener pastures. I couldn't understand that, but at the same time, I completely got it based off my own hormonal stupidity. But as she told me all about the drama that was her early life, I thought only that if she asked me, right there and then, to stay and never leave her, I would do just that. I knew, however, how impossible that was, yet, I secretly wished for it more than anything else. Marci and I could have been very happy together. Not forever; I just don't think that was in the cards for us, but for a long while, we might have been able to find bliss in one form or another.

After her little stroll down memory lane ended in her getting burned for what seemed like the thousandth time, I held onto her and somewhere in there we fell asleep, embraced by one another. It was a nice feeling. One I hadn't gotten to have that summer in any conventional sense. I think I drifted off first. I hope I didn't snore or anything like that.

Second to sleep, first to rise. Marci was making coffee. I could smell the java as it brewed, and it swept into my nostrils, tingling the tiny hairs, making it very hard to not get out of bed, no matter how much I wanted to bask a little longer in our dried, mixed-up fluids. So I rose, found my pants, and walked into the kitchen. "Morning," I said. "How are you feeling?"

"Oh, I'm feeling pretty good," Marci said, placing a cup of coffee in front of me. "Sit down and have some. I'd make you breakfast, but I don't normally eat it, so I don't have anything that could fall into its category."

"I usually will go out and get the food myself. Veps never cooks a damn thing. Don't even know if he could if he wanted." I suddenly remembered what had brought me to Marci's in the first place. "I need to go and find him."

"You drink some of that first. Then you can go. Where do you think you'll start?"

"Our place first, I suppose," I said, drinking. "Then, well, I don't want to go back to the Bronx."

"I've seen that God awful flophouse that Denham keeps hold of."

"He owns it?"

"Ya, not directly, but, ya. He's been using that place for years now. I had to go there once, but I refused to get out of the car."

I reached into my pocket and held tight the driver's license I had found the night before. As I was about to pull it out to show her, a loud knock came from the apartment door. Then another. A series of poundings followed until Marci and I ran over to see who was making that racket. I stood next to her as she opened it up. I couldn't believe what I saw. It was Veps. Dirty, disheveled, smelling like week-old garbage, and a little bloodied up. He rushed around Marci and hugged me before rambling on. "Holy shit, holy shit, God up in heaven, holy shit," he said. "Ash, my lad, my boy, my comrade, how long have you been here?"

"All night," I said. "I came here after I heard the gunshot."

"I didn't know what happened to you. One second all was going fine then Eckstein went and said some things he shouldn't have. Fucker is dead now."

"Wait," said Marci, "Eckstein is *dead*?"

"Yes, ma'am, dead as can be. Saw him go down for the count myself."

"Does Denham know?" I looked at her as she said that. Just hearing him say that asshole's name made me angry.

"That's where I've just come from. And boy, oh boy, is he ever pissed off to the high throne of Christ. But, hey, guess what? Those bastards back at the warehouse didn't get the score. I ran out of there faster than an Olympian with the duffle bag."

"The boss must've been proud of you," I said.

"Happier with me than I've ever seen him, but he's still sore about the whole thing. He spent three hours on the phone with me just sitting there, sweating, experiencing mental projections of insanity the likes of which would give Charles Manson himself nightmares."

"Let's not get that extreme," Marci said. "What happened with the deal?"

"Too much to go in on. I just came here for Ash," he said, glaring at me. "What is wrong with you, coming here?"

"I don't know," I said, nervous now because I knew Veps was angry with me. "This was just the first place I could think of."

"And not our loft?"

"Leave him alone, Veps," Marci said, coming over and putting her arms around me.

"Oh, *fan-tas-tic*. Why can't the two of you just stop it and forget one another? You make my life a constant struggle."

"What are we supposed to do now?" I asked, choosing to allow Marci's public display of affection to continue.

"*I get you* out of here, and then meet with Boss Denham once we've had a chance to wash off the remnants of a deal gone sour," Veps said, walking into Marci's bedroom.

"Hey! What are you doing in there?" Marci asked, rushing in after him with me following.

"Getting my guy's clothes in order. Ash, here, throw your stuff back on. We gotta get outta here with the quickness."

As I put my shirt over my head, we heard the very recognizable voice of Boss Denham. Time stood still. A warzone. This had all the likelihood of becoming a terrible bloodbath with me and Veps smack dab in the middle of it all. Veps, sweating now more than ever, looked to Marci. "Let him in and get him out of here, or I will make up such a lie that you'll need OJ's team to talk you outta it," he said, whispering as loud as he could.

Marci, knowing that none of this looked good for anyone involved, ran out of the room to intercept her boyfriend. Veps and I threw ourselves into her closet. The door, unable to close all the way, remained slightly opened. Just a crack. "No matter what goes on with those two," Veps said, grabbing hold of my wrist really tight, "you keep your mouth shut, and stay in here."

"What happens if he finds us?" I asked, petrified.

"Then we're dead. No talking our way out from this. So be quiet, or it's a death sentence."

I could hear a raised voice. It was Boss Denham's. He'd been ranting ever since he entered Marci's place. I could hear her too, but his booming overpowered all others sounds. "Sons of bitches," he said. "I can't believe those bastards did this to me. I've given them so much business in the past and for them to treat me this way? Absolutely not will I take this."

"Don't start a war over this," Marci said. "It sounds like it was something Eckstein said."

"Eckstein, that stupid piece of trash. He's responsible for all of this. I swear to God that if he had survived last night, I would have killed him myself."

"But you have the ecstasy still, right?"

At this point they had walked into the bedroom, and for a moment, I hoped to all things holy that he suffered from allergic congestion. "Of course I still have it," Boss Denham said. "Ricky, Veps, told me he and his buddy grabbed the stuff and hauled ass to safety."

I looked at Veps with a face that said, "Really? You lied to him to keep me looking competent?"

"Then it's just a matter of finding the ones who were responsible and punishing them, right?" Marci asked, suddenly figuring out where we were now hiding. She walked to the slightly opened closet, blocking it with her body.

"Oh, I'm going to find them," Boss Denham said, lighting up a cigar and filling the room with the essence of a Cuban bar the likes of which not even I was prepared to inhale, let alone Marci.

"Could you not smoke in here?"

"What did you just say to me?" He flicked the dead match to the floor.

"I don't care if you smoke that in front of me anywhere else, even in my kitchen, but not in here where I sleep."

"*Your* kitchen? Hey, sweetheart, *who* do *you* think pays for this place?"

"You know what I meant."

"No, see, I don't think I do. Seems to me that you're getting to be a little ungrateful for all that I do in the department of taking care of you."

"Of course I'm not," Marci said, her voice giving way to a minor cracking.

"No, see," Boss Denham said, sounding like he'd just taken one long drag off that stogie, "I think you are, and I think I need to teach you, remind you, about your manners towards me."

Very quickly, without warning, Marci was grabbed by her front and dragged away from our view. Next thing we knew, Boss Denham had her on the bed, smacking her face with those broadstroke hands of his. I was about to lunge out, but Veps sensed this, and instead of grabbing hold of me all it took was his hand upon my shoulder to remind me that I had to allow this to continue in order to save our own hides.

The hitting didn't elicit any kind of sound from her. Marci, it would have seemed, was used to being taught lessons. But when Denham decided she hadn't had enough yet, he tore off her bathrobe, exposing her to all voyeurs in the room, unbeknownst to him. Then it happened. At first, I had hoped the fat bastard would've just stuffed himself right into her pussy, pumped a little, finished, and left, all the while with my leftover juices slowly crusting over him and that we'd forever be linked, but that's not what happened.

When he had her fully nude, he put her onto her stomach, holding her down. This was when she first started to struggle. He punched her in the back of the head and Marci began crying. Boss Denham then unzipped his pants, found his dick under the roll of fat, and shoved himself directly into Marci's asshole. She begged, pleaded, screamed for him to stop, saying it didn't have to be that way, but he refused to acknowledge her whatsoever. I remember looking at Veps, who simply closed his eyes and shook his head, indicating that this still had to be allowed to go on. I fumed at both the unfair reality and my own spinelessness.

I continued to watch. Like the ones who allowed Jesus to be crucified, watching on without interference, so too did I watch our lamb lay herself down for the slaughter. The woman, who I had been with just hours before, was now being violated in a way that she didn't deserve. To protect me and Veps. Well, herself too. I had to remember that. She was not an innocent in all of this. Was I reasoning this all out to the point of ridiculous? Probably, but, it had to be done in order for me to be able to ever sleep again.

When Boss Denham finished, he pulled out of her rectum, wiping himself off on the sheets. There was nothing immediately said, and Marci didn't make an attempt of any kind to move or speak. He got off her, his cigar having never left his filthy mouth, and walked out of sight, but not before saying, "I hope you learned something, sweetheart. I'll see you tonight for dinner." And he was gone.

Veps allowed me to leave the closet once the apartment door slammed shut, and the hog's aura could no longer be felt. I crept towards Marci and saw the blood that could have only come from her backside. He'd ripped her. Wide-opened. She was crying. I wanted to cry with her, for her, but I couldn't bring myself to do it. "Marci," I said, "can you walk? Can you get up?"

She kept her face concealed and just continued to wail. Veps walked out of the closet, looked at me, saying without speaking that we needed to get out of the place, but I waved him off, signaling to just wait in another room. He threw his hands up in frustration, obeying my wishes under protest. Upon his exit, I tried to touch her, but Marci coiled away from me, presumably scared out of her mind. "Has...has he done this to you before?" I asked, forcing the question out of my head.

"Only when I deserve it," she said.

"You didn't deserve this," I said, dumbfounded by her response. "How could you deserve this? No one should ever have to be treated this way."

This is when she turned over, trying to cover herself in order to maintain some strange form of dignity in front of me. "No one, huh, Ash?"

"Yes, no one should ever have to be a part of something like this."

"So you're telling me that never in your life have you ever treated a girl, woman, female of any age or type, this way?"

She was angry, but, she was right. Suddenly, the entire summer shot through me as if I'd just jumped off the Empire State Building, and my entire useless life had flashed before my eyes. I saw Christie, Tammy, and, last but not least, Kiki. They hadn't deserved what Veps and I had given them, but they got it nonetheless. So without Marci concretely realizing it, she'd been spot on right, but, I couldn't let her know that. Not at that moment in time. No, she had to be lied to in order to feel better, and I had to whip out an amazing performance. "No woman deserves it, especially you," I said, sitting beside her, trying to touch her hand but to no success, for she pulled it from my reach, it shaking the entire time.

"Just leave me be," she said. "You guys are safe. Denham didn't find out about anything."

"I'm more worried about you."

"Don't pretend like I matter, Ash. I'm just another notch on your belt, right?"

"You are anything but. We made love last night. We were together in such a way that I can't recall having ever experienced something like that before."

"You're not a romantic, hopeless yes, but not a romantic. Just leave and don't come back."

"Wait," I said, realizing that this situation had a possibility for resolution, "why don't you do that?"

"Do what? Why are you still here?" she asked, tears streaming down her face in greater abundance.

"Leave here and not come back. Come on, we'll get some of your stuff and you can get outta here."

"Ya, right, are you delusional? Where would I go?"

"I don't know, but you'd start by coming back to my place."

At this point, Veps burst back in, obviously having been listening the entire time. "Are you outta your mind? She can't come back to *my* place."

"She has to get away from him," I said.

"Hey, Marci," Veps said, eyeing her, "you staying here?"

"Yes, I have to," she said, answering like a machine.

"See, problem solved. Now let's get outta here, please."

Veps grabbed me to bounce, but I shoved him off and turned to Marci. "You're doing this all to yourself then. You know that? You're a moron if you stay here."

"You don't understand anything, Ash. You never will," she said. "I have to stay here or I'll have nothing."

"Better to have nothing than to live under Boss Denham's plump thumb," I said, holding up my own digit to emphasize the squish.

"One day, maybe you'll understand why I have to stay and you can leave at any time. You're not as deep as me."

"You should have better than this," I said, pointing to the room, the apartment, her nakedness, and, especially, her now scabbing anus.

"Veps," Marci said, looking at him for the first time. "Get him out of here. Make sure he doesn't come back."

"Will do," Veps said, grabbing me again. "Time to go, old chum."

This time I allowed him to lead me away from her. She knelt there, alone, no clothes, a thin sheet covering her, watching me exit her life. Had we been in love? I don't know. We kept saying that we were making love the night before, and I had reiterated it in our argument, but when it came right down to it, could you really love a person who screwed you in a bathroom? I didn't think so then and a part of me still maintains that belief. No, a girl who allows it in the john shouldn't be the one you take home to meet your mom. Even though mine was dead, the tradition wasn't.

So as Veps brought me out of that apartment, I bid Marci a not-so-fond farewell. My obsession was given the kibosh due to a reality check. It was heart-wrenching for me. I only hoped the same feeling would be within her so that the pain had a chance of being shared. Marci was not the one who got away nor was she the love of my life. But for a time, she was the object of my true, honest, youthful affections. For that, I won't forget about her. For that, I continue to remember her face. It was a beautiful face. Even with that chubby bastard's handprint slapped across it.

August had flashed by us, finally, and the end of it all approached. I didn't miss Marci. I couldn't. If I even felt those kinds of feelings, they were drowned in a sea of weed and cocaine. Veps saw to that. In the days after we'd left her apartment, he had become my de facto psychiatrist. He may not have ever taken a course in the field, but he could definitely prescribe the right kind of drugs. And while the medication worked for the most part, I had to constantly remind myself of the impossibility that Marci and I represented. It didn't even look good on paper. It just made sense once in a while when I'd throw the idea out into the void of the Universe. But reality checks were coming quicker with each passing moment. Veps kept telling me it was all for the best. Even said that for meetings with Boss Denham, he'd make excuses for me. For my own safety, of course. Can never be too sure if or when a girl like Marci is going to go blabby.

So while Veps continued on his work schedule, and me waiting to get my own, all in due time I kept getting told, I drowned my sorrows in television, specifically, *Looney Tunes*. For me, there's always been this overwhelming sense of security knowing that Wile E. Coyote will never catch the Road Runner. To know, beyond a shadow of a doubt, that that high-speed highway sprinter would never fall into that canine's hungry hands gave me a warm feeling down in the pit of my stomach. How many other guarantees does a person get in life? You know, I'm not even sure what would happen if the Coyote actually did break away and go against the will of Warner Bros. only to catch the bird. A part of me sees a break in the space-time continuum and the end of civilization as we know it. Like proving God to be fallible, if the Road Runner fell to the wily one, all that we had worked so hard for would be undone.

Around the fifth hour, and what felt like the millionth time the wanna-be-predator fell off yet another cliff, I heard a knocking on the door. Still in my pajamas, I rose from the tomb that the couch had become and walked to answer. When I opened the door, I saw a short girl standing in front of me. She looked at me as if she knew me, and for the longest time, I felt as if she did. There was something about her that I recognized, but I couldn't be sure what the hell it was. "Ash, right?" she asked.

"Um, yes. Can I help you with something?"

"I'm looking for Ricky or whatever it is that he goes by."

"Veps."

"Sure, whatever."

"What do you want with him?" It was after I asked the question that I finally took notice of her abdomen. A subtle bulge protruded from her that could either have meant she'd been on an all-night bender and had one too many drunken orders of waffles, or, well, you know.

"I'm pregnant," she said, confirming my "you know."

"Who are you?" I asked, trying to remember a face that reeked of familiarity but one I couldn't yet place.

"Cheryl. You guys were at my place a few months ago. After the concert."

That's when it all clicked. This girl was missing the dyed black hair and almost every ounce of make-up. But upon closer viewing, I observed the beat-up Converse sneakers that she obviously couldn't live without. This had been Veps' good time the night of the Ahab's Animals concert. She was the one who had associated herself with that caveman of a female who I had been marked to bother with but who I ended up not having to do anything with. "How are the cat fetuses?" I asked, hoping to make her leave out of sheer hatred.

"Don't get cute with me. Where is Veps. I need to talk to him."

"Yes, I see that. What do you need with him?"

"What are you, retarded? I'm pregnant and it's his."

"Oh," I said, throwing my hands up, "you can't be sure of that. Don't you have a boyfriend?"

"Haven't seen him in a while. No, this belongs to Veps," she said, holding a stomach that just barely revealed a bump, causing me to swear within my mind. "Where is he?"

"He is working right now."

"Fine, I'll come in and wait," she said, pushing me aside, making herself comfortable on my island of self-pity. It was obviously attracting such lost creatures as we evidently were turning out to be.

"What exactly do you want from Veps?" I asked, hoping to God she would not fall to pieces on me.

"I want to see what he'd prefer."

"What does that mean?"

"It means, I'll wait for him to get here and I'll talk to him about it."

"He isn't going to be back for a while. Like, hours."

"Does he have a cell?" she asked, glaring at me with the kind of annoyance only an expecting woman could pull off successfully.

"I don't know," I said, knowing full well Veps still had the phone Boss Denham had given him via the now not-so-dearly departed Eckstein.

"You live with him, and you don't know?" Cheryl asked, I felt, getting ready to go full-on hormonal and kill me with one swift blow to the chest.

"All right, don't get yourself all worked up. I'll go give him a call."

"I want to speak to him."

"I'm not promising you a goddamn thing," I said, walking into Veps' bedroom to make the call.

I closed the door behind me and dialed Veps. It rang a couple of times before he finally answered. "What's up?" he asked.

"There's a problem here," I said.

"What'd you do, back up the toilet? You poop machine, you."

"I wish it were something like that. Actually..." I said, stopping myself.

"Seriously, what's going on? I'm working."

"You remember that weird chick you had sex with a couple months ago?"

"Dude, you've gotta be more specific. You've just described practically all of them."

"Her name is Cheryl. She's here."

"My boy, I don't remember names unless they're capable of doing something for me outside of the bedroom."

"Cat fetuses," I said, having nothing else that might jog his memory.

There was a silence on the other end until he said, "Oh, shit on me and call it chocolate pudding. The one with all those creepy dolls and the gargoyles?"

"The very same one."

"How did she find me?"

"Beats me, but she is here...and Veps...she's pregnant."

"Motherfucker," he said, coughing out a cloud of smoke from the cigarette I knew he'd been trying to nurse in between speaking. "Did she say what she wants?"

"Keeps saying she wants to talk to you."

"Get her outta there."

"I tried. She said she was gonna sit and wait for you to come home."

"Dude, I'm not coming back there while that nut job is lurking about. I'd just as soon sleep on the street. And I'd be one heck of a hobo."

"Well, I can't throw a pregnant chick out on her ass. I don't think I have that in me."

"Who cares what's in *you*. I'm more concerned about what's inside *her*. We might have the makings of a true Damien, dude."

"I guess one can only hope, right?"

"I don't know what to do now," Veps said, frustration sounding out.

Before I could say anything else, I felt a hand grab the receiver from me. Cheryl had invited herself into the room, snatching the phone from me and pushing me aside. Pregnant women have an uncanny strength when they choose to use it. They were like mini Incredible Hulks. Don't make them angry, because you'll get a knock in the mouth. And that would be if you were lucky. The gods help you if they're on a crave fix, looking to score some random, disgusting combination of foods that no sane individual would ever consider mixing. I think my own mother had craved burgers with peanut butter on them. Although, nowadays, that's called urban-gourmet. Of course.

But Cheryl was a determined woman. She told me to get out so she could talk to Veps alone. I walked to the door, but I didn't leave. I wasn't going to be bossed around in my own apartment, even if I didn't actually pay for it. Damn it, it was the principle of the thing. The two of them went at it. She yelled, I heard him reciprocate. He yelled, she told him to shut the fuck up and die. At one point, I'm pretty sure Veps squealed like a pig. I didn't know what to make of that and, evidently, neither did she.

When they were done, I was handed back the phone. Cheryl stood there next to me as I put it to my ear. "Um, what am I supposed to do now?" I asked, hesitating to say anything more in her presence."

"Look in my sock drawer," Veps said. "There's money and an address."

"An address for what?" I asked, obviously still more naïve than I would have liked to have admitted.

"A clinic to take her to."

"Whoa, man, um, I don't think I should be the one to do this."

"You're the only man available at this point in time, my lad. I'm working."

"Why do *I* have to take her to this clinic?"

"Because *I* threw out all of the *wire-hangers* months ago."

"Fuck you," Cheryl said, chiming in after hearing Veps' voice.

"Tell that crazy bitch she's getting exactly what she said she would the night the fireworks went off over the bay, and in her pussy."

"I don't think I can say that," I said, hoping that with his short attention span, he'd forget what he had just asked me to do.

"Go in the sock drawer. Take care of this for me. You live rent free, and I've never asked you for anything. I'm not asking here, Ash."

Knowing full well that he was being completely truthful and honest with me, I agreed to the task.

"That a boy," Veps said. "See you tonight. I'll bring take-out."

I brought the phone to my mouth. "What happens if she wants to come here?" I asked, whispering and pretending she couldn't hear me.

"I'm not sharing the take-out with her," Veps said, hanging up.

With Cheryl watching, I searched through Veps' drawers until finding the cash and piece of paper with the clinic's address. "Are you ready?" I asked, but she didn't answer. We walked downstairs and climbed into a cab in silence.

After I gave our driver the address, he looked at me with such judgment that I wanted to punch him right in the jaw. I refrained. Everyone deserves an opinion. I wasn't, and still am not sure, of what my own is. Women's bodies are their own business. I think. It's a good thing I'm not a registered voter. No use to either side of the spectrum.

When we pulled up to the building, I followed Cheryl onto the sidewalk. She turned, looking into my eyes with a coldness that only someone close to the end of their ropes could. "You're coming in with me?" she asked.

"I figured that it would be the better way to do this," I said, not particularly sure if I believed myself. Veps, without question, would have wanted me to supervise this. He didn't need her going in, changing her mind, and then showing up at the start of the following year with a Ricky Jr. God help us all. But she nodded in approval, and I walked in with her.

It truly surprised me that I had made it as far as I did with Veps before entering any kind of medical healthcare structure. And this hadn't even been for me. Cheryl spoke to the nurse, and we sat down, awaiting her name to be called. The *procedure* would ultimately follow. I love the words they like using in order to dull the blow of the fact of the matter. "Are you okay?" I asked, trying to make time stop from passing slower than a retarded cheetah.

"I don't actually think I want to speak right now," she said, turning her head away.

"Veps had said you've done this before."

"He has a big mouth. But, yes, I have. Really didn't think I'd be doing it again so soon."

"I'm sorry."

"No, you're not," Cheryl said, her voice dropping to a final silence once a nurse came for her. For a second, she, the nurse, looked to me as if I'd been marked as the hand-holding buddy. Cheryl informed her that I was of no importance, and they left me to my own devices.

I've never understood why waiting rooms are always cold. No matter what time of the year it is, you can never find a warm spot. As I sat in that very uncomfortable chair, I looked around at some of the faces around me. Women who were here for one reason and one reason only. Here and there were guys sitting as well. Some of them were with their girls, others, like me, sat solo. This made me think. What in all the world was I doing there? Why me? This girl, Cheryl, had not been with me. She didn't even want to deal with me. But I was the one who had taken her in order to have *it* done.

It should have been Veps sitting in that chair. Would he even have stayed? It made me truly think about what I was doing with myself. From the very start, I wanted to be like him, like Veps. He was the kind of guy who knew what he wanted out of life and did all he could to achieve it. Did he ever consider his future? Who knows? Was this all a part of the initiation process that made a person just like my buddy? These were questions I had tried to ask myself a couple of times over the entire summer. It had been one hell of a time, but fall was on its way. What then? *Veps* should have been sitting in that chair, not me. Never should it have been me. And it made me angry. What I didn't know made me angry. I still had that license in my pocket. I hadn't shown it to him. It might not have even done anything.

That's when I decided that when he came home with the food, I was going to ask him. Going to ask him everything that I needed to know. My role in the whole dealing situation would be addressed. I had to. All the freeloading I had been doing was not going to fly much longer. There had been moments in recent memory where Veps appeared to be losing interest in having me around. These were few and far between, but a person can only take being on edge for so long. Just as Cheryl had been in a small, private room of disgusting suction and cancelation, I too needed to initiate a purge. It was time to take my whole perspective on the situation that was my current place in life and question its validity. Only then could I be happy with myself.

This whole self-reflection must've drowned me out of my surroundings, because the next thing I knew, a nurse was tapping me on the arm. "Sir, are you the one who brought in Cheryl?"

"Um, yes, sorry," I said, coming back out of my thoughts.

"She's going to stay a few more hours. Just until she feels well."

"So the whole thing is over and done with?"

"Well, yes, but you don't have to be like that about it."

"Wasn't even mine to begin with."

"It never is."

"No, wait, it's not what you're thinking."

"Sir, I really have no intention in caring on what the relationship is between you two. She just wanted me to inform you so that you could leave."

"Oh, okay," I said, getting up and handing the nurse Veps' money. "Make sure she gets this, all right?"

"I'll see to it."

As I walked out of the place, I took notice of a jar of free condoms. I wished, right there and then, that stupid men would just slap on a rubber. Maybe then I wouldn't have had to sit in that clinic.

Maybe Cheryl wouldn't have had to have another one. Maybe Veps could save money. And maybe, just maybe, my old man wouldn't have been dealt me. Bastards, all of us, in one way or another.

On the ride back home, I considered how to approach Veps. It hadn't been easy the entire time I had lived with him, and this was liable to start an argument. There was a lot to go over. In what order should I have done it? I continued to think hard on all of that until I found myself turning the doorknob, letting myself in, and smelling Indian food throughout. Veps was home. Dinner was in tiny boxes on the kitchen table, and after the sound of a toilet could be heard, Veps walked out of the bathroom, into sight. "Salutations, my good man," he said. "All went according to plan, I presume?"

"Ya, she did it," I said, circling around him to avoid direct contact, but probably looking all the more weird on my part.

"Excellent, my boy. Can't have little me's running around. God forbid, right? No, not at all necessary at this moment as the earth continues its axial rotation."

"If you say so," I said, looking away from him.

"Ah, Jesus, what's wrong with you?" he asked, throwing his arms up and then to his side.

"Ya know, what you had me do today wasn't exactly fun. Not really a walk through the park."

"You wanna go for a walk through the park? Okay, come on, I'm down."

"You're joking around, but I'm angry, dude."

"What are you so angry about? It wasn't like you had to sit up there on the table and get the nasty done to you. Shit, you didn't even have to force the broad."

"You didn't give her much choice, eh?"

"Don't get into this philosophical, what's right, what's wrong crap, Ash. I'm tired and I have a long morning tomorrow."

"That's not what this is about."

"Enlighten me then, because dinner is getting cold." That's when I held the ID tightest in my pocket. I wanted to toss it onto the floor, right in front of his feet, let him make the effort to pick it up, ask me how I found it, then proceed to tear into his lies. Everything would be confirmed for me.

But I didn't do any of that. Nothing happened. As Veps stood there, waiting for me to make a move or utter a sound, I let go of the ID. What was the point? Why did I need to know about Ray-Ray? It wasn't like I couldn't figure it out all on my own. And even if I'd be wrong in all of my assumptions, who would care? Raymond Duluth, my potential Ray-Ray, was gone. He'd been taken out by the junk. Yes, that's it, the junk. Boss Denham had mentioned something about getting rid of a shooter. Veps even had to show him my arms.

So I kept standing there. Lost in my thoughts. Had I come back to scream at the guy who'd taken me in? Tell him off because there was a part of his life that I demanded he share? Where was my right in asking anything? And none of it would matter in the end. Ray-Ray didn't exist anymore.

"I said to enlighten me," Veps said, breaking me out of my internal struggle. "What do you want?"

I almost asked if he'd been the one to end Ray-Ray's suffering. Would he do such a thing for me? He was my friend. The only real one to my name. But there was just so much piling up. I didn't know if I could maintain. I'd made it so far, and now a buckled feeling began to wash over me. Fight it. That's what I had to do. Fight, win, move on, enjoy the time with Veps. This was a life shared. Don't rock the boat. He didn't kill anyone. He merely liquidated useless assets.

"Yo, Ash," Veps said, giving me a gentle knock on the shoulder.

"Then what am I supposed to do from here on out?" I asked, the words just seeming to generate at random without participation of the brain.

"You're gonna start up a route of your own. I've been pushing the boss man for it."

I wanted to believe him because the alternative, well, there was no alternative. Where would I go? "Fine," I said, grabbing paper towels for us.

"Exactly," Veps said. "No worries. Come on, we'll eat up on the roof for shits and giggles."

And that had been the big, all out, verbal, and semi-physical brawl. I had failed. I would always fail. That feeling haunts me still today. Had I gotten the entire story of Ray-Ray straight up? No. But there was no way I'd ever be able to muster enough courage to bring it up to him again. Secrets. Everybody's got them. I have my share, but I know them. The others, the ones not belonging to my mind, those were the key to my understanding of what I was doing living in New York City.

We went up and sat in two old lawn chairs as the sun began to set over New Jersey. We hadn't spent any time in the Garden State together, but we had managed to fly over to Europe. I think the shaman of all crooners was right about your own being the strangest life you could ever know. Who else's could even come close to yours? But there we were, the two best suited individuals for one another there could be. More than I would like to admit even to this day, Veps left a lasting impression on me. Always the pain in my ass. Sometimes, however, welcomed, oddly enough.

As I took a mouthful of chicken makhani, spicy as Beelzebub's butthole, I just had to ask the question that no one could ever answer, but I did it anyway in spite of myself. "What's it all mean, Veps?"

"Very enormous penis," he said, shoving food into his mouth.

"Wait, what?" I asked, turning and staring right at him.

"That's what it means: <u>V</u>ery <u>E</u>normous <u>P</u>eni<u>S</u>. V, E, P, S. Veps," he said, still not making eye contact and being as serious as ever.

And there it was. The unanswerable answered somehow. Not really the question I'd asked, but the answer in and of itself spoke volumes about the man sitting next to me who I had lived with for over four months. All the mystery had been killed off in that one utterance from him. This was Veps. This was the hero of my summer. He was the one who had once slapped a five-year-old boy in the face for ruining the mother's vagina before she entered into that prime age of sexual escapades that Homer himself would never have been able to orate on. And for that, I had to respect him. Somehow, some way, I loved that guy.

"You working down there tomorrow?" I asked, nodding towards the World Trade Center.

"Yep."

We ate our dinner until the night crept up on us. The sun was now resting its head, setting on what had been our long-running, seemingly unstoppable dawn.

The next day was a Tuesday. *The* Tuesday. Veps, like every week, made his way, suited up, downtown. He always got there early. I had planned to sleep in, but the sounds rocked me awake and at attention.

It was a bad day. I even tried to call him. All I got was voicemail. We didn't have Facebook or Twitter yet. No such thing as a smartphone for the general population. If you didn't get the person via call, well, you weren't getting them at all. Can't even remember if texting existed. Maybe it did, but just wasn't in full swing.

Everything changed that day. Not just for me, the city, the world, no, it was bigger than that. Existence, and those who would come after the inaccessible restore point, had been forever affected by it. I didn't think my summer was going to end that way. I'd come so far, yet with the actions of just a few crazy fundamentalists, it all went down the drain. Didn't even find my old man, although I never really looked. He remains a specter within the confines of my mind. I had intended to build a life there in that time and place. But permission would not be granted.

I left after that. Got up and ditched the city that'd been my adopted home. And they were good times, amazing ones in fact. No chance for me to ever relive them. I don't even know what happened to him. My friend. The only person in all of Creation who took me for my flaws and never expected anything more than what I was. Don't know if he got reported missing. Probably not. Who would have done it when I failed to do so? Boss Denham? No, incredibly unlikely. Hundreds of potential Veps' out there for him, but only one for me.

As much as I lived with my head in a self-made haze of blissful ignorance, my prayers at night are that he took in everything he'd been carrying and felt nothing. For a long while, I dreamed of him, eyes bugging, veins bulging, riding down that smoking fume of pure energy until he became one with all of it. If there is a God who is still somewhat merciful despite our abuse of freewill, I hope He allowed Veps that much at the end. Ray-Ray turned out to be the lucky one. He'd escaped long before the insanity had given birth to a city of carnage; Ys and Iram had nothing on Irving's Gotham, no matter how close to the edge it seemed to constantly teeter on. One day sent it spiraling over. You can regroup, rebuild, reshape, but it's never the same as before. I still keep that driver's license on me.

Looking back, a decade removed, and with my mind cleared up more than ever, I can assess the enormity of the story I've been able to tell. I had said that this would be an honest one, that you'd get it the way it happened. That's what I did, I hope. One can only hope. Pieces were definitely missing, and my memory isn't as good as it could have been. Forgive me for my shortcomings.

Every generation will experience a loss of innocence. Mine's was long overdue. We'd been born, raised, allowed to grow into young adulthood, thinking the world was going to be ours. Somebody stole the inheritance. But why had this happened? It seems that not all questions get to be answered. Countless lives unfulfilled. This is now the norm. Welcome to the 21st century. It was born of death. Do I sound cynical? My upbringing, I suppose.

BILLY TOOMA was born and raised in northern New Jersey. After receiving his BA and MA from William Paterson University, he entered into the world of independent filmmaking, becoming an award-nominated documentarian for *Fly First & Fight Afterward: The Life of Col. Clarence D. Chamberlin*. He lists Ernest Hemingway, Jack Kerouac, and Michael Chabon as three of his literary idols. Currently, Tooma is an Instructor of English Literature & Writing at Essex County College, and a doctoral candidate at Drew University.

CPSIA information can be obtained at www.ICGtesting.com
Printed in the USA
BVOW03s1157121014

370466BV00013B/251/P